TWIN FLAMES

BOOK THREE OF THE WESTWOOD PACK

F.D. FAIR

Foundations Book Publishing
4209 Lakeland Drive, #398, Flowood, MS 39232
www.FoundationsBooks.net

Twin Flames
Book 3
The Westwood Pack

ISBN: 978-1-64583-109-9

Published in the United States of America
Worldwide Electronic & Digital Rights
Worldwide English Language Print Rights

Chapter One

Sophia

"I think he knows that I'm meeting with someone when I come out here," I say to my only friend, Samara, at our secret meeting place in the woods.

"How could he know? You're always so careful."

She's right. I am always careful. I make sure to only come here when he's gone for the day and change my clothes on my walk home, but I can't shake the feeling that he knows.

"I know I am, but he's been saying things lately. I think he suspects that I have a friend, and you know how he feels about those," I wrinkle my nose in disgust as I tell her, as if she doesn't already know.

The one and only time I brought Samara home to meet my adoptive dad in sixth grade was a disaster. He took one look at her and told her to leave and never come back. What she doesn't know, though, is what he did after that. He forbade me from ever talking to or seeing her again, and he made sure it was a lesson I'd remember by beating it into me. Well, at least, he thinks I learned it. I've just become very good at keeping things from him.

After that, we only talked during the day at school and always made sure that none of my dad's friends' kids saw when we did. There were times when we'd be running and playing at recess, and I would notice the other mage kids looking toward us and quickly plop down on the grass and pretend not to be hanging out with her. The first few times she thought it was part of whatever game we were playing but caught on quickly to what was happening. She tried to hide the hurt that crossed her face each time, but I saw. Each time it was harder and harder. But after that beating, I knew I wouldn't be the only victim if I was caught with her again.

Since we graduated, things have gotten a little more complicated because we no longer have the neutral ground of classes to see each other. Now, we only meet in secret at the dilapidated hunting cabin in the woods behind my house that she's called home for the last decade. She's made the inside comfortable, but she left the outside as it was so that no one knows she's there. I'm not sure she knows just how grateful I am that she's stuck with me through all these years. I don't think many people would've put in the effort it has taken to simply be my friend.

My friend has already given up too much for me, and I will never be able to repay it. Although she is intelligent and beautiful, Samara spends most of her time alone in a shack that is barely livable. We sit facing each other on a broken-down couch that she found on the side of the road and repaired herself. The only light in the room comes from the windows since, as she explained once, "lamps and lightbulbs ruin the 'abandoned' look." She lives like she's in a warzone, and she deserves so much better than that.

"Why don't we just leave? You know, like we always talked about. Just you and me. We'll run as far away as we can," Samara pleads with me, just like she always does. The closer we get to thirty, the more pressure she's putting on us to leave.

I blow out a breath, "You know why, Samara. Where would we go? Who would help us? I have no money and no car. He'd find us and then kill you for trying to help me. I can't let that happen," I explain, repeating the same words that I tell her whenever we get on this subject. She thinks that it would just be so easy to leave, but I know better. I know what this coven of mages is capable of. They've shown me time and time again. They have no problem killing to get what they want, and I refuse to let my only friend get caught in the crossfire... Again.

I know she understands my reasoning, but it doesn't stop her from trying. "I have money. You know that. I have more than enough for us to disappear," she tries to reason.

"We've talked about this. It's not safe for you to use that money. Besides, how far would we get with this?" I ask, tugging on my choker. It is an intricate, silver necklace that fits tight against my neck. Its thick bands weave in and out of each other. If I hadn't spent every day of my life stuck wearing it, letting it siphon power from me, I would be tempted to think it is beautiful.

"Okay. What if we did have help? What if I could convince someone to hide us? Would you leave then?" As tempting as it sounds, it's impossible. She's a lone shifter, the only mountain lion shifter left in Halifax, and she's hiding from the mages herself after they slaughtered her entire pride. So many innocent people died because of me, because she wanted to be my friend and her parents wanted to help me. If she leaves, I would be well and truly alone. I look into her deep brown eyes and sigh. It's not fair of me to keep her here. She deserves a life.

"You could go. There's nothing holding you here. You should go and find another pride or pack or whatever. Go live your life and be free. You don't have to live in this run-down shack by yourself." I go to continue, but she cuts me off, shaking her head no.

"You know I'll never leave you here with them." The way she spits the word 'them' is laced with so much venom I can almost feel it burning through my veins.

Samara is nothing but a short fuse and explosive anger when it comes to the mages. She's been protective of me since we met in first grade. Though, that was before, when she had her family and her pride with her. Knowing I'm the sole reason for their demise weighs on me. After all, if I'd never brought her home that day, the mages never would have had a reason to pay the nearby shifter pride any attention, and they would still be alive. After she left me, she told her parents about my situation and then kept them updated over the years.

By the time I was eighteen, Samara and I had developed a fear that I would soon be given to a mage as his 'coming of age gift.' It was a reasonable fear, given my father's repeated threats, and she must have shared it with her parents who finally tried to step in. It didn't work. The only thing that came from them trying to help was their entire pride being decimated. Though I'm eternally grateful that they tried, the price was far too high. Still, it was nice to know that someone cared.

"I'm a tethered phoenix. I'm not worth dying for, Samara. I never was. I've been tethered since the day I was born, and I'll die tethered. I'm lucky that they don't keep me in a cage anymore." I step closer and grip her warm, strong hands in mine. She chews her plump lower lip angrily, like it is Devin caught between her teeth instead of her reddening lip.

"I love that you want to stay with me, and I appreciate it, but I love you enough to tell you to go. I want you to go live your life. Live enough for the both of us, and maybe this tether will weaken enough that I'll be able to break through it and come find you one day."

I have tears rolling down my face at this point because, although I'm telling her that it's possible, I know it's not. My father, Devin, has already noticed the small flames that lick up my arm when my emotions become too much for me. It's never been a problem before, but a little less than a year ago anger, sadness, and anything else quickly started becoming too much for me to handle. I know he must realize by now that the tether isn't working properly anymore. I'm sure that he will be replacing it any day now with a stronger one.

"No. We leave together or not at all. That was the pact we made, and we're going to keep it. I'll find a way to free you. I promise," she says, grabbing me in a tight hug.

Oh, how I want to believe her. I really want to believe that I have a future ahead of me where I'm not doing chores or getting smacked around for simply existing, but we made that pact when we were eighteen, before they slaughtered her family. Back then, I still had hope of living a life. Now I know that won't be possible. I'm lucky to have even figured out a way to keep Samara in my life for this long.

"I should go before he gets home. I'll need to lie low for a few days, so I can try and throw him off. Maybe you should go into town or another part of the woods. That way, if he tracks me out here, he won't find you," I tell her quickly before turning to stride away. I don't say goodbye. I can't. It gets harder and harder each time to leave her out here. One day, I will end up staying too long or not covering my tracks well enough, and one, or both, of us will pay the price. One day, she'll finally do what she should have done so long ago and leave. One day, I may return to realize I already hugged her goodbye for the last time.

I stop underneath the willow tree a few hundred meters from the back yard and quickly change into the clothes I stashed there so I don't smell like Samara. As I slip the new dress over my head, it gets caught in my hair, making me lose my balance and scrape my bare thigh against the rough bark of the tree. I internally curse and hope that there isn't a mark left in a visible spot.

Even though mages don't have the keen sense of smell that shifters do, somehow Devin has always been able to tell when I've been around Samara. It starts with simple comments that could just be insults toward me. He tells me I smell filthy, like an animal. Once he's convinced himself I am hiding something, he turns to asking where I met a shifter and why I wasn't at home all day. There isn't an answer that will make him happy. From there, it usually gets physical. There are times when I haven't been around a single soul, and he starts. Sometimes I think he just enjoys disciplining me and will make up any excuse to do it.

After quickly changing and rearranging my wavy hair, I stroll back to the house, picking any wildflowers I find on my way to use as my excuse for being outside. I have a gut feeling that he will be home when I get there, and I've learned to trust my gut. It hasn't steered me wrong yet.

My walks back to the house each day are the only times that I allow myself to fantasize about a life away from this place. A life where I don't wear a stupid choker around my neck that I can never take off. A life where I can go to the beach, have friends, and go out to eat. A life where I can maybe even meet my mate and have children. A life with everything everyone else takes for granted.

Maybe I'd build a cabin in the woods near water so I could sit with my toes in the sand and listen to the waves or watch the birds flying from tree to tree. A place where Samara can run free in her mountain lion form without fear that she'll be shot and killed or worse.

As much as I would love all of that, I know it's not possible. Most days, I've accepted it. However, there are times—usually after my time with Samara—when I think maybe, just maybe, someone will come along and save us.

"Where the fuck have you been?" Devin is already shouting at me before I break through the trees into the back yard.

"I just went for a walk to pick some wildflowers for the table."

I knew my gut was right. He's been doing this more and more, coming home early from work to check and see where I am. I'm home most of the time, but there are times, like now, when I've been walking back from seeing Samara, and he's been waiting for me.

"I don't fucking believe you. You're meeting someone out there, aren't you?" He rips the meager wildflower bouquet from my hands and throws it on the ground. "I think you've got some little fucking boyfriend out there." He laughs toward the sky, and spittle flies from his dull, red lips. "Who am I kidding? Ain't no one out there who wants you. And you know better, right? You remember what happened to your last friend?" I can feel the blood drain from my face at his mention of Samara's family. He loves to throw that in my face, that the deaths of her pride are all my fault. She survived, but he can't ever know that.

He's really in a mood today. It's a good thing that I told Samara I won't be able to come back for a few days. I don't want him to find her.

"No, of course not. I just thought it would be nice to have some fresh wildflowers for the table tonight, and it was such a beautiful day," I say sweetly, trying to play the dumb blonde that he thinks I am.

"When I get home, I expect you to fucking be here. Not wandering around the woods like you own the damn place. I have half a mind to send some guys out there to investigate exactly what you've been up to," he says with a sneer, gripping my arm tightly as I walk up to him. I stay quiet. No matter how much I want to yank my arm away from him and tell him to leave me alone, I've learned the hard way that it won't work.

"You hear me, girl? If you so much as look in the direction of the woods again, it will be back in the cage for you. You don't want that, do you?" he spits at me. I simply shake my head and look at the ground. I really don't want to go back into the cage. He kept me locked in there for most of my childhood and claimed it was part of my training so that I learned my place in the family—like a dog.

"Good. See that you remember that. Now, go start dinner. We're having guests tonight."

My body stiffens at his comment for a moment before I get to work on my tasks. This is the worst. I hate when he has guests over. His guests are always other mages that enjoy making my life even worse than it already is. Between the derogatory comments, ass grabs, and slaps every time he has his friends over, I end up in a funk for the next few days. It's foolish to say they are sucking the energy out of me. Of course, they are. That's the whole point, but I prefer it when they are not actually under the same roof while they do it. I can handle a lot, and I know that their comments and actions shouldn't bother me. You would think I would be used to it by now, but I'm not.

My mental health is like a roller coaster. Some days it's up, others it's down. When I am at my worst, I think maybe it would be better if I left this world. Then I think of Samara. She wouldn't know. No one would tell her, and she'd end up storming the gates, so to speak, and end up in the next world with me. I can't let that happen. Not to her. I know this life isn't normal, no one should have to live this way, but unless someone magically appears with the ability to remove this choker from around my throat, I'm stuck dealing with it.

I head inside and begin preparing dinner. At least I'm safe while I'm in the kitchen. I don't think that man has ever seen the inside of a kitchen in his life. If he wants a drink, I am ordered to get it. If he's hungry, I am instructed to make him a sandwich. He's even woken me up in the middle of the night to get him things because, according to him, that is my job.

I see how the other mages and their daughters act, and it seems like there must be something wrong with me. We've all been raised the exact same way, but I'm the only one who seems to see a problem with how we're treated. I made the mistake one time of confiding in one of them, a girl named Janet, but instead of agreeing with me, she defended them. She knew, with the conviction of any indoctrinated child, that however I was treated was what I deserved. At only twelve herself, she informed me I was lucky they even let me out of the house to go to school.

She then tattled on me to her dad, who told Devin, who then had to 'make an example of me' by whipping me in front of everyone in the back yard. That was the last time I made that mistake. The rest of the girls I grew up alongside seem to just accept our fate. Maybe they truly do, or maybe they are forced to hide their true emotions too. They're all married now, paired off to mage boys as soon as they turned eighteen as coming-of-age gifts, and getting pregnant as soon as possible. I have no children of my own, thank the gods. But now that I am an adult, I can see how horrific our treatment was, and I feel sick when I think how the daughters of the abused little girls I was raised alongside are, even now, being raised the exact same way.

* * *

I get lost in my head for the next couple of hours as I cook, thinking about my life and wondering how I ended up here. I know my parents are dead. Devin brags openly that he killed them to get me. There are times, though, when he's had too much to drink and mentions 'the other phoenix.'

I have been alone and tethered since I was born, so I have no knowledge of what it means to be a phoenix really. Still, I am happy to know there's another one out there. More recently, Devin has drunkenly complained about how that "other phoenix" got out because of some incompetent guy named Tanner.

Whoever she is, I am happy for her. If there is someone else like me out there who managed to escape, maybe she'll find me. Maybe if I can escape, I can find her, and she'll help me. I should know better by now. All hoping ever does is disappoint me, but it is a nice fantasy to occupy my mind with. I let out a sad sigh and return to peeling the potatoes for dinner. If no miracles have happened in the last twenty-eight years, there's no use hoping for them now.

Dinner goes exactly how I expected; I am forced to serve rude old men with wandering hands who don't know to not touch what's not theirs. I say nothing, though. If I do, I know it will be another public display of Devin 'teaching me a lesson.' Even though there aren't any physical scars from those lessons, the emotional ones are very real.

I am not sure any of them actually know my name. "Whore" or "bitch" is usually all I get. Sometimes, when they're in a good mood, they'll call me 'girl,' but those times are few and far between.

As usual, they bring up the idea of pairing me with one of the mage boys. Some of them offer their sons so that, if I have girls, they can tether them too. Devin always shoots this down. He does not always bother explaining his reasoning, but they all know phoenixes are famously protective of their offspring. Any children I have would make me harder to manage. I am in the room, ladling food onto their plates while they talk about me like I am a particularly fickle breed of dog. Tonight, though, Devin does not shut down their offers immediately. He stays silent. What does that mean?

I'm just finishing up washing the dishes, hiding out in the kitchen while everyone leaves, when Devin calls for me. Fuck. I was really hoping he would just leave me alone for the rest of the night. He's had too much to drink already, and I don't have the patience to deal with his lectures and bullshit tonight. On top of that, I've been on my feet all day and just want to go to sleep.

"Sophia!" he yells this time, and I hurry over.

"Yes, Father," I say as I make my way to him in the recliner.

The TV casts a moving, unnatural light on his red, round face and familiar, tinny voices come from across the room.

"I just wanted to let you know I spoke with some of the other men, and we decided that maybe it's time to put you to better use by giving us some phoenix babies."

I suck in a breath. He's threatened it before, passing me around like livestock for them to breed with, but it's only ever been a threat. My thoughts are racing, but I try to avoid giving him the satisfaction of surprising me.

I simply nod and turn back to the kitchen, hoping he doesn't notice the change in my posture, the hitch in my breathing, the panic in my stomach.

I can't let this happen. I need to find a way to escape before it does.

As I return to the kitchen, drowning my hands in the too-hot water of the sink for distraction, I let my mind stray to the places I usually avoid.

I'd rather die trying to escape than become a broodmare, giving life to daughters who will live and die in cages like I have.

If they catch me trying to run away, the worst they can do is kill me. The tether will keep my regeneration from saving me, so I may find peace either way.

Chapter Two

Darren

I wake up a few minutes before the alarm I set, feeling more alone in the quiet of my large cabin than I usually do. Although I should be exhausted, I jump out of bed to get ready for the day.

In the last two weeks, our pack has hosted two births, two mating ceremonies, and one alpha challenge for another pack. That's not even counting the fact that I stayed up all night cleaning up after the celebration for the newly mated alpha pair of the Ironwood pack. Everyone else is ready to rest and relax, but I cannot settle down with them. There's a longing, a hole in my chest, and I cannot figure out what is missing. I do have this strange feeling, though, that the only thing that will fill it is somewhere on the adventure I'm about to go on.

I still need to head over and let Alaric and Phoebe in on my plans before they start making their own. It is, after all, Phoebe's sister that I am trying to rescue, and Alaric has been worrying for days that Phoebe will take off on her own to find her twin. Alaric is able to hide his anxiety from most of the pack, but I could feel it through our familial bond. That is the advantage of being the alpha's brother and beta. It makes both jobs easier. Although, when he's feeling stressed and there's nothing I can do about it, it is absolute hell for me. Like when Skarlyt was missing. Did I mention that there was a kidnapping? It really has been a hell of a week.

I pull out my phone and do a quick check of the weather in Halifax. It shows it's supposed to be T-shirt weather. Good. Nova Scotia isn't like Ontario. Their summers are short, and winters are extremely long. I'm glad that I'm going this time of year rather than in the winter. I throw some clothes into a bag, adding in a few hoodies just in case it gets cold at night or rains. Once I'm packed, I grab my bag and keys, lock the door on my way out, and head over to the alpha house.

"Hey, Uncle Darren. Why are you here so early?" Phoebe, my brother's mate and my pack's luna, shifts the tiny bundle that is my niece to mime a wave at me. She looks tired—dark curls tucked into a falling bun and tired dark eyes—but effervescent, swinging the porch swing softly as she sits with Aurora. I drop my bag on the step. She looks at it, then back at me with a raised eyebrow. "Going somewhere?"

"Morning, Phoebe and my little princess," I say, walking up and placing a soft kiss on Aurora's head. "Yeah, I am. But I wanted to talk to you and Alaric first." I step back, pulling up a chair to sit across from her. "Where is Alaric anyway?" I want to get this conversation over with so I can take off. I think I'll feel less jittery if I'm making some progress, even if it's just waiting at the airport, and I know he's not going to be thrilled about my decision.

"He's just grabbing us coffees and will be out in a minute." Ordinarily, I'd be grabbing a coffee as well, but my nerves are shot. I think drinking a coffee might make it worse, so I nod and wait for Alaric to come out.

"Hey, bro. You're here early," Alaric says, coming out of the house to sit on the swing with Phoebe and Aurora while handing her a cup. "Did you want one?" He gestures to the coffee.

"Not this morning, thanks." He raises his brow at me. I know what he's thinking. I've never turned down a cup of coffee before, even at midnight. I love me some java.

"Okay, what's wrong?" Phoebe is the one who asks. She's gotten to know me so well over the past nine months, she fits into our family like the missing piece we never knew was missing. She and I have grown so close that it's hard to picture her ever not being here with us.

"Well, I wanted to talk to both of you. I'm hoping that you'll hear me out before you make any decisions." I pause a second to ensure that I have their full attention before continuing. Or maybe it's because I'm too chickenshit to start this conversation with Alaric.

"You know how Joe said that your sister is in Halifax, right?" They nod, so I keep going. "Well, for some reason, I feel like I need to be the one to go and get her. I have this powerful pull, like this is my quest to take. I don't know how to explain it," I say, looking at them both. As I expected, they're shocked. I've never left Ontario before, and I never expected to. I've been happy my whole life staying in my small section of the world.

"Well, that's unexpected," Alaric shifts into his alpha voice easily despite the sweatpants and morning hair. "Are you sure you want to go? We don't have any leads on where in Halifax she could be. It could take you months to find her."

My brother is always logical, but I know that whatever this pull is will lead me straight to her. It's not going to take me months. It might not even take me days. At least, that's my hope.

"Yes, I'm sure. Seb's going to come with me. Pheebs, if we could take a couple of strands of your hair or a drop of blood to use as an anchor for a locator spell, that would be helpful." She has a mixture of shock and excitement written all over her face. I know if I found out I had a twin and that twin was being kept hostage by a group of mages, the same evil assholes who made my life hell, I would want to be out there finding them. I also know the only reason she isn't right now is because of the beautiful girl sleeping in her arms.

"It seems like you have it all figured out already. I'm not sure why you even bothered coming here to talk to us." I can tell Alaric is peeved by the tone in his voice, but I was expecting it. As his beta, I should have cleared any travel plans with him well in advance. I know I never really get a "day off" from being a beta, but I didn't expect him to be petty about it. Something defensive in me makes my hackles rise at his tone.

"Don't be like that, Alaric," Phoebe says, slapping his arm. "He's doing this for us—for me. You know how much I want Sophia here with us and safe. If I could get her right now, I would, but we talked about it. I agree I can't leave Aurora right now, and we can't take her with us."

His dark, pinched eyebrows begin to soften, and he lets out a breath. This is one of the reasons I'm happy that she came into our lives. She has a way of getting through Alaric's overly stubborn head and making him see reason.

"It's not that I don't know that, love. It's just he's my baby brother. These are dangerous mages we're talking about, and they have a tethered phoenix. It took an entire pack and coven of witches to take down Tanner and his men when you *weren't* tethered. But I am going to send Darren and Sebastyn? Just them? No offense," he directs this last part toward me, and I nod in acceptance. "I simply think we should come up with a plan before rushing headfirst into danger."

I sigh, looking into his eyes. "Alaric, I understand you're worried, and it's probably not the smartest thing I've ever done. Despite all of that, I need to do this. I don't think I'll be able to just sit back and wait for us to come up with a plan. I can feel it in my soul that I need to go, and I need to go now," I plead with my brother, hoping I can make him understand that I need to go to her.

"Have you seen something?" Phoebe asks, looking worried. "Is something wrong?"

"Not like that," I explain apologetically. "I don't get dreams and prophetic feelings like you do. I just know that I need to go." I turn back to Alaric, putting some steel into my voice. "And I am going. Seb and I have already booked our flights, and we are leaving tonight. I wasn't coming here to ask permission. I was coming here to tell you I am going, and I hope to get your blessing. If you don't want to give it to me, that's fine. We can work it out when we get back. If it were you who was having this feeling, what would I say to you?" I've successfully got him thinking now by the look on his face.

"You would tell me to trust my gut, and that you would help in any way possible," he says, blowing out a breath with a look of defeat. He's right, I would. Heck, I'd drive him to the airport and drop him off, even if I was scared shitless the entire time.

"I would. Now, I need you to trust in me when I say that I need to do this. Be my big brother. Give me a hug, tell me to be safe, and drive me and Seb to the airport tonight. Maybe even get me a lock of your mate's hair and a couple drops of her blood," I say the last bit with a laugh, trying to lighten the mood. Thankfully, it works, and Phoebe passes Aurora to Alaric as she gets up, I'm guessing to go get the hair and blood. I'm not sure if we will even be able to use it, but I know some locator spells require something close to the person you're looking for. You can't get much closer than a twin.

The six of us—Alaric, Phoebe, Aurora, the boys, and I—use the rest of the morning to spend time together. Alaric seems to think that I'll be gone for a while. He keeps reminding me that I don't have to do this, that I can come home at any time, and we will try again once we have a plan. I can tell he's trying to convince me not to go, but it's not going to work.

"What about classes at the academy?" he asks, and I'm sure he's hoping that bringing it up will deter me.

"I've already spoken with Heydon. He's going to take them over until I return," I tell him, proving that I've thought this through more than he believes.

If it were anything else, though, bringing up my classes at the academy would have stopped me. It's my baby. Alaric helped a lot with the planning and coordinating with the other supernaturals in the area, but all of the day-to-day tasks are mine. It's been a dream of mine since we were small to have a school just for supernaturals where the shifters didn't need to fear losing control mid-class, witches could practice their magic openly, and even the vampires can feed if needed. Each class is a mixture of all races to teach them how to work together rather than apart.

This is the first year we have allowed students under the age of eleven to attend. Because vampires and witches are born with their abilities, they do not get the luxury shifters do of attending human school until puberty forces the shift to start. At the beginning of summer, we reached out to packs around the country and invited them to join us, as did the bears, mountain lions, vampires, and witches who are already allied with us, but few were interested. One day, though, it is my hope that not only supernatural children from Canada but also all around the world can attend. It's why I had such large dormitories built and left room to expand.

At five o'clock, Seb shows up.

"Are you ready to go?" he asks me, checking Alaric's face and then mine for any lingering signs of tension.

"Yup. Alaric said he's going to give us a ride," I reply, grabbing my bag and turning toward the driveway.

"No need. We're going to teleport." What? I don't want to teleport. What if I get lost somewhere in the middle of nowhere?

The shock must show on my face because Sebastyn bursts out laughing. "Oh, my mother...Are you scared? Big bad wolf. Afraid of a little teleport," he taunts between his laughter.

"Of course, I am! I'm a shifter, not a witch. We're not meant to do magic. What if you drop me somewhere, and I can't find my way back?" I know I'm being irrational, Seb's never done anything that would put me in actual danger, but I'm not sure I want to teleport anywhere. I mean, what's wrong with just driving?

"It's perfectly safe. I promise," Seb states, a lithe, tattooed hand over his heart.

"Yeah, like you promised that if I stuck my tongue to that pole, you would help me get it off in fifth grade? Or like the time that you promised it was just a chocolate shake, and it turned out to have Ex-Lax in it? Or is it like the time you promised not to tell anyone about the Ex-Lax thing and then announced it on Christmas morning? Is it like any of those promises? Because forgive me if I don't trust your promises anymore." By the time I'm finished, everyone is red in the face, dying with laughter.

"Come on, Darren. We were kids for all of those things. We've grown up now. Of course, you can trust me," Seb says, trying to convince me.

"The Ex-Lax thing was just last Christmas!" I half shout at him, which just causes more chuckles to break out. I'll admit, thinking about all the crazy stuff he pulled on me is quite comical, but it doesn't make me want to teleport with him. Not one bit.

"This is different, and you know it. I've never pranked you when it was important like this." He's right, he hasn't. Even so, how do I know something won't accidentally happen?

I'm still standing with my bag in my hand, staring Seb down, when he walks toward me, grabs my hand, and teleports us. Before I know what's happening, we arrive in the men's bathroom at the airport.

"See, that wasn't so bad, was it?" he asks.

Ugh. I feel like shit. "Why do I feel like puking?" I ask with a groan.

"It will pass in a minute. It happens to everyone the first time they teleport." He's right. It passes about a minute later, but it doesn't stop me from punching him in the arm.

"That's for not warning me," I say, then punch him in the arm again.

"What was that one for?" he asks, looking wounded.

"That was for not letting me say goodbye." I pick my bag up off the floor where I dropped it when we landed and stride out of the bathroom to find our gate.

As we are waiting in line to go through customs, the last of the nausea wears off.

"Why didn't we just teleport all the way to Halifax? I mean, if you were going to make me do it anyway?" I lower my voice to ask the question, but Sebastyn doesn't worry about who may overhear when he answers.

"Well, it's tricky. First, I've never been to Halifax. I am pretty damn good, but I still can't go somewhere that I haven't physically been before. Apparently, that takes years of practice. Even if I could, it is still too far for me. It's the same reason I couldn't just zap myself home when Skar went missing. I've been home plenty of times, but Egypt is a hell of a long way away."

The woman behind us in line coughs an accusation and covers her son's ears. He appears to be about five, and she seems more taken aback by the use of profanity than anything Seb actually said.

We both shrug and are silent as we pass through the metal detectors. On the other side, he begins again.

"Think of it like a muscle. You have to work out to build the muscle up. The more I teleport, the less it drains me, and the more I can do."

I know he's kind of bragging, but I guess it makes sense. It's like shifting. In the beginning, the shift is slow and painful, but the more you shift, the faster and less painful it becomes.

By the time we go through customs and find the right gate, our plane is already boarding. Four hours from now, we'll be in Halifax. Four hours from now, the real search begins. I just hope my gut is right.

I know that this is my mission, but I hope it doesn't get us killed.

Chapter Three

Sophia

It feels like I've only just fallen asleep when I wake up, startled and in a pool of sweat, with the overwhelming feeling that something or someone is coming. I don't know what, but something big is going to happen.

The strange dream that woke me hovers at the edges of my memory, a series of images that I search for an explanation for the pounding in my chest. I was flying high with another phoenix and talking with a black wolf. I have never flown, never even seen myself as a phoenix. The wolf, a mystery with eyes so intelligent that he must have been a shifter, was no danger to me.

Whatever else lived in that dream slips away like water between my fingers. It almost felt like a premonition. I look over at the small clock in my minuscule room and see it is just after four. Ugh, I've only been in bed for five hours, and I don't know if I'll be able to go back to sleep now. My stomach is doing flips like it's in the Olympics, and my hands are itching to move, to do something. This anxious rush to move, to work, to do anything has been steadily getting worse since the moment Devin told me that he plans on letting the mages have their way and use me to produce phoenix children. A shudder flows through me at the thought of any of those men touching me. I wince away from the image of rough, disgusting hands that have already taken too many liberties.

No way. Not going to happen.

My gut is telling me that something big is going to happen soon. I have to hope it's something good because I don't know how my life could get any worse at this point. Although my first thought is that it has something to do with Devin's big revelation last night, for some reason, that doesn't seem true. No, this is something else. Or maybe it's telling me that I need to do something. It is not comforting to have a dream warn me that this is a defining time in my life. Stay and become a slave for the rest of my life, ensuring that any children I have live the same way, or leave and chance both mine and Samara's lives.

It's almost the exact same feeling I got nine months ago when I woke up with flames dancing up my hands and arms. Luckily, there are no flames this time. Devin has never denied who I am, so I've known that I am a phoenix my entire life. Because of the tether he made for me when I was a baby, I never experienced any of my so-called powers until that night. I have practiced calm, controlled breathing to hide them when they make a rare appearance. Not because I'm afraid to hurt myself or someone else—that might actually work in my favor—but because I know Devin will throw me back in the cage the second he thinks they are out of control.

I don't know what's changed, but I know Devin has noticed a couple of times before I could smother the flames, and I'm worried. No cage yet, so that's a positive. Is that why he's changed his stance on me having children suddenly? If he's losing control over me, he'll just start over with my child?

My child. *My* daughter. The word enters my mind with little weight, but it immediately ignites my anger in a way I do not expect.

I do a mental face-palm. That's probably exactly what Devin is hoping for. If the tether fails, there is nothing holding me here any longer. He thinks Samara is dead, so he can't use her against me. A child, any child, is leverage to use against me. Ugh, why couldn't I have had a normal father, adoptive or not?

When I was little, every other child at school traded stories about the things they did with their parents. They would boast about camping trips or vacations, and I always felt left out because I never had a story to tell. I didn't understand why I didn't get to experience any of those things, so I started making them up, building this picture-perfect fantasy family in my head.

Every now and then, Devin would get a little too rough, and I'd have to stay home from school for a few days to let the bruises heal. Instead of telling the truth—because I learned my lesson about that early—or saying I was sick, I started making up stories about these grand adventures I had been on.

I knew we'd never actually go anywhere, so I pulled ideas from the things I saw on TV. I had to stay home, and Devin had to go to work or coven meetings all day. That meant I stayed home alone, watching old sitcoms and cartoons, daydreaming and selecting which plot would make a reasonable story for my classmates.

Samara was the only one who knew the truth, although, I've still never told her the whole truth of just how bad it got at times. She's extremely protective and loyal to those she cares about, and she would not have been able to simply stand by. As it was, I had to beg her not to do anything. The only way I could convince her was by explaining that it would make it worse for me. Even as a child, she knew how Devin treated me was wrong and wanted to fix it. Although she didn't like it, she understood why she couldn't do anything about it yet, so she helped me the only way she could—by being my friend.

There was this one time when Devin had taken me to the grocery store, and I really wanted this ice cream, so I started begging him for it. I knew I shouldn't have asked, but my only lessons in being a normal child came from my cartoons and my classmates. On TV and at school, I'd seen other kids harmlessly push their parents to get something they wanted.

I decided to try. He got so angry with me right there in the middle of the store that when he moved toward me, I flinched and backed away. Someone must've seen and called child protective services because, by the time we got home, there was someone waiting to talk to us.

She was such a nice lady, and she made me feel safe and comfortable. When she pulled me aside to talk, I wanted to tell her everything, and that's exactly what I did. I told her about the cage and the beatings. I even told her that he would keep me home from school because of the bruises. It appalled her. She was so angry on my behalf, and I thought for sure she was going to take me away and save me from him.

Instead, after she talked to Devin, she looked at me differently and explained how it wasn't nice to make up stories about a man who opened his home to me. She said if I were older, I could get in real trouble for doing it. I didn't understand. I wasn't lying, and I still don't know what Devin said or did to her. He's got the charisma of a sponge, so I assume magic was involved. After she left, I got a beating that I'll never forget.

He whipped me for hours that night, until my back was raw and bleeding, before throwing me back into my cage. He told me to remember that feeling the next time I even thought about telling someone. I was eight years old. That's the night I lost all hope. That night, I realized that no matter who I told about the abuse I suffered, nothing would ever be done. No one would be coming to save me. It took a week before the wounds healed enough that I could go back to school.

Tired of reminiscing over a past that I can't change, I decide that sleep is not going to be my friend tonight, so I might as well do something I enjoy. I lift the side of my mattress and pull out my sketchbook and pencil. I have to hide it so that Devin doesn't know there is actually something in my life that I enjoy because he'll take it away. He tells me it's for my own good. If I have nothing I enjoy, I'll start finding joy in smaller things like cleaning and cooking for him. I am prone to excess, and he's training me to temper myself. I think it's just because he's a controlling asshole.

I sit and draw for what seems like hours. By the time light from the sun is poking through the crack underneath the door, I have drawn the most beautiful landscape, with tall trees surrounding a large cabin overlooking a lake. There, taking a drink from the pebbled shore, is the most beautiful wolf I've ever seen. I never use colors when I draw, but I can tell that it's midnight black with beautiful ocean-blue eyes sparkling in the moonlight.

This happens a lot. When I start drawing, I have no clear idea what it will end up being. When I am done, I am astounded by the results. It's as if I am not really there while the image forms, so I can be surprised by the finished product. Nine months ago, around the same time my powers started manifesting, I started drawing the most beautiful phoenix, flying high above the trees with a pack of wolves running beneath her in the forest.

I don't know what it means or where these images come from. I've never even seen a wolf in person before, and the forest I keep drawing is the same each time and differs vastly from any that I've seen around here. I can't help but feel it's an actual place, and it's where I'm meant to be. Maybe that's the other phoenix Devin has mentioned, and maybe it means she's going to help me. If only I knew where she was, I'd say yes to Samara, and we'd head there. Maybe I should slip her one of the drawings to see if she can search for it on the internet. I rip one of the pages out, fold it up, tuck it within the pages, and make a mental note to bring it to her the next time I head out to the hunting cabin.

I slip my book and pencil back under my mattress and begin getting ready for the day. Devin will be here to unlock my door any time now so I can get him his breakfast, and he gets upset if I'm not ready when he does. He doesn't like to wait.

Right on cue, I hear Devin's footsteps getting closer to my door before the locks click and the door opens.

"Come on. We have a lot to do today, and I don't want to be late." What the hell does that mean? Usually, he just goes to work and leaves me here to clean and cook his dinner so it's ready when he gets home. *We* never have a lot to do.

"Of course, Father..." Do I ask him what we are going to be doing today? No. Well, not like that anyway. "Is there something, in particular, you wanted me to get done today?" I ask. Yes, that's better. That way, it doesn't sound like I'm expecting anything.

"Yes, actually. I will be taking you to the doctor today to get your annual checkup and ensure that you're fit to get pregnant. We can't have you giving us sickly children now, can we?"

I stop mid-stride on my way to the kitchen. What the fuck? Annual checkup? I haven't been to the doctor once in my entire life. Not even when I broke a bone. All the blood drains from my face. I knew he meant what he said last night about me giving them children, but I thought I would have time to plan an escape. If we're already going to the doctor, it means he's had this plan in motion for a lot longer than I expected.

I can't help the slip that comes out of my mouth. "But..." He spins around to face me, making me stop before I can even find my words. I know I shouldn't have said that. I know I'm going to pay for it.

"But what? You ungrateful little bitch," he snarls, grabbing me by the shoulders tightly and shaking me. "You're lucky that we've waited this long. You should have been married with ten kids by now. I could've left you to rot after your parents. Instead, I gave you a home, clothes, and food. Hell, I even let you go to school. What more do you want?" I think I would have rather been left to rot. I don't say anything, even though I want to. If I'm lucky, he'll only use the leather whip on me instead of his enchanted one.

He lets me go, and I head to the kitchen. I make quick work of his breakfast, and he tells me to go take a shower and get changed into nicer clothes before we go out. That's something to be grateful for, I guess. I can't remember the last time he let me have a shower. He even locks the bathroom door when he leaves so I can't do it while he's at work. I usually have to just use a washcloth and bucket, or the sink.

I allow the silent tears to slip down my face while I'm in the shower, allowing myself a moment of weakness. Once I'm clean, I slip out of the shower, wrapping the towel around my thin body, and stand in front of the mirror. I use my hand to wipe off some of the steam and take a long look at myself, noting all the protruding bones in my face. Although I'm not starved, I am only fed the bare minimum required to keep me alive. Alive and weak.

My eyes land on the silver tether around my neck and, for the first time in an extremely long time, I bring my hands up, running them along the braided metal surface, looking for a way to remove it. Finding none, I bring my hands back in front of my face and beg my flames to come to life. If I can make my fire come at will, I can escape, perhaps even remove the tether. Angry tears prick at the back of my eyes when they don't show, and I quickly finish getting ready, ensuring I leave the bathroom with no trace that I was ever here.

After dropping off my dirty clothes and towel in the hamper in my room, I head to the living room to find Devin. At the sight of his pale, wrinkled face, I flex my hands again, wondering if the flames will choose now to appear. What, if anything, would I do if they did? Would I apologize and hide them? Would I put my burning hands on his face and see how long it took for him to become ashes? Would I keep burning everything in front of me until I burned up myself?

Feeling hopeless but determined to find a way to escape, I follow him to his truck.

Chapter Four

Darren

The flight is long and uncomfortable. My wolf wants to be safe on the ground and won't let me rest while we are in the air, but the drive would've been excruciating. It would have been a full day of non-stop driving or two to three days if we stopped to sleep. A few hours trying to keep myself from shifting in a plane is much better than being stuck in a car for that long with Sebastyn and his questionable music choices.

By the time we land in Halifax, just after midnight, I can feel the jitters finally starting to subside. This is it. This is where I'm supposed to be.

"What now?" Seb asks, grabbing our bags from the baggage claim with a grunt. Sebastyn is strong, but he's not shifter strong. Why he insists on carrying our bags when he knows I'm physically stronger, I'll never know.

"Either grab a taxi or rent a car, then check into the hotel."

"Sounds good to me. Better to rent a car so we can get around ourselves." That's a good point. It's definitely going to be easier to find Sophia if we can drive ourselves wherever we need to go.

I step outside of the airport to look around while Seb goes to complete the paperwork to rent our car. It's a little chillier here than I expected but still beautiful. In the near distance, tall buildings, speckled with lights, illuminate the surrounding city. It looks amazing, but I can't help noticing how I can't see many stars. As beautiful as this is, it makes me miss my forest. I feel a sense of urgency starting to grow, replacing the jittery feeling. I know, for whatever reason, we need to find her and fast.

Seb pulls up in a black SUV, and I place my bag in the trunk before hopping into the front seat. "To the hotel, Seb. I think we need to pick up our pace a bit. I feel—I don't know—I feel like we need to find her fast."

"If you feel that way, we need to trust it. The Mother is giving you a sign. We'll go to the hotel and try one of the locator spells to see if this will be easy. Hell, we might even be on our way back home tonight," Seb tells me as he pulls away from the curb and drives to the hotel. I can hear the hope in his voice, and I feel a pang of guilt. He just got home after years of traveling only to have to leave again to help me. Maybe I should've just come by myself.

A churning in my gut begins, and I wince. Along with the urge to find her, I have a new feeling that this isn't going to be as easy as we originally hoped. Before meeting Phoebe, I used to brush off any gut feelings, but her freakishly accurate gut has convinced me to listen more to my own. The quicker we get started, though, the faster we will find her.

We picked an upscale hotel because Seb, who is used to traveling comfortably, said that I should celebrate finally leaving Ontario by experiencing traveling at its finest. I have to admit it's nice.

Walking into the lobby, it feels like I've been transported into a life of luxury. Even the white floors gleam without a speck of dirt on them.

"Are you sure this is the right place?" I ask, spinning around in a circle to take everything in.

Seb claps me on the back. "Yup. Nothing but the best for my best friend." I turn and scoff at him. He picked it for him. He knows this is way out of my comfort zone. I'm terrified as it is that I've tracked in mud on my shoes and am dirtying up this perfect floor. I turn and look back the way I came, not seeing any dirt, and breathe a sigh of relief. The second of inattention causes me to bump into a table, knocking something off.

Using my shifter reflexes, I spin and catch what is probably a very expensive vase and place it back on the table, looking around to make sure no one was watching. Thank Mother Moon, if anyone saw, they're now looking the other way. It would be just my luck to get us kicked out before we even check in.

I rush over to the reception area but freeze just before I get there, distracted by an unfamiliar scent in the air. Inhaling through my nose, I catch a slight whiff of mountain lion shifter. It's so faint that I wonder if it is even really there. As Seb seamlessly takes over checking us in, I walk around the lobby and put my nose to work searching out other shifters. I am careful to be mindful of my surroundings. I don't want to bump into anything else. If we could network with other supernaturals in the area, it could be invaluable to our search. Unfortunately, other than that slight scent, there's nothing. There's not even a hint of magic.

Well, that's just fucking weird.

"Anything?" Seb asks, walking toward me with the room keys. He already knows what I was doing. I am thankful to have a partner who knows me well enough that I don't have to explain anything.

I shake my head. "Nothing. Absolutely nothing. No shifters; no magic. There was a faint scent of a mountain lion, but it's faded so much it could've been days ago. This is weird."

Seb looks around as we make our way to the elevators, his dark, groomed eyebrows pinched in confusion. "That is weird.

Normally a big city like this would be overflowing with super-naturals."

"I know. You can't walk a block in Toronto without encountering one species or another. There's something else going on here."

Seb nods. "I'll reach out and see what I can find."

We stop the elevator at the eighth floor and find our room quickly. We reserved a regular room, but when Seb is finished, it is more like a two-bedroom apartment. He did his magical juju and basically recreated his small cabin back home. He then surprised me by teleporting back home a few times, bringing more and more things with him. No wonder he had been able to pack so light. By the time he's done, it looks almost as cluttered as his cabin. Everything he brought probably has a use, but I question the sheer amount. There's no way he needs that many books, beakers, or vials. Who needs four mortar and pestles? That's excessive.

I like things a little more organized than Seb does, but, somehow, he always seems to know where everything is. He calls it his organized mess. "Okay, I'm going to try a couple of different spells to see if we can find out where she is. Hopefully, we'll get lucky. If not, we might have to search the old fashion way," Seb tells me as he begins to pull out maps and ingredients.

I watch him over the next couple of hours as spell after spell comes up with nothing. It's as if she doesn't exist. "I don't understand why it's not working," I say, exasperated with the lack of results.

"She's probably cloaked by the mages that have her. I had hoped that Phoebe's blood might give us some luck, but we don't know if they are identical twins. If they are fraternal, we'll need something stronger.

"Either way, we aren't going to find anything tonight. Let's get some sleep and start fresh tomorrow," he says with a yawn.

It's three o'clock in the morning, so I should be tired. Instead,

I'm hopped up on adrenaline and worry. I need to know why, ever since I heard her name come out of Joe's mouth, I've had this pull toward her. What does she mean to me? So many thoughts are running through my brain that I don't know if I will be able to sleep. Maybe I should ask Seb for a sleeping potion.

Just as I'm about to ask, he hands me a cup.

"What's this?" I ask, taking a whiff of the cup. Mmm, it smells like blueberries.

"Sleep," he explains simply with another dramatic yawn before falling backward onto the bed. "Your fidgeting is going to keep me up, and you know how grumpy I get when I don't get enough sleep."

"Do you know why I'm feeling like this?" I ask him, allowing the vulnerability I'm feeling to surface. That's one of the things I love about our friendship. We may prank each other and goof around a lot, but we are both comfortable enough with each other to share our feelings without fear of judgment.

"I have some theories," he admits with a smile toward the ceiling.

"Like?" I probe. I've never been the anxious type. Okay, maybe I am a little anxious when it comes to the pack but never about anything personal.

"I think I'll keep them to myself. I don't want to influence anything." His eyes sparkle with mischief, and I wonder if I truly even want to know his theories. I know that Sebastyn loves me. Hell, we've been best friends since we were in diapers, but that doesn't mean he doesn't love torturing me every now and then. Since he's been gone so long, he probably feels that he has some catching up to do.

I drink down the cup in a single gulp. It tastes even better than it smells. Let's just hope that it does what it is supposed to.

"Thanks, Seb," I say before heading to bed. "I appreciate it, you know. Everything."

He acknowledges me with a growl before rolling over, and I try to make myself comfortable in my own bed.

I don't remember falling asleep, but I'm instantly overtaken by dreams.

I'm running through the forest in my wolf form, howling at the moon with my pack behind me. I can feel the wind through my fur. In front of me, Alaric is jumping over logs in a full sprint. Two phoenixes are flying above us. I skid to a stop, staring at the sky in awe. I can immediately recognize Phoebe because her coloring is darker than the other.

As if she senses me looking at her, the lighter phoenix screeches and comes to land in front of me, shifting into a beautiful woman with strawberry blonde hair and bright blue eyes. I can immediately see the resemblance to Phoebe, and I know instantly that this must be Sophia. Although their skin tone, hair, and eye color are contrasts, the shape of their faces and eyes are so similar that only a fool would not see the resemblance.

She walks up to my wolf, stroking a hand through my coarse fur. "Beautiful," she whispers, and I nudge her hand with my snout, encouraging her to continue.

She sits down on the ground, not caring or not noticing her naked-ness, but I do. I'm all but drooling at the sight of her milky white skin. I try to keep my gaze from her intimate parts. Dream or not, I don't want to give her a reason to leave.

"You know I've never even met a wolf shifter before," she says, still stroking my fur as I lay down with my head on her lap. "Unless you're not a wolf shifter? Are you a real wolf?" she questions, looking into my eyes as I raise my head.

I give her a wolfy nod and lick her hand. She giggles, and—goddess —if that's not the most beautiful sound I've ever heard.

"No licking," she scolds, but the smile on her face tells me she's not going to stick to it, so I slowly reach my tongue out once more and

lick at her hand. When she giggles, I do it again and again until she is rolling on the ground laughing while I lick her face. "Okay. Okay. I give up. You can lick me but only my hand," she concedes, and I nod moving back allowing her to get up.

I don't know why I don't shift so I can talk to her, but something deep inside me feels like I need to stay like this for now. I do not want to risk breaking whatever fragile dream I have fallen into. Her soft, blue eyes are dreamy, drawn toward the surrounding forest —my forest, I realize—as she absentmindedly strokes my head. When I see a tear streak down her face, I let out a whine and rub my head on her face. She wipes away the tear.

"I wish this was real. I wish that I was really here with you rather than locked away in my nightmare of waking life."

I let off a growl without thinking and smother it quickly, but she wraps her arms around me instead of being afraid.

"It's okay, big guy. I'm alive, and we still have our dreams," she says, although it's muffled against my back.

She sits back up and dries the rest of her tears.

"I'm Sophia, by the way. I probably should've told you my name before I started crying all over you."

I rub my head into her neck, nuzzling her, trying to convey that I don't mind. Again, I don't know why I don't just shift back., Then I could talk to her. But it is as if there is some unseen force stopping me from shifting.

"You know I had a really hard night last night. My father, Devin—" she stops and braces herself with a deep sigh, staring off into the distance. The way she says his name is venomous, and I suppress another growl. I want her to open up to me.

No, I need her to open up to me. I do not understand what is happening and do not feel entirely in control of myself, but—if we are really meeting in a dreamscape—I need any information she can give me to help me find her.

I do not know if we are in her dream, mine, or somewhere in between. *Wherever we are, I do not think she's aware that I am really here with her.*

She lets out a deep breath and continues.

"Devin had his friends over, and they were assholes." This time, I let the growl free. "They always are. They didn't hurt me. Not last night anyway." Those last words are so soft that I only hear them because I am a shifter. Despite my urge to rip out the throats of these assholes, I stay silent and let her continue. "They want me to have their babies. Pass me around—I guess—until they have enough phoenix babies to keep them happy."

I cannot hide my surprise and stand quickly on four paws, a whine escaping my mouth.

"I won't do it," she assures me. "I can't stay and let that happen. I won't give them children and allow them to raise and treat a baby— my baby—the way they treated me. But I don't know how. I have nowhere to go, and no one to help me."

She sniffs, and I reach inside myself to shift but nothing happens. Dammit. I need her to know I'm here. I need to tell her that I will help her and she has an entire family waiting for her.

She looks behind her, into the hazy distance, like a faraway voice has called her name.

"It's time for me to go now, my beautiful wolf," she says and places a soft kiss on my head. "Maybe I'll see you tonight in my dreams," she whispers as she begins to disappear. I sit and whine in the spot hoping, praying that she will return. After what feels like hours, I turn away, running in the direction the pack went, watching the sky for a sign of fire.

I wake with a start, the amazing dream beginning to fade from my mind. I quickly grab a pen and paper, writing as much of it down as I can. Maybe there's a clue in there to help me find her. I need to ask Sebastyn. He may know what is happening or at least how I can shift in my dreams.

I rush to his bedroom, throwing the door open and jumping on his bed. "Sebastyn," I prod, shaking his body awake.

"What? What is it?" he asks, sitting up quickly with a panicked look on his face.

"Is it possible for two people to meet in dreams?"

"What? You woke me up from *my* dream at," he turns and looks at the clock, "six in the morning to ask about dreamscaping? Are you crazy? We just went to bed!" he exclaims, laying back down and pulling the covers over his head.

"This is important," I say, pulling the covers off his head. "I need to know if it's possible."

"Yes, it's possible," he growls at me, but I don't stop there.

"How? Why? Can you control it?"

"Why all the questions?" he asks, opening his eyes and turning toward me.

"Because something happened..."

"In your dream?" he asks, sitting up quickly and leaning against the headboard, suddenly more interested. I nod. "Tell me."

And I do. I tell him everything I can remember from the moment I was running through the forest, to not being able to shift, to her talking to me. I have to look at the notes I made because the dream started to fade from my conscious memory the moment I woke up, but I think I remember most of it.

He throws the covers off and rushes to his workroom, and I follow hot on his heels. He rummages around before pulling out a book and something that looks like a crystal ball. Without explanation, he holds the ball up to my head and whispers, "*Capere somnia.*" Suddenly, it feels like there is pressure in my brain—an immediate and intense headache—but it fades as quickly as it came.

"What the fuck was that?" I question, but he shushes me.

"Look." He holds up the crystal ball and there, in front of me, is my dream. From start to finish. Her words are faint and hard to make out, but Sebastyn moves his hand in a circle around the ball, and they get louder.

He replays it three times, watching, listening, and making small notes on a pad of paper before turning to me. "This is very strange."

"What is?" I ask, both panicked and excited to hear what he has to say.

"Somehow the two of you are linked. You're right. This wasn't just a regular dream. This actually happened," he says, a mixture of shock and awe on his face.

"But if it was real, why couldn't I shift?"

"I'm not sure. Mother Moon has linked you, but she hasn't given you the ability to shift in that link. Or maybe something is blocking her influence? Tonight, I'm going to cast a spell to record your dream. We recorded this memory quickly, but there are still likely parts that slipped away too fast. If we want to save her…"

"Soon," I growl, remembering what she said. They want to force her to have their children.

He nods in agreement.

"If we want to save her soon, then we need all the help we can get."

Chapter Five

Sophia

We make our way to the doctor's office in the city and park in the underground garage. It's been a quiet drive. Neither of us say anything on the way. I've been too busy trying to remember the amazing dream I had and thinking of ways to make sure that I'm not fit to have children. I didn't come up with any ideas to fool the doctor, though, and each time I reach for the dream, it seems to slip further and further away. I can only remember the woods, unfamiliar and beautiful, and a wolf waiting patiently by a lake. I'm not sure what Devin's reason for being so quiet is, but it gives me an uneasy feeling in my gut.

"Sophia, you know the drill," he says, putting the car in park and turning to me. "You don't speak unless spoken to. You don't try to go anywhere I can't see you." He repeats this to me every time we leave the house—which is almost never. Still, it's not like I'm stupid. He really doesn't need to remind me what to do to avoid a beating when we get home.

"I know, Father," I reply. Satisfied with my answer, he gets out of the vehicle at the same time I do, ushering me into the building.

I am surprised to find the office's lobby completely empty except for the older lady working at the desk. All the doctor's offices on the TV have a bunch of people in the waiting area. This just feels off, and I keep looking around. Devin must notice because he turns to me.

"We took precautions to make sure you'd have some privacy here." A frown slips onto my face. With my inability to magically make my body seem unsuitable for pregnancy, I was hoping there would be at least one person here that would recognize I need help. But that's what I get for hoping again. A whole bunch of disappointment. It makes sense for Devin to have arranged for this though. If I were to make a scene with a bunch of humans around, he wouldn't be able to use his magic. No witnesses means that he doesn't have to worry about that.

Instead of replying, I just nod and take a seat. He goes up to the secretary and tells her we're here for our appointment before sitting down next to me. It's not long before an older man with salt and pepper hair comes out to greet us.

"Devin," he says with a big smile on his face, and they clasp hands. Great, just what I need. Even if I had thought of a way to fake my tests, he's obviously friends with Devin and would tell him if I got caught.

"Sabien," Devin replies and gestures to me. "This is Sophia." Sabien allows his gaze to roam up and down my body slowly. I suppress the shudder that is trying to travel through my body. This guy gives me the creeps. His eyes, dark and shining as they study me, wrinkle unnaturally with his too-bright smile. His attention makes me feel embarrassed and sick.

"Sophia." Even the way he says my name is creepy. It's like he's picturing bending me over and fucking me right here in the waiting room. Gross.

Devin clears his throat, and Sabien snaps out of whatever dirty fantasy he was imagining, clapping his hands together and gesturing toward the door.

"Just through here." I follow behind him into the exam room. Thankfully, Devin waits in the waiting room.

"Have a seat on the bed there. We just need to take your blood pressure, temperature, and a couple of vials of blood, then you can be on your way. Your father doesn't want a pelvic exam until you're given a clean bill of health otherwise."

Thank fuck I don't have to have a physical exam. There must be some higher power out there looking out for me. I wasn't worried about it before, but now that I've met him, I don't want the man near any part of my body—let alone my vagina.

It goes almost as quickly as he said it would, and, despite his obvious looks of lust, he doesn't try anything with me. He's probably scared of pissing Devin off. If I were him, I would be. Hell, what am I saying? I *am* terrified of pissing him off. Nothing like being whipped and thrown in a cage to ensure compliance.

"Everything looks wonderful," Sabien puts off reporting any of the findings to me until we rejoin Devin in the waiting room. "We just need to wait for the blood tests to come back. In my opinion, she should be fine to start trying as soon as next week."

He claps Devin on the back in a type of congratulations.

Next week? No way! I can't let that happen. It's time for me to finally agree with Samara and for the two of us to get out of here. We just need a plan. I'm even willing to let her use the money her parents left us if it means we can get away from here.

How am I going to get a hold of her? I told her to go lie low in the city for a few days, and I know I can't escape on my own. Maybe I can sneak and use the phone, but then I don't know her number. Or maybe I just leave her a note at the cabin and start walking. If I pack enough food and leave right when Devin leaves for work in the morning, it will give me a head start.

Lost in thought, I don't realize we're already home until Devin is opening the door for me. I slip out as if on autopilot but come to a stop when I see a long line of men waiting on the porch.

"What is this?" I ask, turning to look at Devin's smirking face.

"Applicants to father your baby, Sophia. Apparently, you're very desirable," Devin responds, obviously loving the amount of interest. If he wasn't already the coven's high priest, I'm sure this would increase his standing. As it is, I'm not sure what he's getting out of this aside from more power from any phoenixes I may produce.

I scan the men who are queued up so patiently to force themselves upon me. Most of them are familiar. Some are young—probably just turned eighteen—and the oldest man has more salt than pepper in his hair.

"But surely…" I begin, but Devin turns to me with a scowl.

"You will keep your mouth shut. Go inside and prepare something for our guests."

I want to respond, but the look in his eyes gives me pause. I know what will happen if I fight this, and it will be nothing good.

Wordlessly, I walk up the porch steps and inside the house, feeling the disgusting gazes of the men roaming my body. Even the men that could be classified as handsome make my body recoil.

I spend the rest of the day in the kitchen, baking cookies, making dinner, and serving up coffee. Devin brought me in to meet each man as if hoping that one of them would catch my eye. As if that would ever happen. As if he would even care.

As the last one leaves, I turn to Devin. He brought me in to meet them. Maybe that means I can offer him an opinion without punishment.

"I don't want to take any of those men as a mate," I plead with him.

He laughs, clutching his stomach. "Oh, Sophia. You are not fit to be their mate. You are to birth their children—not be their mate. Most of them already have a mate at home."

"But then, why?" I question, unable to hide my shock.

He walks over to me and grips my shoulders. "It's very simple. Being the father to the next generation of phoenixes will put them in a very powerful position. You're not fit to be anyone's mate."

With that, he walks away, still laughing while I stand rooted to my spot. I don't know whether to take his words as a blessing or a curse. If my attempt at escaping fails, at least I won't be tied to someone for the rest of my life. On the other hand, I'll be passed around like a toy. I didn't allow the beatings to break me. Hell, I didn't even allow being put in that cage to break me. But this...

I suppress a sob, clutching my chest and rushing to my room.

This will break me.

What must be hours later, I hear Devin lock the door of my room from the outside. For the first time since I woke up, I actually feel safe. Even though I can't get out, I know none of those men can get in either—not without Devin's permission. Until the test results come back, I know that's not going to happen.

I should be grateful that they're even waiting for the test results to come back before breeding me. There are more complications with interspecies children. Miscarriages happen, but the mothers can be lost too. They can't risk losing me to childbirth before they have my replacement here in chains.

As my tears dry up, my body relaxes. I try to calm myself by conjuring the scene from my dream the night before. The forest—unfamiliar trees and water in a hazy, golden glow—and the wolf drinking by the lake. I can almost smell the trees, their scent sharper and cleaner than the ones outside my window now. As I let the images develop, I feel myself falling into a deep sleep. Didn't I pet that wolf? I remember his fur—impossibly soft and warm on my bare skin. Instantly, I'm pulled into the same dream as the night before.

Once again, I'm flying high above the trees with another phoenix soaring beside me. I can't see my own form, but hers is beautiful. Deep, crimson flames lick up her body. She soars above the trees, weaving back and forth in a playful dance before shooting straight down to the ground, landing in front of a black wolf. For a moment, a pang of jealousy flows through me at the thought of it being my wolf, but the small red patch of fur on his chest shows me it's not. I search the forest for my wolf, finding him quickly at the edge of the same lake I drew in my sketchbook. I land beside him and feel my flames settle and extinguish.

"There you are, my beautiful wolf," I whisper, and he rushes over to me, licking my hand and pushing me down on the ground gently. He nuzzles my face with a whine. "I missed you too," I coo, wrapping my arms around his neck and pulling him into me.

We lay there on the ground, my arms wrapped around his neck for what feels like forever before I push him back and sit up, turning to face the most beautiful lake. It is perfectly calm, with the moonlight shining down on it. There's no place I'd rather be. My wolf comes and sits beside me, and I wrap my arm around him, leaning against him.

"You know, meeting you in these dreams almost makes the hell I'm living during the day worth it." He growls softly at my words as if he's worried it will scare me, but it doesn't. The rumble of his chest only makes me feel safe, like nothing can touch me when he's near. "I wish you could talk to me," I tell him, and he whines. "I've never felt this safe before. Here with you beside me, I feel like I can take on the world."

He nuzzles me again, and I take that as agreement.

I let out a soft sigh. "There were interviews today with men who want to be the father of my children, but, like with everything in my life, I get no say. One of them was old enough to be my grandfather, if you can imagine." He growls at that, and I giggle. "I know, right? Gross. But I'm not going to let that happen. I'm going to escape this place or die trying."

He turns toward me with a menacing growl, but I know it's not directed at me. I don't know how I know that, but I do.

"Silly wolf. I don't plan on dying, but I would rather that than the alternative." He swipes his tongue up my cheek, and I melt back into his side. "I wish you were real. That you could somehow find me and help me escape this place. But my life isn't a fairy tale. There's no prince charming coming to save me. I need to save myself."

He lays down next to me, placing his head on my leg, careful not to get too close to my exposed center. How I wish he could shift and become a man so I could talk with him, hear his voice, look into his beautiful blue eyes and what I'm sure is a handsome face.

As if my wish is heard, his wolf body slowly begins to fade away and is replaced by the most handsome man I've ever seen. Just like his wolf, his eyes are the brightest blue. My eyes roam his face, making notes, cementing it in my memory. A day's worth of stubble is on his chin and cheeks; his thick black hair matches the color of his wolf and is styled perfectly with the top a little longer than the sides. I move my eyes downward, noting the tattoos that cover his muscular upper body. I itch to peak even lower but stop myself and bring my eyes back to his.

"Sophia," he whispers, and my body shudders at the huskiness of his voice.

I reach up and place my hand on his cheek, and he leans into it, closing his eyes. Feeling brave, I lean forward and place my lips on his. They're soft and instantly move to meet mine in a passionate kiss. Sparks fly between the two of us, and he pulls me into his lap, wrapping his arms around me. I moan as wetness begins to slip out of me, and I pull back in embarrassment.

"I'm Darren," he says in a whisper, leaning his forehead against mine.

My embarrassment is forgotten as the tingles spread throughout my body.

"Darren," I respond.

He pulls his face back, searching my eyes. "Where are you?"

"I'm right here. What do you mean?"

"No, where are you in the real world?" he asks with an urgency that makes my brows furrow in confusion.

"Why? This is just a dream."

He shakes his head. "No. It isn't. I'm real; you're real, but we can only meet in our dreams. The goddess has linked us. I can find you and keep you safe."

I scramble back off his lap, covering my exposed body with my hands. "Is this some kind of trick? This isn't funny."

Devin has done it before, placed dreams in my head to make me feel safe and then laughed maniacally when he transformed them into nightmares.

He stands up, walking toward me with his hands out, but I step back.

"I promise, Sophia. This is real. Devin has nothing to do with this. Just let me help you." The vulnerability in his voice gives me pause, and he takes my hands in his. "Please. Just tell me where you are."

Something in his eyes makes me feel compelled to answer. "Halifax, Nova Scotia."

"I know that. I am too. I came to find you."

"But why?" I ask.

"Because your sister is my brother's mate. Because the goddess commanded me to. Because I needed to."

"But I don't have a sister," I tell him, even more confused than before.

"You do, and you have two nephews and a niece. Her name is Phoebe, and she is searching for you," he says, and I step back once again.

"I have a family?" I ask in a whisper.

He nods and pulls me into an embrace. "You do, and we will stop at nothing to find you."

"I'm..." I begin to tell him where I am, but I can feel myself waking up.

"No, Sophia. Don't go," he pleads, trying to grab my already fading body.

"Please," he begs, falling on his knees as I fade further.

I wake with tears in my eyes.

I have a family, and they're searching for me.

Just like the day before, the dream unravels as soon as I try to look at it again. There's someone—my wolf—he's waiting for me. My wolf is by the lake.

The images stick with me best, and I recall the drawing from the day before. I am flying over unfamiliar trees, and I land to greet my beautiful wolf. If I can get to that lake, I will be safe.

In mere moments, I am left with nothing but the feelings. I am heartbroken but hopeful. I know there is something important that is just out of my memory's reach.

The locks on my door jiggle, telling me that Devin is letting me out. My dream is thrown to the back corner of my mind as I jump up, quickly throwing on my clothes so that I'm dressed and ready when the door opens.

"Come, Sophia. We have a full day of interviews scheduled. You need to get to work."

With that, my day of hell begins once again. I can't wait for him to go back to work so I can check and see if Samara is back at the cabin. We need to leave. The more men he parades through here, the more urgent the feeling in my gut becomes. Goddess, I hope she's there.

Chapter Six

Darren

"Well, that was interesting," Seb says to me as I wake up from my dream of Sophia.

"But it wasn't enough. She was going to tell me where she is," I growl, hopping out of bed and throwing on some clothes.

"At least we know we're in the right place," Seb supplies.

"Yeah. Did you miss the part where she's going to escape or die trying?"

He nods sullenly. "I caught that, yeah. It just means we need to find her."

"Damn right we do," I say with a growl, heading to the small kitchenette in our room and pouring myself a cup of coffee before waking over to the worktable to look at the maps. Seb must have started the coffee and the search while I was sleeping.

"She's been in Halifax since she was a kid, so I figure we start with the schools," he says, sipping from his own steaming cup.

"You start with the elementary schools, and I'll work on the high schools," I tell him, pulling up a list of nearby elementary schools on my phone. "Holy shit," I whisper when I see the sheer number of results. This is going to take forever. That is if they even give us the information.

"This is going to be a long day. I'm ordering breakfast," Sebastyn says, sitting down at the desk with his open laptop.

I dial the number for the Halifax Regional Centre for Education, the school board for the public schools of Halifax, hoping that maybe I will only have to call one number.

"Thank you for calling the Halifax Regional Centre for Education; how may I direct your call?" The woman's voice is polite and practiced.

"Yeah. Hi. I'm hoping you can help me. I'm looking for my sister—information about my sister. We were both adopted as babies, and our adoption papers were just given to me, but all I have is her name." I begin pacing as I tell the story that we came up with on the flight over.

"I'm sorry, but I don't think I can give you that information over the phone," she begins, but I interrupt her.

"Please. I know her first name and date of birth. I've been looking for her since I was a teenager, but the adoption was just unsealed this year."

I hear her sigh on the other end of the phone. "I'm sorry. I can't give out any personal information on past or present students." She says this loudly but then lowers her voice and continues. "But they may be more helpful if you can call the school directly."

I groan. That's what I wanted to avoid. It is going to take too long if I don't have a clue where to start. "Is there any way you can send me a list of the schools?"

"The schools and phone numbers are all listed on the website. I'm sorry I couldn't be more help, and I truly hope that you find your sister."

"Thank you," I whisper before hanging up.

"Any luck?" Seb asks hopefully.

"No. They won't give me any information over the phone. She

didn't even ask for her name," I groan. "But she said the individual schools may be more helpful. So, I guess that's what we're doing today."

The rest of the day is a wash. I spend a maddening amount of time listening to hold music and suspicious questions from every school's office staff. Every school searches their records without finding anything about a girl named Sophia with a February 29 birthdate. When each secretary finally agreed to do the search, I let hope flutter in my chest. It didn't take long, though, for that hope to shrink. I leave my number with each office and ask them to let me know if anything turns up, but I know my quest will get lost in the everyday work of their lives.

"This is useless," I growl.

"I struck out too. You don't think they have a supernatural school here, do you?" Seb asks, and, not for the first time today, I get a glimmer of hope. Maybe this time it won't end in disaster.

"It's a big city," I shrug. "Do you have any way to find out?"

"I will email a few contacts to see if I can," Seb says, immediately logging into the Supernatural Online Network and sending a broadcast message looking for information. "It's probably going to take a while. Maybe we should go out for dinner."

"I can't. I need to keep looking for her," I tell him and begin searching online for high school graduation pictures from Halifax for someone fitting Sophia's description. It would be almost too simple if she had any type of social media, but I have no doubt that Devin has prohibited that. I'd be surprised if she even has a phone. I still check, scrolling through every Sophia in Halifax without finding her picture anywhere.

"Darren. You need to eat. If you want, we can bring the laptop, but I think we both need to get out of this room for a few minutes," Seb pleads with me, and I nod. Maybe I could use some fresh air.

Just as we're leaving the hotel, my phone rings. Hope blossoms in my chest but fades when I see Phoebe's name on the screen.

"Hey, Pheebs," I say.

"How's it going? Any luck yet?" She sounds just as stressed as I am.

I sigh. "None yet. But we're not giving up."

"Oh. Okay," she says sadly, and the urge to comfort her is strong.

"Sebastyn had an idea that maybe they have a school for super-naturals here too, so we're looking into that right now," I tell her, letting any hope I feel come through my voice.

"That would make sense. Sarah told me mages don't particularly like to have their children in the same school as humans, but they also don't like to have them around other supes either, so I'm not sure if that will work. My guess is if they do have a school for their children, it will be only for mages, and you won't be able to find it."

Sarah. I didn't even think of her. She was raised as a mage. Surely, she could know someone from the coven here.

"Do you think Sarah knows any of the mages here?" I ask, and I hear her sigh over the phone and know I'm not going to like the answer.

"I asked her. She said Joe's uncle is the high priest of the mages there, but she said she only met him once and has no idea how to contact him. Some guy named Devin."

I can't suppress the growl that slips out. Devin. That's the asshole that Sophia mentioned. If he's any relation to Joe, I know he's bad news. Shit.

"Does she have a last name for Devin?" I ask hopefully.

"I'll check back with her," Phoebe sighs, "The families weren't close, but she said she'd look through some papers and try to find something."

"It was a long shot. Thanks anyway, Pheebs," I say sadly.

"I'm going to reach out to some of the mage wives in Morpeth to see if I can get any information," she says, and I hear Alaric growl loudly in the background.

"I don't think you are," I chuckle.

"Pssh. As if he can tell me what I can and can't do," she responds, and I can practically see her rolling her eyes.

"No, you will not," my brother growls. "We have a rare moment of peace where someone is not trying to kill you or kidnap our children. You will not be reaching out to anyone in that goddessforsaken coven."

I sigh. "He's right, Pheebs. It's too dangerous."

I hear the difference as she puts the phone on speaker. "You two are ganging up on me, and it's not fair."

"No, we're not. We just want to keep you and the kids safe," I tell her, and Alaric grunts in agreement.

"But what about Sophia? Who's going to keep her safe? Who knows what they're doing to her. We can protect the kids, but who's going to protect her?" I hear the sobs in her voice and know that she's crying.

"Love. Trust in Darren and Sebastyn. They'll find her," Alaric says, trying to soothe his mate.

"Exactly. We're not going to give up. I promise. You gotta have some faith. We've only been at it for a day."

She sniffs. "Okay. For now. Be safe, Darren, and bring my sister home."

"I will. Talk to you soon." I go to hang up, but my brother grabs the phone.

"Darren?" I pull the phone back to my ear.

"Yeah?"

"Are you okay?" he asks, and a small smile graces my lips.

"I'm frustrated at the lack of results, but if you are asking if I am safe, yeah, I am."

"If you need anything..." he begins, and I roll my eyes.

"Yeah. Yeah. I know."

"I love you, little brother. I just want you safe," he says, ever the alpha, worried about his family.

"That's how Phoebe feels too. Sophia is her little sister. You need to remember that."

"I know. That's the only reason you're there with no back up."

"The pack deserves this break. We can't ask them to fight battle after battle, especially when we don't know when the next one will be."

He sighs once again. "I know that too. But you should know there's been a lot of people offering to come and help."

"You said no, right?" I ask. As much as I would love for more boots on the ground, there's no point until we know what we're up against.

"Of course. Seb explained there's a lack of shifters of any kind around there. So, I know a bunch of wolves coming to town would raise some flags."

I blow out a breath I didn't realize I was holding. "Thank you. I promise I'll keep you guys updated."

"Sounds good. Goodnight, Darren."

"Night, Alaric," I say before hanging up.

I join Sebastyn in the elevator, and we make our way back down to the lobby. Once again, there is a faint scent of mountain lion, but it fades so quickly I question if it was even really there to begin with. So weird.

"Is Phoebe upset?" he asks.

I nod. "Yeah. But I told her we're not giving up."

He puts his hand on my shoulder. "We're not. We'll find her." The confidence in his voice almost makes me believe him. Almost. But that's not something we can know for sure.

We eat dinner while doing more searches for women fitting Sophia's description. There has to be a picture of her somewhere. Everything is digital now. If I had a picture of her, perhaps I could show it to the schools to see if they recognize her. Maybe Devin changed her birth date, and that's the problem. I know he didn't change her name because that's what she introduced herself to me as.

With office hours over, we can't make any more calls, but that doesn't stop us from reaching out to as many contacts as we can to try and find any information. I call all the east coast alphas and betas that I have in my contact list, but none of them know any packs in the Halifax region. It seems to be a strange blind spot for everyone—almost like there are no supernaturals in this area at all.

"Seb, can I get another of those sleep potions? I'm too wired to sleep but want to try connecting with her again." I glance at the clock and see that it's just before eleven. I hope she goes to bed early and will be waiting for me.

"Comin' right up," he says, quickly getting to work making the potion before walking over and handing me a cup.

"Thanks," I say, quickly downing the blueberry-flavored drink. I have enough time to make my way to the bed and strip out of my clothes before I fall into a deep sleep.

Like every night for the past three nights, I find myself in the forest outside the Westwood pack land on a run with my pack. I glance around, recognizing the pine, maple, oak, and spruces that live within our forest. It even smells like home. Unlike before, only Phoebe is flying overhead, and my heart sinks a little. Where is she? An invisible force pulls me toward the lake, and I leisurely make my way there, stopping briefly to shift and throw on some clothes from one of the stashes randomly placed throughout the forest. I know it is there in the real world, but I am glad to see it present in the dreamscape as well. As I break through the trees, I catch sight of strawberry blonde hair blowing in the wind and break into a sprint. "Sophia!" I exclaim, and she turns toward me. She's fully clothed this time in a simple blue dress. If it's possible, she's even more beautiful tonight.

"Darren!" she shouts, running toward me. I catch her in my arms, pulling her close, placing my head in the crook of her neck, and inhaling hard. She smells the same as usual, like freshly cut grass with a hint of honey.

I push her back so that I can look into her eyes.

"Where are you?" I ask again.

This time there is no hesitation. "We don't have an address since the road doesn't show up on any map, but we are about fifteen minutes outside of Halifax, surrounded by forest. If I had a map, I could show you the area."

"That could be anywhere," I say, feeling defeated.

"Don't worry. I'm leaving tomorrow afternoon. I'll find you."

"But..." I go to protest, but she merges her lips with mine, wrapping her arms around my neck. I slip my tongue through her lips, and she breathes out a moan. Her tongue pushes back to do a seductive dance with mine. I gently pick her up, wrapping her legs around my waist before lowering us both to the ground.

Her hands roam my bare back and chest, clutching at me, as if she is unable to get close enough. As she grinds her hips into me, I can sense her excitement, her arousal. My wolf is demanding that I take her here and now. Reluctantly, I pull back, grateful that I was able to find clothes before meeting her. I am not sure my restraint could hold out otherwise.

"How will you find me?" I ask, but she places her fingers on my lips.

"Shh. No more talking. Find the forest, and I'll meet you there. I trust in the goddess. She linked us for a reason," she says, before pulling my mouth back down to hers. We stay like that, kissing and fondling, but never more, for a blissful while.

She's the first to pull back. "Can we play a game?"

"What kind of game?" I ask with a smirk.

"I was hoping you'd have an idea..." she says sheepishly.

"When I was little, I used to play this game with new people I met

*to see if we would get along. We take turns. I'll ask something, and
we both say our answers."*

*"Okay." She nods, clearly familiar with the concept. She taps her
chin thoughtfully with one thin, perfect finger. "What's your
favorite food?"*

I blurt out, "Lasagna."

While she says, "Spaghetti."

We both chuckle. "Well, they're both pastas," she giggles.

*"My turn," I begin, tapping my finger on my chin. "Favorite
drink?"*

*This time we both say, "Coffee," and we instantly fall into a fit of
giggles.*

*"That says it all. We're meant to be together..." She says with confi-
dence, quickly putting her hand on her mouth as if she didn't mean
to say that.*

*I clasp her hand in mine. "I feel the same way." We don't say
anything else, mouths crashing together and hands roaming each
other's bodies. We stay that way until I feel the tug, telling me it's
time to go.*

*"I need to go," I tell her, sadness lacing my words. "I wish I could
stay here with you forever."*

"Me too. But soon we'll be together in real life, right?" I nod.

*"I won't give up until we are," I place one last ghostly kiss on her
lips.*

"Me either," she whispers, but I'm already fading away.

Damn it.

Why do I have to wake up?

"That was a lot more information than last time," Sebastyn
says as my eyes begin to flutter open.

"You know that's really creepy," I tell him, pulling the covers
off and heading to the bathroom.

"What is? Me watching your dream while you sleep?" he asks,

and I return to the doorway to nod with the toothbrush hanging out of my mouth.

I spit out the toothpaste. "Yes, that."

He waves a hand in the air. "What's a little dream spying amongst friends?"

I finish rinsing my mouth. "Whatever. We need to figure out what forest she was talking about."

"Already on it. I had plenty of time to do a cursory search while you two were...getting to know each other." He motions toward the open laptop and the map pulled up there. "There are two spots that show nothing on satellites fifteen minutes outside of town surrounded by forests. We can try one and hope for the best..." he begins, but I cut him off.

"No, we split up. You go to one, and I'll go to the other," I tell him adamantly.

"I don't think that's a good idea," he says, coming to stand in the doorway of the bathroom. "We shouldn't be splitting up, especially if the mages realize she's gone and are after her."

"I understand what you're saying, but I can't chance it," I say, beginning to pace. "What if we go to one and it's the other?" I mumble more to myself than to Sebastyn who is staying silent during my momentary freak out. I shake my head. "No. We need to split up. She could be at one while we're at the other."

He looks in my eyes and must see the determination there and sighs. "Fine. But we meet back here at five o'clock whether we find her or not."

We quickly grab breakfast before heading on our way. We make a plan to drop Sebastyn off at his forest before I make my way to mine. With his teleportation, he doesn't need the car. He can have both him and Sophia back at the hotel with no issues.

Even though I am desperate to find her, I'd be happy to give him the honor if it means she is safe as soon as possible.

Chapter Seven

Sophia

Each morning, I wake up in a great mood with no idea why other than an inkling that something big is happening. Today, though, is special. Not "special" meaning exciting but "special" meaning today is going to be important. The results of my tests are supposed to be in today, and Devin will get approval to start pimping me out to the mages.

Samara and I have talked about sex in the past, and I know she's met and "hooked up" with men before, but I have been so sheltered that the only person I've been with sexually is myself. I can't imagine my first time being gentle with whomever Devin gives me to, and I've always pictured my first time being with someone I truly care about.

I work silently in the kitchen, hoping and praying that Devin leaves for work soon. My small bag is already packed, and I'm itching to go. I need to get out of here. I glance at the clock and my heart drops. It's ten, already after the time he normally leaves for work. If he doesn't leave the house, I'll have no chance of getting out, and that's not an option. I rummage through the cupboards, thinking of possibilities.

Could I use something to poison him or to put him to sleep that will act quickly enough that I won't get caught? Ugh. I really wish I had access to the internet. I pull out different herbs and spices, smelling each as I do, as if I would be able to recognize a poison by smell. I've thought about this so many times but never had the courage to act upon it, now though, I'm not sure I have a choice. I open up the cupboard under the sink, bleach, Lysol, and Windex can all be deadly, but it would be impossible to mask the smells. The chance of me getting enough in him to cause any kind of damage is minimal. I pull out the muffin trays, flour, baking powder, and sugar and begin baking a large batch of chocolate chip muffins to give me an excuse for being in the kitchen while I continue my search.

I've just about given up when I hear Devin on the phone with someone. I glance at the clock, realizing that I've wasted almost two hours baking and searching for some miracle herb, spice, or chemical that doesn't seem to exist.

"Sophia, I have to run into the city to meet with Sabien. Stay in the house and don't leave. I'll be back in a couple of hours." His words sound almost giddy before he rushes out the door. That's weird. I wonder why he has to go in person to get the results—at least that's what I'm assuming he's meeting with Sabien for. Is there something wrong with me after all?

You know what? It doesn't matter. He's gone, and I can go to the cabin to meet Samara. I hope she's there. We need to leave today.

I sneak to the window, and I watch as Devin's car pulls out of the driveway, then I wait another twenty minutes to make sure that he's really gone before grabbing my bag and rushing out the back door toward the cabin.

My heartbeat is in my throat, as I try to reason myself into something like calm. He can't have even made it to the doctor's office yet. He'll need time to get there, meet with that asshole doctor, and return. As long as Samara is there and ready to go, we will have a head start.

Samara, please be there, please be there. I keep chanting that plea in my head for the whole fifteen-minute jog there.

"Thank Mother Moon," I hear Samara say when she sees me. She meets me in the overgrown lawn, catching me in her muscled arms.

"We need to leave," we both say at the same time, and she gives me a puzzled look.

"They're going to make me have their babies. They want another phoenix to tether," the words rush out of my mouth.

"They're what?" she roars, and I can hear her lion coming out in her voice.

"I'm not going to have their babies. I'm finally ready to go. Let's go and never come back," I say, pulling her arm toward the edge of the woods closest to the road.

"I already got a car and a place for us to go. If we drive all night, we'll get there tomorrow. I have a friend who's willing to help us."

I stop in my tracks and turn to look at her with concern. When did she meet this mystery friend who is supposedly going to be helping us? What if it's a trap?

"It will be fine, trust me. I know you don't trust anyone, but, for some reason, I trust him. Even my lion trusts him, and that's saying something," she says, looking into my eyes. I can see the honesty in them.

I do trust her judgement, and I trust her lion even more. If she's on board with this, I'm going to have to be too. After Samara's pride was slaughtered, her lion doesn't trust easily. It's made Samara's sex life difficult to say the least. Especially being as dominant as she is, allowing herself to be in a vulnerable position with someone else has caused problems in the past. I could see the haunted look on her face the first time it happened, and I knew without her telling me that, whatever it was, was bad. I've never pressured her to talk about it, though I can't help but be curious exactly what happened...Did she hurt someone? Or worse...

"Okay, let's go," I say, and we're off again.

It doesn't take long before we break through the trees and find her waiting car. I can see that she's packed it up with clothes and food for our journey. I pause briefly, feeling inexplicably like I have forgotten something important. I am leaving something behind, aren't I? I shake it off, turning back toward the car.

"How did you know I was going to come with you?" I ask, genuinely curious. I've said no every time she's asked. Why did she think this time would be different?

"I wasn't planning on giving you the option to say no this time," she says in complete honesty. She was going to kidnap me. Oh, my goddess. I recognize the very serious look on her face. Before I can stop myself, I break out in laughter.

"You were going to kidnap me?" I say between chuckles. This is too funny and sweet. She didn't even know what was going on, but she obviously knew that I needed to go. That's what I call divine intervention. She nods, admitting she was planning an actual kidnapping before she joins in with my laughter.

"Okay, where are we going?" I ask when we finally settle.

"Ontario," she says, starting the car with the press on a button. Its semi-electric engine hums to life.

"Why Ontario?"

"Because I met a Fae online about a year ago. I have been talking to him whenever I stay in the city on the secure Supernatural Online Network I told you about, and he offered us protection."

Wow, a Fae? I've heard they can't lie. If he's offered to help us, he must be telling the truth. Or maybe that's just something they tell people to make it seem like they're trustworthy. Either way, I am not sure I really have a choice here.

"Okay. If you trust him, then I will too, because I trust your judgment but also because I don't think we have any other choice. I guess we'll go get his help." I turn on the music for our long drive.

I turn back toward the forest, once more feeling that I forgot something. Samara is still driving slowly, the unpaved road below us passable but uneven. I pull my bag up from between my legs and rummage through it. Clothes, toothbrush, sketchbook. Nope, I have everything. Weird. Why am I feeling this way?

"Do you ever get the feeling that you forgot something but don't know what it is?" I ask her, turning the music down a little.

"Sometimes. I mean, that's what forgetting is, right? Why?"

"I don't know. It's so strange. When we were leaving the forest, I felt like I was supposed to wait for something. Now, the further away we get, I feel like I forgot something important."

"You checked your bag?" she asks.

"Yeah. That's the weird thing. I don't own much, so I would notice if I forgot something."

She hums in agreement. "Whatever you forgot, we'll buy you a new one."

I nod but, for some reason, I feel that I can't just buy whatever it is I left behind.

I shake my head, trying to clear the strange feeling and turn to her.

"So, this Fae?" I wiggle my eyebrows at her, and she giggles.

"His name is Trevan."

"Oh, *his* name..." I tease.

She nods and blushes. "You should see him, Soph. He's so freaking sexy. His hair is like this baby blue, and his eyes match. His face looks like it was sculpted by the gods themselves."

"But he's Fae, right? Is that—is that a problem?" I ask. I should probably know this. Samara tried to teach me as much about the supernatural world as she could throughout our friendship, but I really didn't think I'd ever need it. I thought I'd always be stuck in that house. I wouldn't need information about all the other super-naturals out there, and it only hurt to know what I was missing.

"Not for me. Of course, there are always assholes. Mages won't mate outside of their race, but the rest of us don't usually care. If Mother Moon gives us the opportunity to meet our true mate, whether they're the same or different, it doesn't matter."

"What about kids?"

"Slow down, now. I haven't even met him yet." She laughs, turning her face toward the open window. "It can be more difficult to conceive. Which can be a concern if you are—you know—mated and settled and ready to reproduce," she stresses this thoroughly. "Usually, kids take after one parent. If the mother is a shifter and the dad is Fae, the child will come out one or the other. You could have five kids with three of them showing Fae powers while the other two are shifters or vice versa."

I nod. "So, you really like this guy?"

The smile on her face widens, and I know my answer already. I've never seen her get that look on her face before.

"I can't wait for you to meet him. He's smart, funny, hand-some, and caring. He's been trying to convince me to convince you to run away for the past year, but I keep shooting him down."

"You *have* been trying to convince me to run away for the past year." I roll my eyes at her. "Why did you think I was ready to leave now?"

"It wasn't me. It was Trevan. He said he had a feeling that something bad was coming, and that we needed to leave. If you didn't come out to the cabin, I was going to come and get you in the middle of the night."

My mouth drops open in shock. "You would've been caught."

She smirks at me and waves her hand. "Please. Do you know how many times I've scouted around that place without being caught? Those mages think they're so smart, so untouchable, that they don't even ward or patrol the area."

My mouth forms a thin line. "Still. That was reckless. I don't know what I would've done if anything happened to you. I can't lose you, Samara."

She glances over at me with a serious look on her face. "I know. I'm sorry. I just needed to make sure they weren't locking you in that damn cage again." Her lion flashes in her eyes, and she lets out a growl.

I sigh. "I know you were worried, and that's one of the reasons I love you so much. You're my only friend Samara."

"Not friend. Sister," she corrects.

"My sister from another mister," I giggle. "So does this Trevan have an idea of how to remove my tether?" I ask, pulling half-heartedly at the silver braided ring around my neck. I don't want to go back to a serious conversation, but I need to.

"Yes. He said he has some spells he can try, and if they fail then he has some contacts he can reach out to. He is confident that it won't be a problem. Though he doesn't know what type of supernatural you are. I left that part out for now."

I nod, turning around as we get on the highway to look back the way we came. My chest feels tight, like there is an elastic band wrapped around my heart, tugging me back.

"Do you think the tether could be making me feel like I want to go back?" I ask her. It would be particularly devious to make me wear a spell that makes me want to run back to that terrible house.

She thinks for a moment before nodding. "It's possible. Maybe they used a spell to make you feel like you forgot something just in case you ever ran away."

"Yeah. Devin took me to the doctor the other day, and I didn't feel like this. He leaves me to go to work all the time, and I feel nothing. It's so strange."

"You went to the doctor?" she asks, shocked, then shrugs her shoulders. "We will see once we get that tether off. If you stop feeling it, then we know. If you keep feeling it..." she pauses, looking at me, "I guess we'll need to figure out what you forgot."

I giggle, though it's forced.

"Yeah. I guess we will."

I turn the music back up and look out the window as the scenery changes. I get out my sketchbook, opening to a drawing of the forest from my dreams. The familiar foliage of the forest soon gives way to busier city streets and, finally, less familiar paths outside Halifax. This is the farthest I've ever been from home. The lake and trees in my drawing could be anywhere, but I compare them to what I see from the passenger window, wondering if I will know this place when I see it.

Despite the feeling of forgetfulness and urgency to return, my body is buzzing with excitement.

Chapter Eight

Darren

We are on our way to Sebastyn's designated stop, and he is scrolling through his phone, eyebrows pinched in confusion.

"What is it?" I ask, knowing it could be bad news, just some video of a cat, or anything in between.

"Huh," is all he says and continues scrolling.

"What?" I finally ask again after waiting for him to elaborate.

"I finally heard back from someone on the Supernatural Network. It seems that mages have claimed this city and the surrounding area as 'their territory' and pushed out or killed any other supernatural group located here over the past ten years. It's strange because territory is more of a shifter thing, and witches and mages rarely care...unless..." He stops and scrolls through his phone more, faster this time.

"Unless what?" I try not to snap at him, but it's fucking frustrating when someone stops talking in the middle of saying something important.

He raises his head and looks at me in the eyes. "Unless they had something or someone that they wanted to keep hidden from all the other supes."

"So, you think this Devin guy and the rest of the mages that have Sophia are the ones who forced out all other supernatural groups so they could keep her hidden? That's fucked up." Seb nods and goes back to scrolling on his phone.

Seriously, this is the weirdest thing I've ever heard. A group of supes claiming an entire city and forcing out all others? It's unheard of. Sure, shifters tend to claim territory, but we coexist mostly in peace and can have many species in one city. In Parry Sound alone, we have our pack, a bear shifter sleuth, a mountain lion pride, a coven of witches, a coven of vampires, and an entire court of Fae, and we all get along just fine. We have boundaries for each territory and peace treaties set, which makes it easy to avoid conflicts. I'm sure not all supernatural factions function as well as we do, but to have mages as the dominant species is just plain weird.

Until recently, we had thought they were all killed by the last phoenix shifter fifty years ago. As that thought crosses my mind, I have to correct myself. Not the last phoenix shifter, we've found two in less than a year. Well, almost found. Who knows how many others are out there, either in hiding or waiting for someone to rescue them.

"One of my contacts says that mages wiped out an entire mountain lion pride around ten years ago and started pushing the rest out. No one knows why they did it. It's like a switch flipped, and they didn't want any other supes around. He told me to get out of the area as quickly as possible. That it's dangerous for any supes to be here, even witches."

"Okay, tell me this isn't the weirdest thing you've ever heard of. A city this big with only one type of supernatural? It has to have something to do with Sophia. Someone must've figured out what the mages were doing and tried to stop it, so they either killed or forced all others out to keep her a secret. It's the only thing that makes sense."

"Ten years ago," Sebastyn ponders aloud, "would have been when Phoebe and Sophia turned nineteen."

"Exactly," I nod. "It's when they would have come into their phoenix powers if they hadn't been tethered."

"Here. Drink this," he says, handing me a vial of a green-looking liquid.

"What is it?" I ask, wrinkling my nose.

"Scent Blocker." He responds, shoving the vial in my face.

I eye it warily. "The scent blocker Skarlyt gives us is in a spray bottle."

He shakes his head and sighs. "That's because she doesn't know this recipe. Trust me." I raise my eyebrow at him remembering the Ex-Lax incident last Christmas. "I wouldn't do that. Not when I'm going to be stuck in the car with you anyway."

"How'd you know what I was thinking?" I ask before I down the vial. "Ugh. That tastes like shit."

"Because you always bring up the time I gave you Ex-Lax."

"Always?" I question.

"Either way," he shrugs, "I didn't do anything to that potion."

"It's too late if you did anyway."

"You think I packed Ex-Lax on this trip?" He rolls his eyes. "But I promise there was nothing except scent blocker in there. Today is going to be dangerous enough," he says, his playful tone disappearing and turning serious.

The teasing smile slips from my face. "I know, but it will be okay." We are silent the rest of the way. It is unusual but, given where we are headed, it's warranted.

I pull into a secluded drive in the forest and come to a stop.

"Be safe," I tell him, and he nods.

"You too. Remember. Five o'clock—whether you find her or not," he says before closing the door.

Goddess, I hope this goes well. There's a churning in my gut that wasn't there this morning, getting stronger the further I get from Sebastyn. Forty-five minutes later, I'm driving down the road connecting to the forest on this side of Halifax. I glance at the clock, and it flashes eleven-thirty-six. I hope she hasn't left yet.

I pull the SUV into an opening in the brush, quickly getting out and pulling some of the branches in front to hide it from view. As I turn, I immediately detect a slight scent of mountain lion, and I lift my nose to the air, ready to follow it. Other than the times at the hotel, it's the first sign of a shifter I've seen in this area.

Using my nose, I follow the well-used trail. I hear some rustling in the brush. Even with my enhanced hearing and smell, though, I sense nothing that shouldn't be here.

"Well, well. What do we have here?" A voice calls out, and I spin to find a group of about five men carrying hunting rifles as if they're out on a hunting trip. However, there's something about them that makes me doubt that. How didn't I realize I was being followed? They shouldn't have been able to get that close.

I choose to go for ignorant. "Thank god. I set out on a hike and got myself turned around. Do you know which way is back to the road?"

They all eye me with skepticism but remain silent until an older man, who I would peg as the leader, steps forward. Immediately, the scent of magic wafts closer to me. It's so strong I almost choke, but I manage to keep it in.

"Where's your pack?"

"My what?" My throat tightens.

"Your pack. If you're hiking, wouldn't you have a pack? Some supplies?" he asks, and I exhale some of the tension in my chest.

"I really wasn't planning on being out this long, so I didn't bring one." I shrug my shoulders and pray to the goddess that they point me in the direction of the road and leave.

"Why don't you follow us back home, and we'll give you a ride to your car?" He says exactly what I was hoping he wouldn't. I assess each of the men. I might be able to take on one mage. Five? Definitely not. Especially if they're all as powerful as their spokesman smells. It has to be because of Sophia and the siphon they have on her. I've never met anyone with magic this strong. They make Sebastyn and Skarlyt seem weak—and I know they're not.

"That's not necessary, but I appreciate it. My girlfriend is waiting for me at the hotel. I should've been back by now. If you just point me toward the road, I'm sure I can make my own way." I keep my voice even and calm.

"We insist," he snarls, and a growl begins to bubble up in my throat, my wolf feeling threatened. I manage to cover it with a cough and nod.

"Okay," I agree and follow their lead through the trees. Shit. Shit. Shit.

This is the absolute worst place for me to be, surrounded by shifter-hating mages and heading back to their home. I wish Sebastyn was a shifter so we could communicate through the pack link. Maybe I should've had Alaric send a couple of shifters up here to us; that way we could've been in pairs. Damn it. The only silver lining that I can see is that maybe these assholes will be too busy dealing with me to look for Sophia, giving her more time to escape.

After a short walk, we break through the trees into a small village that is swarming with activity, but that's not what I focus on. What I focus on is the twenty men standing in front of me, all with snarls on their faces. They don't have weapons. But, then again, with magic as strong as theirs, they don't really need any.

I stop in my tracks and take a few steps backward, but the assholes behind me grab onto my shoulders.

"What's going on?" I ask, not even bothering to hide the panic in my voice.

"You'll see. We have some questions for you," the leader says, stepping in front of me.

"Questions?"

He nods. "What were you doing in our forest?"

"I already told you. Hiking."

"Why don't we believe you?" He raises an eyebrow.

I shrug my shoulders. "I don't know. It's the truth."

He shakes his head and begins pacing in front of me. "This can go one of two ways. You tell us why you're here, and we kill you fast and painlessly. Or you don't tell us what we want to know, and we extract the information from you, slowly and painfully, after which you will still die."

The growl comes out of my mouth so quickly, I don't have time to smother it.

The evil smile on his face widens. "Shifter. I knew there was something about you."

Well, if the cat—or, more accurately, wolf—is out of the bag, I might as well shift and try to get away. I quickly call on my wolf, shredding my clothes, slipping from the mages holding me, and turn to run into the forest.

I don't get far before I feel something stick into my hind leg, sending me tumbling to the ground. The last thing I see before everything goes black is asshole number one staring down at me grinning.

"This is going to be so much fun."

Well, shit.

Chapter Nine

Sophia

After about six hours of driving, we are both completely exhausted and need to stop for a couple hours of sleep. We agree it will be safest if we stop somewhere public yet secluded and settle on a provincial park in New Brunswick. It's close to the border of Quebec, and, if we can get some sleep, it will only be one more day of driving to our destination. We debate getting a hotel room but quickly nix that idea, knowing that it will be faster to escape if we sleep in the car. It should be comfortable enough. Samara really spared no expense with this thing. It's a luxury SUV hybrid that runs on both electricity and gas.

After parking in front of the charging port for the car and plugging it in, Samara gets back in the driver's seat.

"I'm going to log in and tell Trev to expect us in the next two days. If we need to, we can drive straight through, but it doesn't seem like we're being followed—yet," she says while opening her laptop. The evenness of her voice makes her seem confident. I know she's wrong, though. By now, Devin would have come home, realized I'm gone, and started tracking me.

I can only hope that they put an anti-tracking spell on my

tether to stop other supes from tracking me—from coming to help me—and I can only hope it will work against them now. Devin never told me much—only enough to taunt me after they attacked Samara's family. So, I do not know if all their magic will help hide me or give them a map straight to me.

"Okay, but let's only take three hours. I don't want to stay in one place too long," I say as I get out of the car to stretch my legs. Three hours should be short enough that, even if they left a couple of hours after us, we should be long gone before they get here. At least, I hope.

I love being in nature. The smell of wet leaves and the sound of birds singing and crickets chirping give me a sense of peace. It's like my own personal playlist in surround sound. I find a picnic table close to where we parked and lay down on top of it, listening to the sounds.

Even though I know I shouldn't, I can't help but feel some guilt for leaving Devin. As fucked up as it is, he's the only family I have ever known. I do care about him in the sense that he has raised me, even though I definitely do not agree with most or—let's be real—all of his methods.

It must be like a version of Stockholm Syndrome. The only reason he raised me is because he literally killed my parents to get to me. At the end of the day, he's all I've ever had, so I can't help but care about what happens to him. It's a long time to spend with anyone, and there will always be the occasional good memories that make you hope things can get better. I shake my head to clear those thoughts. I'm never going back to him, so I need to push those feelings away. My eyes close involuntarily, and I'm sucked into a dream.

I'm walking along the shoreline of the now-familiar lake, staring out at the glass-smooth water. I take a deep breath of the clean air and center myself in the moment. The day's events flood into my mind. I slow my strides, questioning the ground under my bare feet as I try to consolidate my waking memories with my dreaming memories.

Darren. I was supposed to meet Darren.

I realize that I do not remember the dreams about Darren when I wake from them. These dreams feel real; he feels real. But only when I am in this forest, already dreaming. I curse myself and wonder why—how—I could forget him.

I look for him now, hoping to explain, but as I get closer to the edge of the forest, the moon shines down on a dark mass beside a fallen tree. I strain my eyes to see what it is. It's not a rock because the surface isn't smooth. It's not a bush because there are no branches. I take a few steps closer, and I realize it's a wolf. No, not just any wolf, but my wolf. I rush to his side, lifting his head up, placing it on my lap while stroking his fur.

"What happened?" I whisper, but not even a flicker of movement flows through him. I move my hand down to his chest and can feel the 'thump, thump' of his heartbeat, so I know he's alive, and I blow out a shaky breath. Suddenly, this sweet dream has turned into a nightmare. My hands roam over his body to search for wounds but find none. Tears prick my eyes with worry for him.

"I am sorry," I say, but he cannot respond. "I am so sorry, Darren."

I pull him close and bury my head in his fur and let loose a sob. Today had started so well. I had hoped it would end with us finding one another, but I left without him. Did Devin get to him because he was waiting for me? Is this my fault? And now another sob breaks free.

"Soph, we need to go, and we need to go *now*," Samara whispers in my ear.

I am ripped from my sleep suddenly, and it takes my eyes a few blinks to adjust to the darkness. In front of me, Samara has her fingers over her mouth, warning me to be silent. I nod and follow her back to the car quietly.

Once we both get in and half-close our doors to avoid making noise, we slowly begin to drive forward. "Thank goddess I got an electric car. It's so quiet that no one would've been able to hear us leave, not even a shifter," she says to me, and I raise an eyebrow at her. "Okay, maybe a shifter could, but those mages definitely couldn't."

"Okay, now that we're further away, what happened?" I ask her, while getting comfy again in my spot. "Wait. I have to tell you something before I forget."

She looks at me in question, and I take a breath. I close my eyes, trying to pull the details of my dream to the front of my mind. "I had a really weird dream, and I need to tell you about. I need to remember it." I can feel the urgency of that need in my rapid heartbeat, but the memory is already too faded to hold onto. "There is a black wolf. I was sitting and...I was so upset...stroking his fur..." I try to pull more details about why I thought it was important to tell Samara, but they slip away once again.

"You think this wolf is important to you?"

I nod. "I do. I think I've been dreaming about him each night. When I wake, I don't remember anything other than an inkling that something is different. The first time I saw him, I drew a picture." I search for my sketchbook and offer the torn-out page to her. She looks at it only briefly and returns her eyes to the road stretching before us.

"But you can't remember the rest of the dream or why this wolf is important?" She questions, and I shake my head. "Do you remember what happens?"

"I wish I did," I say sadly. "Okay, now what happened to you?"

"I slept for three hours and got up to let my lion run for a bit, but I caught the smell of magic. I thought nothing of it at first, but then I caught a scent I recognized and took off back to find you. It was some of Devin's men. I'd know their stench anywhere. They are following us, and we can't stop again. We need to drive straight through."

"Shit," I curse, looking at the clock in the dashboard. "How did he get so close already?"

"When I was talking to Trev last night, he said to let him know and he could send someone to meet us when we get there, if we feel the need." I still don't know what to think of trusting this guy we've never met, but we really don't have an option now. I can't go back anymore, even if I wanted to. Now that I've run, if I ever end up back there, they'll make me wish I was dead.

"I think that's probably for the best," I say, pulling up the GPS again and selecting the last saved address. The custom entry says "Supernatural" with a heart emoji and a street address in Parry Sound.

Thirteen hours, thirty-two minutes.

Maybe we can cut some time down if we go a little faster.

* * *

We pull into Parry Sound fourteen hours later. We stopped a few times for food and bathroom breaks, but we still made pretty good time. It's still light out, so the bar is easy to find.

As we draw near, I can't help but feel like we are rushing toward a finish line. Safety waits on the other side. If only we can race here, arrive before Devin, we will be safe. I know it is false, but it feels like a game that we are so close to winning.

I don't know why, but entering Parry Sound feels like I am coming home. I've never felt like I belonged anywhere, but I've also never allowed myself to dream about how it would feel to actually be free from Devin, so I'm not sure. If I had to guess how it feels to be somewhere you belong, this is it.

"There it is," I say and point to a beautiful building made

entirely of black bricks. The sign looks worn, but it makes it look more charming. It reminds me of a haunted warehouse. Outside, humans pass by without sparing it a glance. The building is nice, but unassuming. Since Trevan is a Fae and this bar caters to supernaturals, I bet the inside is going to be nothing short of spectacular.

Samara pulls over and parks in one of the parking spots on the street. She looks up at the building and chews at her bottom lip as she studies the club's door from the rearview mirror's reflection.

"Are you nervous, Sam?" In all the time I've known her, she's never been anxious about anything. She's been pissed off, upset, angry and maybe scared once or twice, but she's never looked this edgy or worried before.

"A little, I guess. It's weird. I've been talking to Trev online for a year, but I never imagined actually allowing myself to meet him in person, no matter how much I wanted to. Now, he's on the other side of that door, and I don't know what to do." Words are tumbling out of her with the same quick, manic energy of her hands trying to smooth her perfectly curled hair. I gently pull her hands into my own and try to help.

"Did I tell you how smoking hot he is? He's my own personal fantasy. I showed you the picture, right?" Her eyes meet mine and go wide for a moment. "And I've been in the car for a day. No sleep. No shower. How do I look?" Oh man, she wasn't kidding about really liking this guy.

"You look hot as usual. I'm sure this guy is hot, but he's got nothing on you." I catalogue her features, counting them off on my fingers like I know them as well as my alphabet. "Flawless dark complexion, perfect curly hair, and luscious plump lips. You're stunning, and you know it! Let's go." I stop at the doors, waiting for Samara to catch up after fixing her hair in the side mirror.

Walking inside feels like being transported to a different world. There is so much green everywhere. I turn in a circle, looking around. There's a giant tree in the middle of the bar, and its branches spread over the entire ceiling, making it seem like the whole building is part of the tree. Oh, my gods! I love it! Maybe I can convince this Trev guy to help me set something like this up in whatever home I end up in.

My eyes trace the path from roots to branches, and I am completing a full turn when I notice Samara is standing extremely still, staring at something over my shoulder. I follow her line of vision and come face to face with an extremely handsome man with the bluest eyes and hair I've ever seen. He's got to be over six feet tall and full of muscle. He's not bulky like a shifter, but he's still covered in smooth, toned muscles.

Samara obviously isn't going to say anything since she's standing there like a statue, so I stick my hand out toward the man. "Hi, I'm Sophia; you must be Trev."

"Mine!" Samara growls and pulls me back. What the fuck? Shocked by the possessiveness in her voice, I turn to look at her. I don't know why she just claimed I was hers. She's the one who wanted to come here, but she's not looking at me. She is still staring at Trev, who takes a few slow steps toward her.

Once they're close enough, he reaches out his hand and traces her face. "I've searched forever for you," I hear him whisper to her.

"Mate," Samara or, more accurately, her lion replies. I've learned to tell the difference in the twenty years we've been friends. That explains the growl, I guess.

It looks like they're having a moment, and I really don't want to interrupt, but I don't want the mages to find us here and put everyone in danger either.

"Uh, guys? Sorry to interrupt whatever is happening here, but we kind of need a plan in case they follow us."

That seems to snap Samara out of her staring contest with Trev.

"Shit, you're right. As much as I want to explore this, Trev— and I do. I really do—we need to figure out how to hide Sophia and take off her tether. Is there any way you have something that can help us?" she asks, turning from me to Trev.

He shakes his head, seemingly to clear his thoughts before pulling his eyes away from Samara toward me. A look of recognition crosses his features, although I'm sure I've never met him before. His gaze goes back to Samara, far more comfortable there.

"Yes, of course. Come through here."

He leads us through the bar. It gets even more magical the deeper inside we go.

"What are those berries hanging from the tree?" My hand is already reaching for a bunch of the beautiful purple berries that look like a cross between a mulberry and a grape. I want to reach up and pick one to see if they taste as delicious as they look.

"Those are elderberries," he tells me, catching my movement toward them. "Don't eat them unless you want to be drunk off your ass for the next few hours. We use them in our Faerie wine. It's the only thing that can get a supe drunk."

"Maybe another time then," I say, pulling my hand back with a chuckle. Samara just shoots me a smirk and shakes her head. She knows how I am, so she's not surprised. I have always been curious, but I have never been allowed to ask questions. I obviously couldn't ask the mages anything and, even in school, there was always a risk the other students would tell on me. Now that I am free, I am going to ask every question that comes to mind.

We enter through a door in the back, and it's like we've stepped through a portal to an entirely different building. Although there is still a lot of greenery around, it looks more like a greenhouse and workshop than a bar and club. The white walls and black tiled floor are flawlessly clean despite the pervasive humidity and smell of dirt. I recognize some of the plants growing in pots scattered throughout, but many are unfamiliar as well.

"This room is warded, so no one will be able to track your location as long as you are here. Let me take a look at that tether to see if there's anything I can do," he says as he comes closer to me, examining the choker around my neck.

"Hmm...how long have you had this on?" he asks, trying to test the tight fit against my skin.

"All my life. They've done extra spells on it over the years, but it's never been off my neck."

"Samara said that it's been malfunctioning lately. She didn't go into details; she didn't even tell me what type of supe you are," he gives her a pointed look, and she shrugs. "So, what sort of malfunctions are we talking about?"

I share a look with Samara, and she gives a brief nod. Okay. She trusts him. If he's her mate, it looks like he's going to be in our lives for the long haul. Might as well tell him.

"I'm a phoenix," I announce, and he sucks in a breath, "Over the past nine or ten months, my fire has been bleeding through when I have strong emotions."

"I knew you looked familiar," he says, stepping back from me. "I need to make a call."

"Wait, what do you mean I look familiar?" I don't know much about my biological family except that they are dead, so there's no one he could know. My eyes narrow with suspicion. "Who do you need to call?"

He looks between Samara and me and, with a placating gesture, tells us to both take a seat. My heartbeat kicks up, thumping so hard, it's almost all I can hear as panic begins to grip me.

"Your twin sister is the mate of one of my good friends, and they live just outside of town. I'm going to give them a call to see if they know how to get the tether off of you since they removed Phoebe's with no problems. Come to think about it, it was around nine months ago that they did that."

Wait...What? Twin? Sister?

My heartbeat is still impossibly fast, but I am now filled with excitement—not fear. I have a sister. She removed her tether nine months ago—the same time that my powers started going wonky. That has to mean something, right?

Samara and I look at each other and share a small, excited smile.

"Okay, call her. Please." If he's right, I could be getting ready to meet my sister. A sister that I didn't know existed before today. Wait. What if she doesn't want to know me?

I am flooded by a variety of emotions and anxieties that I barely know how to fathom. It is, first, that Trev must be incorrect. He got the wrong girl—wrong phoenix. Second, that I may have a sister, a power, an entire life, that I am not worthy of. She's been free for nine months already and is mated. I try to pull my mind away from the spiral, but I am left with the same nagging feeling that I have forgotten something important.

Trev dials a number on his phone before pulling it to his ear. "Hey Alaric, you and your mate need to come down to Supernatural." I don't hear what the other person is saying, but, by the pinching in Trev's brows, it's some sort of argument.

"No, you don't understand. There is someone here who your mate has been searching for." I'm not sure why Trev is being vague, but I assume there must be a reason. It would be easier to just say who I am, but maybe it's like Samara not telling him about what type of supe I am. Maybe he doesn't want to be overheard by the wrong person.

"Yes. That is exactly what I'm saying," Trev says and then looks down at his phone in confusion.

"He hung up on me," he sighs. "They'll be here soon."

I nod, chewing on my lip as the new anxiety churns in my stomach. I never imagined having any family. If she doesn't want anything to do with me...I don't know if I'll survive.

I share a look with Samara, and she must be able to tell what

I'm thinking because she gives me a reassuring nod. I blow out a breath as she squeezes my hand in hers.

Whatever is going to happen will happen no matter my feelings.

I might as well try to relax.

Chapter Ten

Sophia

With the deep breaths, the anxiety begins to fade quickly, replaced by excitement. I have a sister, and she's coming here! Oh, my goddess. I can't believe this! "What's she like?" I ask Trev.

"I've only had the chance to meet her a few times," he explains with a frown. "She hasn't been here long, and they've had more than their fair share of mage attacks. Pack land has been locked down for most of the last year. Then Phoebe was pregnant, and now they have a newborn daughter." He shrugs and offers a musical, light laugh. "I guess their first priority hasn't been visiting my club."

She has a daughter? A baby phoenix? I have a niece. Worry begins to worm its way into my gut. Is me being here, bringing the trouble that I am, going to put them in danger?

"I have a niece?" I ask, wanting more details.

"A couple nephews too," he offers, shaking his head as if he can't believe his own foolishness. "I don't know how I didn't recognize it immediately. You are so much like her. Or—I guess—she is like you."

Trev leaves us then to get some drinks ready for "the big reunion."

"You have a sister. A twin sister," Samara says in disbelief.

"I guess so. And a niece, apparently. We have to make sure Devin doesn't get his hands on that baby. Maybe this was a mistake." As I say the words, my burgeoning anxiety turns to terror. What if I brought danger here, and she got hurt? Or worse, what if I lead them here and they take her and raise her the same way they did me? I can't let that happen.

Just as I turn to Samara to voice all my anxieties, I hear Trev come back through the door with two men and two women. One woman stops mid-step and stares at me. Trev was right. She looks just like me in shadow. Her skin is tanned and bronze, her hair is a mess of caramel brown ringlets, and her eyes are like pools of dark chocolate. I am her with the pigment leeched out: peach-pale skin, dirty-blonde waves, and grey-blue eyes. We both take a step toward each other at the same time. Oh, man. There's no denying that we are twins. We are even the same height, but she is a little thicker than me—evidence of her recent labor and likely a health-ier, more complete diet.

"Hi," I say to her with my eyes starting to mist up.

"Hey," she replies, with moisture showing in her eyes as well.

I can't hold it back anymore, so I throw my arms around her and pull her into a hug. I feel complete for the first time in my life. I feel loved. She hasn't even said anything to me, but I can feel all of her emotions through her hug as if they were my own. Weird. Sobs begin to wrack her body, and mine follows suit. Both of us cling tightly to one another.

I can hear introductions being made between Samara and the others in the room. I'm grateful that they're giving us a few minutes to ourselves, but I know that I need to introduce myself, so I pull back.

"I'm Sophia," I tell her, and she smiles, lifting a vial to her face and capturing her tears. I raise my eyebrow at her in question.

"I'm Phoebe. I don't cry very often anymore, so I started bottling my tears just in case someone gets hurt."

Ah, I forgot our tears are supposed to heal. I've worn this tether so long that my tears have never had healing properties. Mother knows I've had enough reasons to cry and enough wounds to test them on.

"You may need a second one," I say, and we both laugh. I'm not even sure what we're laughing at, but I have so much joy in my heart right now I need to let some out.

One of the men walks up and puts his arms around Phoebe.

"This is my mate, Alaric," she tells me, and he sticks out his hand to shake. I meet his bright blue eyes and a flicker of recognition flows through me, but it's gone as quickly as it came. Weird. I slap his hand away, causing his eyes to widen in shock before I lift up on my tiptoes and wrap my arms around his neck.

"It's so nice to meet you," I whisper in his ear. I can't help it. I'm a hugger. Samara always jokes that they deprived me of physical affection my entire life, so I make up for it with hugs. Usually, she's the only one I have to hug though. In this case, I feel such a strong connection to this man that a hug seems more suitable than a handshake.

"Another hugger," he says, a deep chuckle moving through his wide chest. "You and Skarlyt will get along just fine."

I step back to ask who that is, but I am engulfed in another hug a moment later. A beautiful woman with soft, black hair wraps her thin arms around me.

"Oh wow, that's a super strong tether," she says, jumping back from me just as quickly as she had approached. I look over at Samara, but she just shrugs her shoulders.

"How come Alaric and I didn't feel anything when we hugged her?" Phoebe asks, turning to the woman with black hair.

"I'm more sensitive to magic than you," she explains simply before turning to me. "I'm Skarlyt, by the way, and this is my mate Lennox." She gestures to the last man, a tall, muscular shifter with long, blonde waves pulled back from his face. I step toward him and wrap my arms around his muscled abdomen in an embrace. He stiffens momentarily before wrapping his arms around me as well.

"It's very nice to meet you, Sophia," he says, with halting confidence.

"You'd think that you'd be more used to hugs by now, Skarlyt says with a chuckle at her mate as I step back.

Lennox shrugs his shoulders. "You'd think. But I'm still not sure I'll ever be used to anyone other than you or my family hugging me."

"Can you remove it?" I interrupt, hopeful. I've waited almost twenty-nine years to get this thing off my neck. I'm so ready.

"No, I'm sorry. I can't," she says, and I feel my entire body deflate. "But..." she adds quickly, turning to Phoebe, "maybe you can."

"Me? How am I supposed to remove it?" Phoebe draws her brows together in confusion.

"Your phoenix fire should be able to burn the magic of the tether the same way you can burn the barriers that the mages build," Skarlyt answers. "Think of it like overloading a circuit. You're going to pump so much power into that thing that it explodes." Her elegant hands splay into something similar to "jazz hands" as she excitedly announces this outcome.

Everyone gasps, and Samara growls. No one seems to like the sound of this test.

"Not literally. Jeez." Skarlyt waves their concern away with an impatient hand.

"What if I burn her?" Phoebe asks, her voice laced with anxiety.

"You won't, love. Your fire won't burn her any more than it burns me—we're your family," Alaric reassures her.

"Are you sure?" she directs the question to Skarlyt.

"It shouldn't. Especially because she's a phoenix as well."

She turns to look at me, and I share a look with Samara. We've come this far to try to get away from Devin and his cronies...In order to stand any kind of chance, I need this tether removed.

I turn back to Phoebe. "Do it." I steel myself for the burn of her flame. "I want this thing off, and this is the best chance I have ever had."

"If it starts to hurt, you need to tell me right away. I just found you. You haven't even met your niece or nephews yet. I don't want to lose you already."

I give her a nod to go ahead, and she raises her hands. She places them delicately around the tether, around my neck. Her small hands can barely cover the entirety of the collar.

I close my eyes, readying myself for pain. Instead, I feel a warmth spread from my neck throughout my body. I feel a sort of popping sensation and, when I open my eyes, both Phoebe and I are completely engulfed in flames. Beautiful wings have sprouted from her back. At first, I only see her dark crimson flames. When I look closer, though, I can make out the fine details of the wings that surround me. Like an angel's wings, but they are made of dancing flames instead of downy feathers.

She looks like a mystical fire bird. She's beautiful. I wonder if I look like that. I turn my head and see the same wings protruding from my back as well. I have only felt my own fire a few times, and it has always been suffocated by the tether. Beside Phoebe, though, I become a creature of flame myself. Just like our coloring in human form, my flame is a shade lighter, almost a deep orange instead of red.

"Oh, my Mother," I hear someone whisper as Phoebe's flame starts to die out and mine follow suit. When we are finally back to normal, I'm tackled and wrapped in a hug. I'd know that scent anywhere. Samara.

"You are so beautiful, Soph. I knew you would be," she says, tears dripping onto my completely naked shoulder. I raise my hands and feel my bare neck for the first time ever, before I wrap my arms around her as well.

"I'm free. Oh gods. I'm finally free," I whisper. The sudden realization sends tears springing to my eyes. Samara nods into my shoulder, clutching me tighter.

"Yes, you are," she responds.

I feel fabric being wrapped around me. I don't know who's doing it, but I'm so grateful. I've been around Samara long enough to know that shifters don't see nakedness the same way most people do, but it doesn't stop me from being shy when it comes to being naked around a group of people I just met—family or not.

"Okay, I think we should head back to pack land just to be safe." Alaric's words break through the excitement of the moment and remind us that we are not only still in danger but also still in Trevan's workroom. When I step back from Samara's embrace, still clutching to her hand, I notice scorch marks on the floor and ceiling in the spots where Phoebe and I were standing.

"I'm so sorry, Trevan," I say, turning to look at him. He just waves me off.

"It's nothing a little magic can't fix." I watch in awe as he waves his hands in a series of patterns and, before my eyes, the marks are gone. The room looks exactly the same as it did when we arrived. "The plants got a bit of a shock. That will take longer to fix, but they'll understand." He nods toward some now-wilted plants that were within our blast radius.

Well, okay then. He then waves his hands over Phoebe and I, morphing the blankets around our necks into matching toga-style dresses. The alteration is shockingly simple, and the resulting dresses are quite flattering.

"I need to learn how to do that," Skarlyt says in awe.

"You probably could. It's not much different from your transformation spells," Trev replies.

Alaric starts to gather everyone together to head back to his pack, Samara included. Trevan speaks up, coming to put his arm around Samara.

"I'll be coming too if it's okay with you, Alaric." Both Alaric and Skarlyt turn as one, mouths open, gaping at Trev. Guess that's not a normal thing for him to do. I watch as Skarlyt puts two and two together, her eyes bouncing between his arm around Sam and his face.

"Oh, my Mother!" she screams and starts bouncing on the spot. "You met your mate?" she asks him, with an enormous amount of excitement. I watch as he looks at Sam with a smile before turning back and nodding at Skarlyt. She throws her arms around both of them.

Alaric looks excited, but he simply clasps Trev on the shoulder.

"You know you're always welcome with my pack—as is your mate." With that said, he turns, leading us back through the club and out to a waiting SUV.

"Let's go home," Phoebe says, clasping my hand and leading me into the back seat.

Home...I am home. With my family. If anyone had told me last week that I'd be here now, I would have called them crazy. Now I'm sitting in a car with my twin sister, heading to my new home to meet my niece and nephews. I'm not sure how life can get better than this.

I look around for Samara as I climb in the car. I don't want her to feel like I'm leaving her behind now that I found this family. I find her in the arms of her mate, looking at him with stars in her eyes. She looks like he hung the moon, and he looks at her the same way. I feel an unexpected pang of jealousy, but I push it away. She deserves this. More than anyone in the entire world, she's earned the right to be happy.

As if sensing me looking at her, she turns in Trev's arms and meets my eyes with a big smile on her face. With a simple nod, she shows me that nothing from our past or in our future will change our relationship. Sisters for life. Now, we can actually have a life.

With the biggest smile I've ever felt on my own face, I climb into the SUV beside Phoebe while Samara takes Trevan, Skarlyt, and Lennox in the one we came here in.

Chapter Eleven

Sophia

I watch out the car window the entire way to make sure I don't miss anything. This is the first real taste of freedom I've ever had, and I'm not going to waste a second of it. Sure, the car ride here was technically the first taste of freedom I've had, but we were constantly looking over our shoulders. This time, I'm truly free. No collar around my neck; no tether siphoning my power. I can feel the power slowly begin seeping through my body, and it feels amazing. When my flames first showed up nine months ago, I thought that was a lot. I had no idea. Now, my entire body feels like it's buzzing, as if I had too much caffeine.

I want to see and smell and taste everything all over again, to experience it without that choker around my neck to make me feel like I'm on borrowed time.

Instead of trying to make small talk or distract me, Phoebe simply holds my hand in silence. From the little of what Trevan told us about her removing her tether, she must know how this feels as well—to finally be free.

My eyes mist up with happiness. I can't remember there ever

being a time in my life where I was happy enough to shed a tear, but here I am on the verge of ugly crying.

I watch as we turn onto a lane way almost completely hidden by trees. This is it. The forest I've been drawing. All it needs now is the lake.

I watch as we pass by cottages that have been built into the forest, as if they simply grew from trees. As we start to slow, I see the most beautiful lake come into view. That's it. This is where I've been dreaming of. My subconscious must've been leading me back to Phoebe this whole time.

I turn to her. "You don't turn into a large black wolf with brilliant blue eyes, do you?" If my dreams have been leading me to my twin, then what does the wolf have to do with it?

"No," she says with a little chuckle. "I've really only got the one trick up my sleeve. Why do you ask?"

"Okay, this is going to sound weird...Over the past nine months, since my tether started malfunctioning, I've been drawing this lake and forest every day. Like *this* forest. But each time, I see a large black wolf sitting at the water's edge, and I get the feeling he's waiting for me. Sometimes he is taking a drink, and other times he's looking right at me, but I feel that there's something about him that's special." I really hope she doesn't think I'm crazy.

She shares a look with Alaric once we come to a stop. What's that about?

"What?" I ask them.

"Maybe..." Phoebe starts.

"Why don't you come in and meet everyone? Once you're settled, I'll take care of the kids while you and Phoebe have a couple glasses of wine on the deck and talk," Alaric interrupts.

"That sounds amazing." Sister time. Wow. I can't believe that's a thing in my life. I always imagined that the only person I'd ever have to confide in or talk to would be Samara.

We step out of the car at the same time Samara and Trevan are stepping out of theirs, and I see the same look of awe pass over Sam's face that I'm sure is on mine.

The house, if you can even call it that, is large. I would almost call it a mansion. It's built out of wood and set back into the forest like the others, making it look as though it naturally formed there. A large porch wraps around the entire building, lined with benches, Adirondack chairs, and hanging swings. It's gorgeous and welcoming in equal measure. There's a balcony on the second floor that is mostly out of sight, facing the lake.

"Look at this place!" Sam says, her eyes wide with amazement as she walks beside me.

"Yeah, it's amazing, isn't it?" I ask, still looking around, soaking in everything.

Next thing I know, two little boys run out of the house and tackle Alaric. These must be my nephews, and they're absolutely adorable. Once they notice me, they become frozen in their spots with their mouths hanging open. I give them a small wave, hoping to break the ice.

"Mom, why does she look just like Riley?" the younger boy asks. I take a closer look at both boys as Alaric sets them down. The younger one looks like a spitting image of Phoebe, but he's right. The older boy looks just like me, but his hair is a clearer, lighter shade of blonde.

"Well, boys, this is Sophia. She's my sister and your aunt," Phoebe tells them, and their mouths hang open even further. I look at her in question. What do I do? Do I approach them or stand back and let them approach me? She gives me a smile and a nod, so I take a few steps closer to them.

"Hi," I say to them both, and stick my hand out for them to introduce themselves. Ordinarily, I'm comfortable meeting new people. These boys, for some reason, are daunting. I want them to like—no love—me, and I haven't spent much time around children in my life. I find myself more nervous and worried about their perception of me than I was about anyone at Supernatural.

Obviously, I was worried about nothing because, next thing I know, both boys reach over to me and wrap their arms around my waist in a hug.

"I'm Ryker, and this is my brother Riley. I'm eight, and Riley is eleven," the younger boy says as he steps back and gestures to his brother.

"I'm Sophia. It's so nice to meet you," I say, bending down and wrapping my arms around them both once more. This feels so nice. I think my heart might burst from being full.

When I left Halifax, my biggest hope was to find a place to call home and make a family for myself. Now I find a family that I already have, and they seem incredible. It's everything I've ever wished for and more.

I start pulling back from the boys and wipe the stray tears of joy that are making trails down my cheeks as Phoebe steps up with a baby.

"This is your niece, Aurora," she tells me, holding her out. I quickly stand up and reach my arms out, cradling the baby and bringing her up to my chest. I've never held a baby before. She seems so small, so fragile, so perfect. I lean my head down and smell her. She smells like home, like soap and forest with a hint of fire. I've always wondered what the obsession is when people say they like the smell of babies. I get it now. I don't think I'll ever get enough. I inhale her scent once more, closing my eyes and enjoying the feeling of rightness that falls over me.

I look up at Phoebe and notice how she is watching all three of her children and me interact with a soft smile on her face. I wonder if she feels how I do right now. Complete.

"She's perfect," I say, looking back down at her before glancing beside me at Sam. "Isn't she perfect?" Samara's eyes trail down to the bundle in my arms.

"She really is. They all are. They're everything we've ever dreamed of for you. You found your family, Soph," she says.

"No, *we* found our family," I tell her, looking around at everyone around me. I know they're my blood family, but Samara is my chosen family and I'll never let her go. She looks up at me in surprise. She should know by now that we're a package deal, her and I. Different emotions flit across her face, shock, happiness, and acceptance.

Alaric steps up behind Phoebe, wrapping his arms around her and Trev does the same with Sam. That's all that's missing in my life now. My mate. Although now that I'm finally free, I'm not in a rush to find him. Besides, I have two little princes and a princess to keep me company for the foreseeable future.

"Okay, let's get everyone settled, then you two can get to know each other," Alaric says, breaking the touching moment we're having. "Trev, you can stay in the guest cottage. You know where it is. Samara and Sophia can either stay there with you or in the main house, whichever they prefer."

I sneak a peek over at Sam and Trev and notice the unspoken conversion they are having. I think they need time alone, but I don't want to say it in front of everyone. I'll find time to pull her aside.

"How about a tour before we decide?" I ask them. Phoebe quickly agrees, appearing to have noticed the same thing as me.

"Come on in," she says, leading us up the stairs, onto the porch, and through the front doors. If I thought the outside was gorgeous, the inside is even more spectacular. The entire main floor is open and large with tree trunks holding up a high ceiling in place of beams. You can see right through the main floor out to the back deck that overlooks the lake. I can see myself loving living here, swimming in the lake, soaking up the sun on the small beach. I haven't seen the guest cottage yet, but I can't imagine not staying here with Phoebe and the kids now that I've met them and seen this house.

As Phoebe and Alaric walk further into the house, I hear the whispered conversation happening between Samara and Trev.

"Trev, I want to explore this too, but I need to stay with Sophia tonight. I'm sure she's freaking out." She's not wrong about me freaking out, but I understand the pull between mates. She's been talking about meeting her mate since we were kids. What kind of friend would I be if I got between that? She's been so supportive of me. She deserves to have some time to herself, to celebrate her own life changes.

"Trev, is there any way I could have a minute with Samara?" I say to him as I turn around. He looks from me to her, giving her a kiss on the head before going to the kitchen to join Phoebe and Alaric.

Once he's gone, I turn to Sam. "Listen, Sam, I love that you want to be here for me and support me, but I also want to be there for you and support you too. You don't need to stay with me tonight. Go to the guest cottage with Trev. Phoebe and I have a lot of catching up to do anyway, and I'll fill you in tomorrow."

I adjust Aurora in my left arm, so I can place my right around her shoulder.

"Are you sure?" she asks nervously.

"I'm sure! I want you to be happy. You've only been talking about meeting your mate since we were kids. Now you've met him, and you want to stay here with me? You want to paint your nails with my twin while your mate—that hot piece of Fae—sleeps alone in the guest cabin? No. Go enjoy a night with him. Seal the deal so that we can start planning a mating ceremony."

"I had given up on ever having a mating ceremony after I lost my pride," she says, her dark eyes wandering back to Trevan. "I guess I can have one now. I didn't even think of that." A smile grows across her, and she wraps her arms around me. "Thank you."

"You don't need to thank me. I expect repayment when I meet my own mate." I step back and give her a wink. We hurry to the kitchen together to continue the tour.

"Everything okay?" Phoebe asks. Of course, she noticed we stayed back to talk.

"Yup. We were just discussing the sleeping arrangements. Sam is going to stay at the cottage, and I'm going to stay here with you— at least for tonight," I reply and watch as Phoebe's face lights up with excitement and Trev's goes from a look of shock to gratitude.

"Aunt Sophia, come see our room next," Ryker calls to me as he grabs my hand and drags me up the stairs. *Aunt Sophia.* Oh goddess. As they lead me up the stairs, they are bouncing with excitement. It's infectious.

"You can sleep in our room if you want. We each have bunk beds," Riley says. I don't want to shoot him down right away, so I just giggle. This is how normal kids are supposed to act. They are rambunctious and excited, living without fear of being locked in a cage if they say the wrong thing. I get a small pang in my chest at the thought of what my life could've been like, but it's quickly replaced with gratitude that these children are here, able to live free and happy. Somehow, these boys and Aurora have already claimed my entire heart, and I know without a doubt that I would do anything to keep them safe and happy.

They aren't kidding about their room being amazing. They lead me into what I guess is their bedroom first. There are two sets of bunk beds, one on each side of the room, a large picture window with a bench underneath, and toys strewn throughout the room. One of the boys presses a button, and a TV slides out of the ceiling, displaying a cartoon I am not familiar with. That is so cool. They then lead me through the bathroom attached to their room, glossing over it as if it doesn't matter. It does to me; I pause within the bathroom, spinning in a circle to look around. I've never seen a more beautiful bathroom. Double sinks with a large walk-in shower. It's a bathroom I've only seen in my dreams, almost double the size of my bedroom growing up. I find out why they gloss over it as we walk into the next room though.

It is a large toy room, the same size as their bedroom, with all the video game consoles you could think of, gaming chairs, arcade machines, and a pool table. It looks more like a grown man's ideal man cave than a toy room for children.

"This room is incredible, boys," I tell them, and it's the truth. I wish this was something I had when I was younger. All I had to play with was the pieces of wood I brought in from the forest that I pretended were my dolls or my sketchbook and pencil to draw.

"Alaric had it built for us when we moved here," Riley says proudly.

"But we'll share it with you if you want," Ryker adds, getting a big smile and nod from Riley. These boys are just the sweetest.

I do not entirely understand their living situation. Trev mentioned Phoebe has only been in town for about a year, and the boys are obviously too old to have been born here. It is possible that Alaric is their stepfather. If he is, I am even more thankful for the love he's shown them.

"Well, if Alaric had this whole room built for you, he must have been so excited to have you here," I say, lowering my voice conspiratorially, the boys giggle and agree.

"I most certainly was excited," Alaric laughs, using his large hand to ruffle Riley's hair. "This room is mostly thanks to your uncle, though. That'll teach me to set him loose with my credit card."

"If I recall his account of events," Phoebe laughs, quoting a clearly well-worn argument, "he was instructed to 'get things ready' to 'spoil them silly'."

"He's nothing if not thorough," Alaric shrugs, but I can tell he doesn't really mind.

"If you don't want to stay in our room, there's a guest room right across the hall. Or I'm sure Aunt Skar will let you stay in her room downstairs. She never uses it anymore because she got married," Riley says, taking over the tour and offering me every room in the house.

"She got mated," Ryker corrects, looking proud.

"She got mated," Riley agrees.

"Shifter vocabulary takes some getting used to," Phoebe shrugs in explanation.

The guest room Riley leads me to is also the size of the entire main floor of Devin's house, with an open concept bathroom and walk-in closet. It's painted in a neutral gray color and has a beautiful red bedspread laid out on the largest bed I've ever seen. I don't know how I'm going to sleep in that thing all by myself. My bed was barely big enough for me to fit in; I could roll over at least five times without ever falling off this one.

I walk around the room, touching everything, trying to absorb these memories before I wake up from the dream I must be having. My hand pauses in its trail over the smooth headboard, and my mind goes silent for a moment—like I have lost track of something important.

There is no way this is my life now. You can't go from being a captive and slave to living like a princess in a fairy tale in a matter of forty-eight hours. It just doesn't happen that way.

"We can change anything you don't like," Phoebe says from the doorway, making me jump. I didn't even hear her approaching. She holds out her arms to take Aurora back, but I snuggle her sleeping form closer.

"I'm not ready to let her go yet. Everything is perfect! This is like a dream I never want to wake up from," I tell her, and I can see she understands exactly what I'm saying.

"Boys, say goodnight to Aunt Sophia. She'll be here in the morning, but it's time for both of you to get ready for bed," Alaric says from behind Phoebe.

"Aw, do we have to?" both boys ask, earning a stern look from both of their parents. They groan in displeasure but come up and give me a hug, each promising that we will spend some time together tomorrow.

"Why don't we go get comfy on the porch and talk," Phoebe suggests, leading me out of the room.

I think that is a wonderful idea.

Chapter Twelve

Sophia

Heading back to the porch, where Alaric and Phoebe are talking, I snuggle Aurora into me a little more. Her soft auburn hair tickles my cheeks, but her eyes stay closed. Once I reach them, Alaric reaches out his arms for Aurora, and I give her one last squeeze and a kiss on the head before handing her over.

"Good night, ladies. Have fun, just please don't find any trouble while you're out there," he adds before heading back inside. Phoebe scowls in the place he was just standing, and I chuckle.

"So," we both say at the same time and burst out laughing. Phoebe grabs the wine glasses and bottle, pouring us both one, gesturing for me to start. I wish it were her starting. I'm anxious to hear her story. I want to know everything. Everything that has led to her being here. I'm sure I'm going to want to kill someone by the end, but I have no doubt that she's going to feel the same by the end of my tale.

I take a sip of the wine, feeling tingles spread throughout my body from the alcohol and blow out a breath, steeling myself to relive the past. "I guess I'll start at the beginning. I was always told that Devin—that's the man who raised me—had killed my parents in order to abduct me. He had hinted about another phoenix shifter, but I didn't know or dare to even hope that there was any relation. Not until we met Trev, and he told me about you.

"What I'm going to tell you is probably not going to be easy to hear, but I need you to know that I don't let my past define me. I let it help make me into the person I am today, but I didn't let it break me. I just need you to keep that in mind when I tell you."

I wait for her nod before I continue.

"I was raised by the man I mentioned, Devin, the head mage—or high priest—of the coven in Halifax. I spent most of my childhood in fear that when I 'misbehaved,' I would be locked in a cage for days or weeks on end. I was on the receiving end of multiple beatings regularly and didn't understand why or what I did to deserve any of it, not until I was older and realized it had nothing to do with me and everything to do with him.

"There were some good things too. When I got to go to school, I met Samara. The cruelty of my family didn't scare her away. She stuck by me and helped me any time she had a chance. She even went to her parents about me, and they tried to help. It didn't do anything except get her entire pride killed, which I still blame myself for even if she doesn't."

"I'm glad you had someone, and I'm sure it wasn't your fault," Phoebe says, placing her hand on top of mine.

I look down at our hands and shake my head. "If I hadn't brought Samara home to meet Devin, he wouldn't even have known there was a pride living close. If I hadn't told Samara about the beatings and the cage, she never would've told her parents. They wouldn't have involved themselves. Any way you look at it, if I were removed from the equation, they would still be alive."

"You can't think like that. They did what they thought was right."

I nod as tears spring to my eyes. "Samara was the only survivor. There were children in that pride—so many children. The mages didn't care. They went in and killed every last one."

Phoebe lets off a small growl and grabs my face. "Now you listen to me. That is not on you. That is on the mages. They were evil before you, and they will be evil after you. You are not responsible for their actions at all. They are to blame for their awful actions. Not you."

The fierceness in her tone reminds me of Samara and makes me want to believe her. I try to. I'm not fully there, but maybe one day I can be.

When she sits back, I take another drink and let out a shaky breath before continuing.

"When I turned nineteen, I remember being terrified that Devin was going to marry me off to one of his friends or their sons like all the other mage daughters, but my birthday came and went without a mention of it, so I thought I was in the clear." I pause to take another sip of wine, letting the tartness wash over my drying tongue.

"After that, the years passed without much to set them apart. Once we graduated, I rarely left the house. I'd do all the housework and chores. Basically, I was a live-in slave, doing everything in my power to ensure that he didn't have a reason to punish me. I tried to be as invisible as possible.

"About nine months ago, apparently at the same time that you came into your full power, my own powers started flaring up despite the tether. It seemed to be malfunctioning and when I experienced extreme emotions, my flames would start on my hands." I look at my hands now in the pale moonlight, flexing my fingers experimentally. "I tried to hide it as much as possible, but he noticed and started paying closer attention to me. He began getting suspicious about me meeting with someone in the wooded area behind the house, and I was. I was meeting with Samara on

107

almost a daily basis when he was gone to work. It was the only thing that kept me sane through the years.

"Last week, he seemed to finally hit his last straw. He took me to the doctor to see if I was healthy enough to start birthing children for them. His entire plan was for me to be passed around his coven to give them as many phoenix babies as possible to tether." The shock and rage on her face spreads tingles through my body. Other than Samara, I've never had anyone care for me deeply enough to show those emotions.

"I knew I couldn't let that happen, so I finally let Samara take me away. She has tried for years to convince me to leave and run away, but I was so terrified that he'd find us and kill her. I knew he wouldn't kill me. He needed me, but Samara? He would have tortured her in front of me and laughed just to get a rise out of me. That's why I waited so long.

"They caught up with us just outside of Quebec, and we snuck away without them noticing. I'm sorry if I end up bringing them here. It is not my intention to put you all in danger. If you want, I can leave until the threat is taken care of."

"No," Phoebe exclaims forcefully, standing up and pacing a few times before turning to me.

"I know you didn't tell me everything that happened, and it's okay. You're not leaving. Not now; not ever. You're my sister—my family—and family sticks together," she tells me, slipping back into her seat and taking a drink of wine. "I've brought my share of trouble here as well, so don't feel bad." She takes a deep inhale, seeming to steel herself the same way I did.

"I don't know anything about what happened to our parents. After they were murdered, I somehow ended up being adopted by this amazing couple. I feel guilty for having such a different childhood than you, but I can't change it. My childhood was filled with love. My parents loved me and each other with a passion. We did everything together, along with my best friend, Charleigh, who you will meet tomorrow. I knew nothing about the supernatural world growing up, and I didn't know that she was a wolf shifter or what I was."

My mouth drops open. "It must've been a shock for you when you found out."

She nods with a smile. "Oh, it was. Anyway, at eighteen, I met a man named Tanner, and I thought I fell in love. He was sweet, caring, and so attentive. I thought I had found a love like my adoptive parents, one to last through the ages. Turns out it wasn't, and he was just wearing a mask.

"I quickly found myself pregnant, and we got married soon after. Once we were married, he let his mask fade. He became controlling and emotionally abusive. He convinced me to push away my friends—even Charleigh. He had me so convinced I had no one who cared about me other than him and my parents, and then one day they both died in a freak car accident...Then I had only him."

"I'm so sorry," I say, reaching over and placing my hand on hers. She gives it a squeeze with a nod.

"He eventually agreed to have another child, Ryker. Once we found out he was another boy, Tanner went and got a vasectomy without me knowing so that we couldn't have anymore. Looking back now, it was a blessing because I wouldn't want to subject any more kids to what those boys had to go through. I didn't see it then. I thought staying with him was the right thing for them, that taking them away from their father, even an abusive one, was wrong.

"I thought he'd never physically abuse any of us and vowed that the day he physically hit either of the boys, I would leave. That's what happened. I met Alaric at a grocery store, and Tanner found out that I had a conversation with another man, got extremely jealous, and lashed out at me. Because he hadn't hit either of the boys, I stayed, expecting it to get better. But, instead, it got worse. One of the boys had told a friend about his dad hitting his mom, and Tanner took offense to that. I was only out of the room for a few minutes, but—That was it for me. My final straw."

I do not interrupt her, but I'm seeing red. Anger is fogging my brain. How dare he? Who could do that to their own flesh and blood?

"Charleigh and Alaric came and whisked me and the boys away from him. I learned about shifters and magic. We still thought I was human at the time, but when Tanner and his coven of mages attacked us. They attacked multiple times, even after we came here.

"He ended up kidnapping one of the boys, offering me a trade: myself for my son. I took it." I nod in agreement. I've only known Riley, Ryker, and Aurora for a little over an hour and would already do the same. "Of course, I did. I'd rather die than let him get his hands on my babies. I fought like hell for the new life I had created for myself. I fought for my freedom, but it didn't work. He killed me. He grabbed at my foot as I was running away, and I fell onto a rock. I bled out." While I look on horrified, she lets out a small chuckle.

"Of course, being a phoenix, we're extremely hard to kill because we regenerate, so I came back. I took my revenge on Tanner and killed him. I didn't want to. I never wanted to take a life, but I knew that the boys and I would never be safe as long as he was alive, so I did what I needed to do in order to protect my family."

"Good," I say, wishing I could bring him back from the dead to kill him all over again.

"After that, things seemed to get quiet for a while. Until they weren't. The mages came back with a new leader, Joe, Tanner's best friend. He was hellbent on kidnapping Aurora to probably raise her the same way that you were raised.

"When we captured and questioned him, that's when we learned about your situation and where you were. Alaric's brother and his best friend left for Halifax three days ago, looking for you, but I suppose you were already on your way here. You must've just missed each other."

"Someone went to find me?" I ask, and my head starts to swim. The kindness of people I have never even met astounds me.

"Speaking of that, I should probably call and tell them to come home." She grabs her cell phone off the armrest of the chair and dials a number, her brows furrowing in confusion. It must've gone to voicemail. I hear the muffled voice from the speaker of the phone, and it prickles something in the back of my mind. Do I know that voice? Isn't that voice important? I shake the strange feeling off once again.

"Hey, Darren, call me back when you get this," she says, and she turns back to look at me. My eyes are misty, and my fists clenched at the horrors she went through before I got here. I pick up my half empty wine glass and take a sip, enjoying the warmness filling my belly. I feel tingles throughout my body. Maybe I should slow down a bit. It tastes so good, and I could probably drink a whole bottle by myself. I am not used to drinking any alcohol, though, and half a glass is already making my head swim. The bottle is probably not a good idea.

"I'm sorry you went through that, and I'm sorry that the boys had to deal with having an asshole like that for a father," I tell her.

"Like you said, it's in the past, and I've made strides to put it behind me. Now, I have an amazing mate, three beautiful children, and my sister all under one roof. It's a dream I never thought I'd see come true.

"Besides, what you went through is much worse than what I did. At least I had my childhood. You didn't even get that. I'm so sorry you had to grow up that way. When he comes for you, and I'm sure he will, we'll face it together." She must see my terror on my face, and she squeezes my hand supportively. "You're no

111

longer tethered. We'll start working on your control in the morning."

"Just because you had a better childhood doesn't change what you went through. You had the boys to worry about. You had to watch them be hurt by a man who was supposed to protect them. If he wasn't dead already, I would be taking care of that asshole myself.

"But we are together now. We have some shit we have to deal with, and I am the one who brought to your doorstep. I don't plan on running anymore if you'll have me. I'm here to stay. I want to get to know my sister. I want to spoil my niece and nephews and eventually start my own family."

Phoebe nods, happy tears shining in her eyes. She wipes the stray ones that fall away, clapping her hands together. "So...you mentioned a dream wolf earlier..."

I chuckle at her change of topic. "Yes... I've been having dreams about a black wolf, but I can't remember all the details. I just have this feeling like I've forgotten something important. In the car, you seemed like you knew something about it...Do you?"

She takes a sip of her wine before placing the glass on the table and turning to look at me. "First, was the wolf all black or did it have any other colors on it?"

I think about it for a second, closing my eyes and pulling up the image of him in my mind. "Pure black. His eyes are so blue they look like sapphires."

When I open my eyes, she has a smirk on her face. "When I first met Alaric and my tether was removed, I started having these extremely vivid dreams. I was flying high, covered in flames, and I would meet with a black wolf with a small patch of red on his chest. Turns out that the wolf from my dream was Alaric, and my subconscious was telling me that he was my mate. I couldn't sense it the way I should have after being tethered for so long. I'm just thinking, or hoping, that if you are having vivid dreams of this forest and lake, and a black wolf...maybe your mate is here too."

"Really?" I ask with a mixture of nerves and excitement. Could it really be possible?

"I guess we will see," she says, with a small smile.

We spend the next few hours talking and drinking wine—her more than me. I kept to my word, sticking to the single glass. We tell different stories about our lives, keeping each as light as possible. Each time we start to get into a darker story, the other lightens the mood with a happy one.

* * *

A while later, a dark-haired man pops up on the front porch seemingly out of thin air, and Phoebe clutches at her chest.

"Sebastyn! Shit! You scared me. Come meet Sophia." She tries to stand and fails, stumbling back into her chair. I walk over and help her settle back down. Sebastyn looks between me and Phoebe in surprise before his brows furrow in confusion.

"Sorry, Phoebe, didn't mean to scare you. Is Alaric or my sister around?" he says without looking at me. Rude.

"It's two o'clock in the morning, Seb. They're in bed. Why?" Phoebe's face morphs to one lined with worry. He opens his mouth to answer, but Phoebe cuts off whatever he was going to say. "Where's Darren?"

He lets out a sigh. "That's why I'm here. We decided to split up to look for Sophia and were supposed to meet back at the hotel, but he never showed up. Now his phone is going straight to voicemail." I suck in a breath. He went missing looking for me?

"You were looking for me? Where?" I ask, hoping it wasn't anywhere close to the coven.

"This is one of the guys who volunteered to go to Halifax to see if we could find you, so that I didn't have to leave Aurora or the boys," Phoebe explains before turning back to Sebastyn. "What do you mean he didn't show up?"

I can see the panic starting to build on Phoebe's face, but I can't move or say anything as dread pools in my gut. What if Devin found him? If he did, I don't even want to imagine what he would do to him.

"Wait here. I'm going to get Alaric, so I only have to explain this once. Call Skar?" The man points to Phoebe, and she nods, already picking up the phone as he blinks away again.

"Skar, I need you to come over," Phoebe says through the phone. She nods a couple of times before hanging up and looking for me.

"I'm sorry," I whisper to her, once again feeling like this is all my fault. I don't want to ruin these people like I ruined Samara's family.

"Hey. Everything is going to be okay. You'll see." She tries to put on a brave face, but I know that one. I do the same thing. That's not something she can say for sure. I thought coming here was a great thing, but now I'm not so sure. I could've already cost this family one member. If the mages follow me here, I could cost them more. I can't let that happen.

Alaric and Sebastyn appear back outside, and Alaric is shirtless and steadying himself, looking like he may vomit. Before he can straighten to his full height, Skarlyt pops onto the porch, looking a little disheveled from having been woken up.

"You've been practicing, I see," Sebastyn says to her, and she gives him an enormous smile and nod, wrapping her arms around him in a hug.

"Okay, we're outside now." Alaric takes a deep breath and demands, "Tell me what's going on."

"Well, you know how we were in Halifax looking for Sophia," Sebastyn says and waits for everyone to nod in agreement, including me. "It didn't go according to plan, clearly." He motions to me, standing on the deck with my twin, hours away from where they were looking.

"None of our locator spells worked to find her. Even your blood wasn't strong enough, Phoebe, so we had to search the mundane way....with no luck.

"Yesterday, Darren had this..." He pauses and looks at me before clearing his throat. What is that about? "He had this feeling that we needed to increase our efforts, so he suggested splitting up. He had good reasons, so I agreed, and we were supposed to meet at the hotel hours ago.

"While I was out, looking for Sophia, I noticed someone following me. Wherever I went, this guy in all black was on my tail. I ducked into an alley and teleported straight back to the hotel room to lose him. I was going to tell Darren that we needed to head home to regroup. We were gaining too much attention in Halifax. There's some extremely fucked up shit going on there by the way," he adds with a pointed look at Alaric.

"But when Darren missed our meeting time, I tried calling him on his cell. I must've tried a hundred times, and it kept going straight to voicemail. For the first hour, I figured that his phone just died. The more time that passed, though, I got a sinking feeling in my gut and decided to do a locator spell on him.

"It didn't work. Nothing did. Then I called the car rental place and had them track the car's GPS. It's parked in the middle of some rural area. Even the satellite maps don't show anything—just a blurry picture of some forest. I don't know what's there, and I didn't want to go without at least telling you guys where to come save us later," he finishes with a wry smile.

I turn to look at Alaric who is practically vibrating in rage. He hands Phoebe the baby monitor and walks down the steps before shifting into his black wolf and letting out a howl. That's going to wake the neighbors for sure.

"Can you show me where the car is parked?" I ask, and he

nods, pulling a paper map out of his pocket. As he spreads it out, a rumpled Samara comes running up the steps with Trev.

"What's going on?" she asks.

"Apparently Sebastyn—that's this guy—and Alaric's brother have been in Halifax for the past few days looking for me, and now Darren is missing. He is going to show me on a map where the car locator said he was. He said it's in a forest area," I tell her, and she sucks in a breath, obviously thinking the same as me.

"That's probably the shifter I smelled at the hotel the other day. Too bad we didn't run into each other. This would never have happened. I should look too. I know those woods better than anyone. I've been the only one living there for the past ten years after all." I glance around at everyone at her words, seeing the shock on their faces. It's not uncommon for a shifter to live in the woods, but they don't live alone.

He places the map on the ground in front of us, and someone shines a flashlight down on it as Seb places a finger. Samara and I look at each other. Oh shit.

"That's your..." Samara says, and I nod.

"That's where I grew up. It's in a small community of mages. It's too dangerous for you to go on your own," I tell him, looking into his eyes, hoping he realizes the danger.

"Shit," he whispers. "How many are there?"

I close my eyes and do a mental count. "There are about one hundred adults living in that community—men and women. About another fifty or so kids."

"But there was that group who followed us. So, there would be less than that there now," Samara adds with hope in her voice.

"Okay, I'm back. What's the plan?" Alaric says, stepping out onto the porch from the front door once again. He's back on two legs and dressed, and he's got murder in his eyes.

Chapter Thirteen

Darren

I groan as I wake up on something cold and hard. I try to stretch out, but my body meets resistance. I open my eyes and see metal bars surrounding me. I sit up and look closer.

I'm in a fucking cage? Fuck! How did I let this happen? The last thing I remember is Seb and I deciding to split up so we could find Sophia and leave this place as soon as possible. I grasp at the memories from the day.

I remember waking up after that dream and needing to meet Sophia in the forest. Then I dropped Sebastyn off and made my way to the forest. There was that scent of mountain lion that I was following and then...the mages. Gods damned mages.

I look through the bars of the cage and around the room, realizing I'm in some sort of basement. Even with the lights off, my shifter sight allows me to see the dirty concrete walls and floors. From the musty smell, there must be water leaking in here somewhere.

I try to investigate the cage to see if I can locate a locking mechanism, but I can't even find hinges to mark the door. What the hell? How did they get me in here without a door? As I'm looking around, I notice small sticks strewn throughout the cage with small scraps of fabric attached to them, like clothing.

I lift one of the makeshift dolls to examine it closer. That smell, like freshly cut grass with a hint of honey..."Sophia." A low growl slips out, but it's not from my wolf. In fact, the more I reach for him, the further away he seems. I glance around the room, looking for evidence that she's here. I must have been taken by whomever had kept her locked up all these years. Maybe she didn't get away to meet me after all. At that thought, my heart sinks.

"No," I say to myself adamantly. Her scent here is fading. Even with my dulled senses, I can tell that much. She hasn't been here recently. For the first time since I woke up, I realize that she must've been kept in this cage often for it to still smell like her. Damn it. What did these monsters do to her?

Footsteps above me bring my attention back to the present. I can hear two distinct sets of steps, both far too heavy to be Sophia. Whoever is walking around up there sounds like a herd of elephants trampling through the house. I get comfortable, well, as comfortable as I possibly can inside a five-by-five cage and close my eyes. If I block off my other senses, I may be able to pick up some of the conversation with my enhanced hearing. With my wolf feeling so far away, it's not going to be easy. So, I close my eyes and listen.

"If Devin didn't wait so long to let us have that stupid bitch, she wouldn't have run off. He should have let us knock her up as soon as she turned eighteen, like the rest of the bitches." My eyes snap open. What the fuck? Are they talking about Sophia? Are they saying she isn't here? That she got away? My heart beats faster at the thought. At least one of us got away. I quickly close my eyes again; I need to get the rest of the conversation.

"He had his reasons; you know that," the other voice answers.

"He doesn't have to consult us on his decisions. Like with that mutt downstairs, why didn't we just slit his throat?"

"Apparently he's been trying to get information about the bitch, so Devin thinks he might come in handy trying to get her back."

"Still, now we're stuck here babysitting instead of being out there searching."

At that moment, I hear both of them fall to the floor and their breath catches. "Fuck, what was that?" one of them gasps.

"Shit," the other says, and it takes him a minute to catch his breath. "That bitch somehow removed her fucking tether. Now what?"

So, Sophia figured out how to remove her tether. Good. Now I just need to figure out how to get out of here to see if Seb can use the tracking spell now that she's away from them. We need to find her and keep her out of Devin's hands.

The door to the basement opens, and a lone man walks down the stairs, flicking on the lights as he passes. He has an average build with salt and pepper hair and a great big bushy beard. It's his eyes that I focus on though. The way they pull at the corners as he comes closer makes me shiver. This isn't a man. The evil coming off of him makes him only one thing: a monster.

"Good, you're awake," he says, pulling a metal chair that scrapes across the floor until he's sitting right in front of me.

I don't grace him with an answer, instead choosing to look down at my fingernails as if they're the most interesting thing in the world.

"Not talkative?" he questions, and I continue to stare at my hands. "That's fine. I have other ways to make you talk." He chuckles darkly, and my breath gets lodged in my throat. I don't plan on giving him any information, but I have to wonder how much pain I can endure without my wolf until I sing like a canary.

I steel myself, intent on giving nothing away. This is all my fault. It was my suggestion that we split up. It was me who told Alaric I didn't want any back up. And it was me who refused to wait to come up with a plan before bringing Sebastyn along on what could possibly be a suicide mission. Maybe if I had waited, I would've had those dreams at home, and we could've been prepared.

Shit. I shake the dark thoughts from my head, looking over at him.

"Why are you looking for Sophia?" he asks me simply. He acts more like he's too busy for this conversation than like he's upset. I study his face in silence for just a moment, sizing up my competition.

He whispers something under his breath, and my entire body seizes up like a strong electric current is flowing through it. The pain is excruciating, and my jaw is locked so hard I worry I'm going to crack my teeth.

After what feels like hours but is likely only a few minutes, the pain cuts off suddenly. The memory of the pain is still humming through my muscles, but I try not to show the pain.

"Why are you looking for Sophia?" he repeats.

I laugh. "Fuck you."

"Have it your way," he snarls, whispering under his breath, and the pain is back.

This time it's not electric shocks. I think I would've preferred that. It feels like there are millions of bugs burrowing through my skin, into my muscles. They are everywhere on my body, even in my nether regions. I grit my teeth through the pain, willing myself to take it, to take whatever he throws at me. I'll never tell him anything. Not if it means my family and Sophia are safe.

As if sensing that this is not working, he stops the spell. I do not bother hiding my relief from the pain, and I let out a heavy breath, turning to look at him.

"I'll ask again, why are you looking for Sophia?"

"It doesn't matter. You'll never find her." I let out a maniacal laugh.

"Why do you care?" he asks, seeming confused.

"Fuck you," I repeat, not giving him the satisfaction of knowing what she means to me or my family.

"Perhaps pain is not the way to make you talk. Don't worry. I have other methods." The way he's smiling at me gives me an uneasy feeling. "You should get your rest while you can, mutt."

His words are nothing, and I don't know if I'll ever fall asleep again without remembering the itch of those phantom grubs in my skin, but my eyes are too heavy to keep open. I try to fight it, but I hear him whisper something and, next thing I know, I'm transported into a nightmare.

The room is the same, only a sliver brighter, but I am no longer in the cage in the room's center. Sophia, a halo of pale hair around her young face, has replaced me.

She must be about six years old, shivering in the corner of the cage, leaning into the dark, metal bars.

"I'm sorry, Father," she whimpers. "I won't do it again."

"No, you won't. I'll make sure of it." A younger version of the man who just tortured me stands before her. So, this must be Devin.

"Please, no more, Father. I promise I won't say anything," Sophia pleads.

Devin doesn't answer. He just laughs, pulling Sophia out of the cage by her hair. I move instinctively to catch her, but I find I'm rooted to the spot. Once he lets go, she collapses on the ground. He whispers under his breath, and she cries out. Not in pain but sorrow. Instantly, I know that he's doing to her what he's doing to me, and he's showing her something to break her heart. I try as hard as I can to rush over to her, to comfort her, to take on her burden, but I can't. I am unable to move and unable to take my eyes away from the beautiful little girl sobbing on the dirty floor.

"Stop," I grit through clenched teeth, but it doesn't stop. If I manage to make any sound, neither of the younger visions before me acknowledge it.

Next thing I know, the nightmare contorts, and an older version of Sophia is standing before me in the basement. She must be close to eighteen. Her normally strawberry blonde hair is matted and so dirty it looks brown; bruises line her cheeks and body. Her clothes are ripped and torn, but she doesn't cry.

Devin approaches her, stepping from the dark somewhere outside my limited view.

"Do you know what you've done?" he asks her.

She nods.

"Tell me," he demands.

"I told Samara about my punishments," she says, hanging her head. "And do you know what you made me do?" he asks with a disappointed look on his face. She shakes her head no. "I had to exterminate that entire pride because of your big mouth." He spits, and her hand flies to her lips as the tears begin to fall.

"Every last animal in that pride is dead because of you, even your precious Samara." She collapses into the cold metal as sobs wrack her body. The pain isn't physical, but it is devious and devastating. I itch to run to her, to take away her pain. Once again, I'm stuck here watching, and my own heart breaks in the process.

The nightmare shifts again and again, each time showing Sophia in some sort of pain at a different age. The hardest ones to watch are the ones where he's physically hurting her and there's nothing I can do to stop it. There are so many that they can't be anything but memories. I grit my teeth further. If he thinks showing this will do anything but cement my resolve not to tell him anything, he's wrong. If this is what he did to her when she was here, before she ran away, I can't imagine what he will do to her if he gets her back. No. He can never get his hands on her. I'd die before I let that happen.

The nightmare fades, and I'm once again sitting in the cage. I cannot know how much time has passed, but I have to force my eyes open through the tears streaming down my face.

"Ready to talk?" Devin dusts his hands together like he's ready to wash up after mowing the lawn. Despite my resolve, I only have enough energy to shake my head.

"Maybe that friend of yours will have something to say. You know, the dark haired one staying with you at the hotel?" he says, and my head snaps up. Sebastyn. Is he saying they have Sebastyn? His eyes take on an evil glint, and he smiles. "Maybe you'll be more cooperative after watching him suffer." I throw myself at the bars, trying and failing to escape.

"I'll kill you," I growl, and his smile widens. Shit. I just gave him exactly what he wanted. Now he knows exactly what to do. I say a silent prayer to the goddess that she keeps both Sophia and Sebastyn safe. I don't want to have to choose between the two. As shitty as it is, I know in my heart that I would choose Sophia.

"I'll be back when our guest arrives," he says as he laughs all the way up the stairs, leaving me alone with my thoughts.

I lay on the ground, trying to get comfortable enough to fall asleep and go to the only place I can escape. Maybe if I can see Sophia, I can give her a message to get Sebastyn safe or get her to Alaric. But try as I might, it's impossible to fall asleep on a cold concrete floor in a cage that I can't even sit up in without tilting my head.

Sometime later, Devin walks back in.

"Come on, mutt. Apparently, your brother has something of ours, and we're going to use you to get her back." He walks up to the cage, reaching his hand through quickly and attaching a chain to something around my neck. For the first time since I woke up, I feel something foreign there and reach to investigate. I move my hands around my neck, feeling smooth leather.

A collar? I'm wearing a collar! Like a dog. I tug at it with my hands, but no matter what I do, it doesn't budge. Now I know why I can't feel my wolf. The collar isn't just decoration. It's a tether. Shit!

And my brother has something of theirs? Does that mean Sophia is with Alaric and Phoebe? Or does he know about Phoebe and Aurora? And Devin never did bring Sebastyn down, so maybe he got away too. Hope blooms in my chest. If I know Alaric—and I do—Alaric will not trade his mate or daughter for anything. If Alaric has Sophia, he's not going to willingly trade her either. Not even for his brother, and I wouldn't want him to.

Shit.

What am I going to do?

Chapter Fourteen

Sophia

I watch as hundreds of men and women make their way over to us from their homes, asking what happened. Alaric simply tells them that he will explain once everyone has arrived, that it's something he doesn't want to repeat multiple times. I watch after he tells the fifth person this and notice how the speed at which everyone is arriving is increasing. Some come running on two feet, others shift into wolves and sprint into the yard on all four.

Once at least two hundred men and women are standing on the lawn, Alaric gives a whistle to quiet them down.

"Okay, everyone, I know you're curious about what my howl was and why you've been called here." I watch as he takes a shaky breath. His brother is missing, and he actually cares. This is not something I'm used to. Devin's nephew went missing last week, and he didn't even bat an eye when his brother called. Said it was his loss and that entire coven were failures.

But to stand here and witness how a family dynamic should actually be...I'm in awe. I watch as Phoebe walks over and places her slight frame into the crook of his arm. They look at each other with such love, and Alaric leans down, giving her a soft kiss on her head before going back to address the wolves in front of him.

"Truth is, Darren was captured." I watch as every single person in the group gets loud, growling and calling for blood, for action. Alaric has to whistle again to quiet them down.

"We all love Darren, and we are making plans to go and rescue him. We need volunteers to go with Seb via teleport to Halifax to get him back." To my surprise, every single person in the group raises their hand. When I say every person, I literally mean every person. What did this Darren guy do to earn this kind of loyalty and devotion? At least two hundred people here are willing to lay down their lives for him.

I sit back with Samara and watch the flurry of activity that happens. "Is this what it's like to be a part of a pack?" I ask her in a whisper.

"This is how it was in my pride." She nods grimly. "They protect their own."

I watch as a small tear escapes her eye. This is what she had? This is what she lost because of me? I look at the people standing around, some raging, other's crying and being consoled by their friends.

A small group of women approach us. Two of them are holding small babies.

"Hi, I'm Charleigh, and this is Felicia. You already know the raven-haired beauty over here is Skarlyt," the petite blonde woman says, offering her hand to me and then Samara.

"I'm Sophia, and this is Samara and her mate, who I guess you guys already know," I say with a small chuckle. I'm glad I'm not the only one who caught onto my petty attempt at a joke because they all offer me a giggle in return. Just as our giggles start to slow down, I'm enveloped on all four sides by these women and Phoebe, who has just rejoined our group. I know they are using me to focus on something good happening when their friend is out there with those monsters.

I can't help the range of emotions that cross through my mind, sadness for their friend and brother, gratefulness for my new family, and finally love for the support that I'm receiving. I allowed Devin and his cronies to make me feel secluded and alone for so long. If it weren't for Samara, I don't know where I would be today.

I reach my arms through a hole in our group hug and grab Samara's arm, pulling her in with us. As much as I love this newfound family of mine, I'm not about to leave my original one behind. I feel her try to protest, but my persistence eventually wins, and she allows herself to be pulled into the hug. Now this feels right. Well, almost. I still feel like there is something missing. It's like there's something I forgot in Halifax, but I feel almost complete. Even with the looming threat of Devin hanging over me, I can't help but feel that I actually stand a chance at a life.

We all pull apart and take seats in the chairs along the porch. "Okay, who are these bundles of cuteness?" I ask, looking between Charleigh and Skarlyt.

Phoebe chuckles and points in the direction of Charleigh and Skarlyt's children. "That is Cybil, and the little man over there is Kayne. Him and Aurora actually have the same birthday. Remind me to tell you the story sometime. It's a doozy," she finishes with a saucy wink toward Skarlyt, who laughs.

Mental note: ask Phoebe and Skarlyt about that when we aren't in the middle of a crisis—maybe when we can share a bottle or two of wine.

Alaric walks up with Sebastyn by his side. "Okay, I think we've got a large enough group ready to go. Seb's going to need two of those potions that replenish his magic, Skar. He's going to be teleporting a large group there and back." Skar gets up and hands her son, Kayne, into Sebastyn's arms before walking into the house.

Once Skar is inside, Alaric turns to me and Samara. "Is there anything you can tell us that might help?" Unfortunately, I have little to say. I give information when I can, but, even though I was their captive for years, I know so little of their daily routines outside of the house. Samara is a much better help with this, as she has observed them for years, trying to find a way to get me away from them.

She starts with the basics. "They live in a community sort of like this one. There are approximately fifty or so houses spread out over a seven-kilometer area, all backing into the woods. The only way in or out of their community—by vehicle—is a single road." She stops and picks up the map, laying it flat and pointing to the area where the road would be located, even though it isn't marked.

"There's a small hunting cabin here, just off the main highway, and it isn't easily accessible. I've lived there for years under their radar. Sophia knows the way back to the houses from there better than me, but it's only a fifteen or twenty-minute walk I would say." She looks at me for confirmation, and I nod.

"Sounds about right," I add, and she continues.

"They don't have any protection wards that I've ever noticed, not even on the houses, and I've gotten pretty close when I've shifted at night, so you should be safe. If I had to hazard a guess though, they're keeping Darren at Devin's house here," she points to another unmarked location on the map. "The assholes probably put him in the basement where they used to keep Sophia."

I suck in a breath. I know I've told Phoebe about what they've done to me, but I don't know if I am ready for others to know.

"What do you mean?" It's Charleigh who asks.

I take a deep breath and begin a short retelling of my situation, shame coating my entire being. "When I was younger, they kept me in a cage in the basement to 'teach me lessons and house break me,' in their words. Samara is right. If I were a betting woman, I would put all my money on them keeping him there. The cage they use has no locks, no door. It's only opened and closed by magic and is able to drain power just like a tether would." When I'm done, I can see looks of pity on some faces and rage on others. Rage I can handle, but the pity I'm not too fond of.

"Okay, so that should be your focus, Seb. Get to that house, mow down anyone who stand in your way. In fact, maybe we should ask the coven if they would be willing to send a few witches," Alaric finishes as Seb hands him Kayne and then blinks out. I'm guessing that he's going to go talk to the coven.

"What do you mean, *his* primary focus? You're not going?" Phoebe asks, stepping up to Alaric.

"No, I should stay here just in case," he says to her. Instead of being happy like I assumed she'd be, she actually seems pretty ticked off.

"Just in case what, Alaric? That's your brother! Your only brother! He's being held captive by people worse than Tanner, and you know how he treated me. Worse than Joe, and you've seen Sarah." Joe? Now that's a name I recognize. I know it's a common name for humans, but...it couldn't be...could it?

Devin's nephew who went missing from Ontario was named Joe. Did Alaric and Phoebe have something to do with that? I file that information away in the 'ask Phoebe later' file and go back to paying attention.

"You need to go. We'll be fine! We have two phoenixes, at least one hundred able-bodied shifters, an entire coven of witches, and that's not including our new vampire allies. Call Drake. I'm sure he'll either send some people with you or come stand guard while you go."

He just stares at her, his mouth hanging open as she talks.

"I watched how you were when you felt torn between finding

Skar and protecting us, and I won't do that again! You need to go. Between all our allies and the protection barrier, we will be fine."

"But..." Alaric goes to interrupt.

"No 'buts,' Alaric." She takes his face between her hands and looks into his eyes. "Am I the luna of the Westwood pack or not? I will take care of them, and they will take care of me. Skar, tell him!" The last she directs toward Skarlyt who has just reappeared, looking like a deer caught in the headlights.

She must see the determination on Phoebe's face because she simply says, "I agree with whatever Phoebe just said." Smart woman. Or not so smart, based on the murderous look that Alaric is giving her.

"Don't you want to know what you just agreed to?" Alaric asks.

"Sure, but I don't think it matters. If Phoebe is this determined, there's no swaying her, and I'm not stupid enough to go against a phoenix. You're still my best friend, but she's scary," Skar replies with a shrug.

"I simply said he should go with the group to find Darren, and that we will be fine here," Phoebe explains.

"You weren't going to go?" She turns to Alaric in shock.

"No. I thought it would be better to stick around here. I need to protect the pack." Skarlyt doesn't even try to hide her laughter.

"Protect us from what, Alaric? Even if the mages attack us while you're gone, we have an enormous amount of firepower here —plus a newly beefed-up barrier. You not going to help find Darren could be the difference between a win and a loss. With your familial bond, you might be able to get through whatever barriers they have in place where a pack bond can't. Don't you want your brother back?"

Damn, she's good. And familial bond? Pack bond? I sigh. Guess that goes in the "ask later" folder too.

"I didn't think of it like that. It's just..." He looks around at the group. "It's just...what if something happens and I'm not here?" Phoebe steps up, wrapping her arms around him.

Skar seems to take pity on him as well and sighs softly. "How about this...When Seb gets back, he can teleport me to the meeting spot and I'll teleport back. That way if we need you to come home, I will teleport to come get you."

Her mate, Lennox, has been silent during the previous disagreement but looks like he wants to protest this decision. He obviously thinks better of it, though, and just wraps his arms around Skar.

Looking around at all the couples wrapped around each other, I can't help but feel a pang of sadness cross through me. I know I said I wasn't sure if I wanted to meet my mate, but looking at everyone here makes me wish I had that. Someone to lean on, someone to love me unconditionally.

"That works," Alaric concedes as Seb returns.

"About twenty witches will be joining us," he explains, and his sister offers him one of the vials in her hand.

"You can thank me later," she says, "I made a few extra, but you're still probably going to feel like shit tomorrow."

Alaric nods and explains Skar's idea of teleporting her to the meeting spot. Thankfully, since they drove down the highway by the hunting cabin while they were looking for me, Seb was able to teleport to the road and back in a matter of seconds.

"Okay, I got it. Let's do a test run. Hold on, Alaric," Skar says and next thing you know, they're both gone and back within a few seconds. Alaric looks terrible when they're finished. He's practically green.

"It will pass in a few minutes," Skar says, rubbing his back from where he's hanging over the porch railing. She has a wicked smile on her face, and I can't help but think that was some sort of punishment. Another mental note: don't piss off Skarlyt.

"Hey, hun, I think I'm going to go with them," Samara whispers to me. My head snaps to her.

"No, you can't go. They know you. You know that if they see you, they will stop at nothing to kill you just because you're my friend," I say, wrapping her in a hug.

"I know, but I know the area better than everyone, and I think I will be able to help." She sighs against my arms. "I never wanted to go back there, but they have a better chance of finding him quickly if I go."

"You're right," I tell her while stepping back to look into her eyes. "I know you are, but I am right too. We're finally free. I can't lose you now."

"I won't let anything happen to her," Trev says, stepping up and placing his arm around her shoulder. I look from Trev to Samara, and I can see the determination and desire for my blessing in her eyes. Relenting, I nod before enveloping her in another hug.

"Okay," I whisper into her hair. "But you better come back to me."

Stepping back from each other, I realize for the first time that we each actually have the opportunity to start our own lives, real lives, with mates and children, houses and outings. We can have everything we dreamed of, and it feels amazing but terrifying at the same time. I don't know who I am without Samara. She's been the only good thing in my life for as long as I can remember. Now, as I look around, I realize that I have a lot more good in my life. I glance up at the windows of the house. The boys are fast asleep, but I think I can pick out which one is theirs. I suddenly have so many good things in my life that I need to protect.

I step back onto the porch and watch, as one by one, Seb zips away the people going to rescue Darren.

When it's Samara's turn, I grab her back and hold her tight for a minute. When we both let go, I can see the mist in her eyes. I feel arms wrap around me as I watch Samara fade away with Seb. I turn and cry into Phoebe's waiting arms. I'm not even really sure why I'm crying. I simply know that my best friend is headed into danger because of me, and I hate it. I'm already responsible for the death of her family. If something happens to her too...

I feel another set of arms enveloping us both and can instantly tell that it's Alaric trying to say his goodbye to Phoebe, so I attempt to step back to give them some privacy. It doesn't work. They both pull me in and hold me tighter.

This is what it's like to have a family.

I could really get used to this.

Chapter Fifteen

Sophia

We head inside as the last people teleport away and flop onto the couches in the living room.

"I'm so tired," Phoebe says from her spot at the end.

"I think we all are," Charleigh pipes up. "We're going to have to take turns with the kids today so we can get some sleep," she adds, and I see Skarlyt and Phoebe nod.

"Josh and I are going to head back to get some sleep. We'll take the kids this afternoon if you three or four can figure out the schedule until then," Felicia says while standing up and stretching.

"I'll be up around eleven to help. Felicia needs her sleep," her mate, Josh, says while placing his arm around her, and she looks up at him in shock and, dare I say, annoyance.

"Why does Felicia need her sleep? She's the only one without kids," Charleigh snaps. I'm not sure if that's their sibling relationship, but I didn't get that vibe from them earlier.

"Not for long," Josh says, moving his hand to her stomach.

The next thing I know, all the girls are up hugging Felicia and jumping up and down. I hesitate to join, still unsure where I fit in with this group.

"Why didn't you tell us?" Charleigh asks with a look on her face that shows her regret for snapping at her earlier.

"We only just found out last week, we wanted to wait to tell everyone," Felicia says, giving Josh a pointed look. "Either way, you know now, and I'm exhausted. So, we're going to go get some sleep and see you later in the day." She gives hugs all around, including me, which surprises me.

As soon as they leave, Charleigh gestures to her mate. "Okay, us next. Ashton and I will be over when Cybil wakes up to feed the boys breakfast. Maybe you could ask Lexi and Heydon to take them for a few hours while Aurora naps."

"That's a good idea. I'll call Lexi when we wake up . She's probably still asleep since she stayed home with the boys during the meeting," she pauses, her hand rubbing her eyes. "We also need to find time to do some training with Sophia too, so maybe the boys can go for a sleepover or something," Phoebe says, getting up and hugging Charleigh. Again, when Charleigh gives her round of hugs, I'm included, and she gives me a little extra squeeze.

"I'm so happy you're finally here!" she whispers into my ear.

"Me too, Charleigh, me too," I murmur back.

"Okay, Lennox, Kayne, and I are just going to sleep in my room downstairs, so we don't have to go all the way back to the cottage," Skar says, grabbing Lennox's hand and dragging him down to the basement. That's convenient.

"Night, guys," Phoebe and I say at the same time. They just give us a little wave, proving how exhausted they are.

"Do you think you could sleep with me tonight?" Phoebe says at the same time I say,

"Would it be okay if I slept with you tonight?"

I don't know why, but I'm feeling a little off right now, with Samara running off into danger and the threat of Devin looming over me. Plus, if I'm being honest, I just got my sister. I'm not ready to be apart just yet.

We both start laughing and head up the stairs. Once we're on the landing, our laughter quiets down in fear of waking up the kids.

She leads the way into her room, quietly rummaging through drawers as I walk over to the bassinet. Aurora is still sleeping soundly inside. She's perfect. She looks like a little angel with a slight glow emanating from her vibrant red hair. I get the urge to reach out and stroke her soft face but stop myself just before making contact. I don't want to disturb her.

I'm still standing there staring at her when Phoebe walks over and hands me a pair of pajamas. She is already dressed in what I'm assuming is one of Alaric's shirts. I head over to her beautiful, spacious bathroom and get changed into the pajamas she supplied.

Phoebe is already laying in the overly enormous bed when I exit the bathroom. She already has the covers turned down on the one side, ready for me to crawl in. I slip into the bed beside Phoebe, and she passes me a large pillow. I watch as she adjusts her own along the length of her body and wraps her right leg over the top, and I mimic her movements. I've never had more than one pillow before, so I watch her for cues on what to do.

Oh, my gods! This is the most comfortable position I've ever been in! Phoebe must see the shock and pleasure on my face because she lets out a little giggle. I snuggle deeper into the pillow, not caring if I look like an idiot.

Once I've gotten myself in a comfortable position, with Phoebe and I facing each other, she reaches out her hand to clasp mine and gives it a little squeeze.

"I'm so glad we found you," she whispers to me.

"Me too," I reply, which is followed by a large yawn.

Sleep comes easily to me while still holding Phoebe's hand, and I dream of the same forest I have been for a while. The same forest that is right outside my window.

I am flying in my phoenix form next to another phoenix. I now know this is Phoebe, and there are two black wolves waiting by the water's edge instead of one. They look so similar. There is no doubt in my mind that they are brothers. I recognize Alaric immediately by the red patch on his chest. My suspicion is proven when Phoebe lands before him and strokes his fur. The other wolf just looks up at me from where I'm flying in the sky. I feel such a deep connection to him.

My memories flood back.

Darren. This is Darren. His big, blue eyes sparkle in the moonlight, and he begins to run toward me as I land. He instantly tackles me to the ground, but he's no longer a wolf by the time he lands on top of me.

"Sophia," he whispers. "Are you safe?"

I nod into his neck. "But you aren't."

"I'm okay," he says, and I push him back to look at him.

"Does Devin have you?" I ask, fearful of his answer.

"He does," he admits.

"Did he hurt you?" I rake my eyes over his body looking for any signs of injuries but find none.

"No..." he begins, but I can tell there's more.

"But?" I question.

"He showed me memories of you in the cage and how he treated you over the years to try and get me to talk."

I suck in a breath. "You saw that?"

He nods, sitting up and gripping my shoulders. "Know that what he did to your friend wasn't your fault. That was one of the hardest things for me to watch. You must've really loved her. I'm sorry."

Immediately, I know the memory he's talking about. It's the one where Devin told me about Samara's pride.

"She survived. She escaped while they were attacking. Her parents made her slip into a secret tunnel. She was the only survivor. She's here with me and your pack. Actually," I say with a small smile gracing my lips, "she met her mate here."

"She did?" he asks, a genuine smile on his own face. "Who?"

"Trevan. He's a Fae who owns Supernatural."

"I know Trev very well. He's a good guy, and if Samara is worthy of the love you have for her, then they'll be a good match. Have you heard from Sebastyn?"

"He's safe. Searching for you. Half of the pack just left to come find you," I tell him.

"They're moving me, I think. They came and pulled me out of the cage with a collar and leash and put me in a truck before giving me some sort of tranquilizer. He said something about coming there. You need to warn them."

"I never remember our dreams," I tell him, and his mouth drops open. "That's why I left you—I never would have—not on purpose. Can you remember? You remember me when you wake up?"

"I do. I thought you did too," he runs his finger through his dark hair, searching for an answer. "Shit."

"I can try though. I'll write it down right away or tell Phoebe or something."

He nods. "It will be okay. There's nothing either of us can do right now except get some rest."

"I wish I could stay here with you," I say, feeling helpless.

"I need to hold you," he whispers, pulling me back into him.

My body melts into his as if we are one single person rather than two. My back is against his muscled chest and his arm fits perfectly across my waist. I try not to think about my own nakedness or his.

"We're going to get you back, Darren," I promise, twining my fingers with his. "We're going to be together soon."

I wake what seems like an eternity later, feeling extremely well rested. I feel a slight panic when I open my eyes to a strange place but quickly recover when I remember the events of yesterday. I'm safe in my sister's bed, in her house. I glance down at myself and note that I'm in the identical position as I was when I fell asleep last night, but Phoebe is no longer in bed.

I throw the covers off and search for a pad of paper and pen to write down my dream, but by the time I'm done searching the drawers closest to the bed, the dream has already begun slipping away leaving a nagging feeling that I'm forgetting something important in its place. I write down one word...Darren. I guess it's not really a word, but a name. But why was Darren in my dream? The only part that remains clear is the beginning: my flying high in the sky with Phoebe by my side, the two black wolves waiting at the shoreline, and then the rest fades. Was he one of the black wolves? I shake my head and concentrate harder, but nothing comes. Damn it. Why can't I remember?

I turn away from the dresser to look out the window and see the sun high in the sky and smile. I can't remember a time where I didn't wake up before the sun and had to jump up to start my chores. Even when Samara and I left, we hardly slept, and, when we did, we had to rush to get up and go before they caught up with us, so I savor this moment. It's always been hard to imagine a life for myself outside of Devin and his rules, but I have to admit that if waking up will feel like this every day, I can't wait to get it started.

My bladder begins protesting, reminding me that I need to get moving. I rush over to the bathroom to do my business and notice that Phoebe left a stack of clothes for me and a towel and tooth-brush on the counter. I look from the shower to the clothes. I really want to get downstairs to help her out. I know she's probably tired, but that shower just looks so inviting. Finally, the desire to feel what must be close to one hundred jets streaming the hot water on my skin wins out, and I jump into the shower.

Oh, my gods! This is absolute heaven.

I stay in the shower for so long that I expect the hot water to run out about twenty minutes before it does, so I take that as a sign to stay in. Once I feel that I've sufficiently experienced the ultimate shower, I step out and towel off before getting dressed and brushing my teeth. I look around the bathroom for something to tame my unruly hair when I notice a sticky note on the mirror in front of a hairbrush, some coconut oil and mousse, and a hair tie.

"If your hair is anything like mine, you'll need this ∼P∼"

Thank you, Phoebe! Normally I just braid my hair and spin it up into a bun. It's not as curly as hers, but it is still wavy and reacts to heat and humidity by puffing. I pull the coconut oil and mousse through my long strands and decide to leave it down. Devin never provided me with anything to tame my hair, so I resorted to using ingredients from the kitchen, which never truly worked. It will be nice to leave it down for once without the frizz.

As I begin walking down the stairs, I can hear the sounds of laughter and smell coffee. Ah sweet java. Coffee should have its own food group because it has been an absolute necessity in my life thus far, not to mention the fact that it just tastes delicious.

I'm attacked by two handsome little munchkins as I reach the bottom of the stairs.

"Aunt Sophia!" they both exclaim, wrapping their little arms around me and squeezing me tight. I squat down to their level, placing my own arms around them both, pulling them in for a lingering hug. I can't describe the feeling that I have right now. Happiness for sure, fullness definitely, but there's something else. Something that I can't find the right word to explain—how it feels to finally be wanted and part of a family.

I feel the boys start to squirm and reluctantly pull my arms back.

"Mom said we get to train with you today!" Ryker says with a giant grin.

"Really?" I ask. I expected for me and Phoebe to work on my phoenix flames today, but I didn't expect the boys to join us since they aren't phoenixes.

"Yup," Riley says before adding, "Aunt Skar has been helping us with being able to produce phoenix flames. I'm getting pretty good at it. Want to see?"

"Of course, I do, but later, okay? Aunt Sophia needs coffee first," I tell them and begin to stand up.

"You sound like Uncle Darren. He needs coffee before he does anything," Ryker says. At the mention of Darren, I am struck by a feeling like I've missed a step in the dark. But I shake my head and inhale the smell of coffee. Ryker grabs my hand and leads me to the kitchen where I find an exhausted-looking Phoebe pouring me a cup of coffee, with Aurora strapped to her chest in one of those baby carriers.

"Milk and sugar?" she asks.

"A little of both, please," I tell her. She adds both and hands me the cup. I take my first sip, and I'm surprised. "Oh, that's the best coffee I've ever tasted," I say as I go in for a bigger gulp.

"It's Darren's idea of perfect coffee. He adds a little of the vanilla-flavored coffee grounds to the regular stuff. He says it just gives it a hint of vanilla without taking away the coffee flavor," she explains with a small, sad smile. I can tell she's worried about him, but I have nothing to say that will make it better, so I give her a small nod.

She lets out an enormous yawn, and I get up off the stool and walk over to her, reaching for Aurora.

"Why don't you go have a nap? Me and the boys can take care of Aurora for a bit, can't we, boys?" I say to Phoebe, before looking at the boys and seeing their big nods. She looks conflicted for a split second before another enormous yawn slips out, and she unstraps Aurora and passes her to me.

"Just an hour or two, okay? And if she gets hungry, come get me," she says.

"We'll be fine. Go get some sleep. You're dead on your feet. I promise we'll come get you if we need to," I tell her, ushering her toward the stairs.

Once I hear the bedroom door close, I turn toward the boys.

"Okay, what should we do?" I ask them.

"We could go to the park," Riley says with an excited grin.

"I'd rather stick closer to home if we could, buddy. Any other suggestions?"

"Oh! I know, we could go walk on the beach, or sit on the dock and skip stones," Ryker adds. Now that sounds like an amazing idea.

"Perfect! Let's do that. But first, do either of you know how to attach this thing?" I ask them, gesturing to the baby carrier.

"It goes on like a backpack but on the front," Riley says, coming and helping me get it attached. He has to stand on the stool to help me get it over my head, but, after a few minutes, we secure Aurora onto my chest, and we're ready to head out to the lake. I quickly jot down a note for Phoebe on the counter, so she doesn't wake up in a panic, and we head out the patio doors.

It's even more beautiful than my dreams and drawings could have ever portrayed. The lake is so calm that it looks like glass reflecting the sun overhead.

We spend the next two hours walking along the beach, picking up cool stones and pieces of sand glass, before Aurora starts getting fussy.

"I think Rory is getting hungry," Riley says, cooing over his baby sister.

"I think you might be right. Let's go see if your mom feels

better after her nap," I tell him as we all casually walk back toward the house.

I see Skarlyt sitting on the deck with Lennox and Kayne as we get closer, and I give a little wave while the boys rush over to them, telling them all about our small adventure. I'm glad they seem to have enjoyed it as much as I did.

"Hey Sophia, we got your note and decided to stay close in case Phoebe woke up," she says.

"Thanks. I wanted to get the boys out of the house so she could sleep but didn't want to go too far just in case. She told me a little about the stuff that happened, so I figured she might panic if we weren't in the house." Phoebe told me about Tanner kidnapping and threatening Riley, and she admitted that, even though it's been a long time, she still has anxiety when she doesn't know where they are.

Aurora decides that now she's too hungry and fussing isn't getting her food fast enough. She gives a full-out cry, and I quickly make my way upstairs to where Phoebe is still sleeping. By the time I'm at the door, Phoebe is pulling it open and reaching out for her.

"I think she's hungry," I say, unbuckling the baby carrier and passing her Aurora.

"Sounds like it." Phoebe looks down at her daughter with a smile.

"How do you feel now?" I ask. She looks like she just woke up, but the bags under her eyes have gone down drastically, and she looks rested.

"Much better. Thank you for watching them. I really needed that." She brings Aurora to her breast to eat, and she instantly quiets. "Who's downstairs?"

"Skarlyt and Lennox are down there with the boys and Kayne," I tell her, and she reaches over for a blanket to cover Aurora up before we walk back downstairs.

"Charleigh and Felicia are on their way over to watch Aurora and Kayne, so we can start training when you're done feeding Aurora, Pheebs," Skarlyt says as we reach the bottom of the stairs.

Training?

Why am I suddenly so nervous?

Chapter Sixteen

Sophia

P hoebe and I sit on the deck while she finishes feeding Aurora. Skarlyt, with the help of the boys, begins to set up for our training. I'm thinking I should just ask about my dream last night. I can't help but wonder if the other wolf is, in fact, Alaric's brother Darren. If it is, why the hell have I been dreaming and drawing him for months? Is it just because I am feeling guilt for getting him kidnapped by Devin?

"Phoebe," I begin sheepishly, hoping she doesn't think I sound crazy. "You know how I told you I dreamed about this place before I ever got here? I think I had one again last night." She just nods her head, looking curious but not shocked..

"Was the dream about us?" she asks. "Were we flying?" How does she know that?

"Yeah, actually," I reply in confusion. "There were two wolves by the lake waiting for us."

"I thought it seemed too realistic." Phoebe nods thoughtfully. "Normally, I dream about Alaric and me in our other forms, but I've never dreamed about Darren—or you for that matter." So, I was right. The other wolf is Darren.

"So, we had the same dream?" I ask. "I feel like I can't remember part of it. Do you?"

"It was just a dream," she says, shrugging. "I remember flying and landing. I remember Alaric and—" she cuts herself off, blushing.

"Okay. I get it." I blush along with her. "The other wolf is his brother, then? Why have I been dreaming about Alaric's brother for months now?"

"Remember how I told you I used to dream about Alaric all the time before I figured out that we were true mates?" She pauses, readjusting Aurora, and I nod. "If I had to guess, I'm betting that you and Darren are true mates. That's why you're dreaming of him and why he felt such a powerful pull to go find you."

"You think he's my mate?"

"We won't know until you two meet for sure," she tells me.

Mates? I've fantasized about meeting my mate, about having a family of my own, but I never thought it would be a reality for me. Now, this potential mate has been stolen by my evil adoptive father. If there is a connection between us, I just hope Devin doesn't realize it. Darren will be dead by the end of the day if he does. It's one thing if he thinks Darren just wants me for my power; it will be another matter entirely if he figures out we're mates. Devin won't just kill him; he will torture him in front of me to gain my compliance.

"What is he like?" I ask with curiosity. We might not even be a good match. He might be a complete and total asshole, even though everything I've heard about him tells me the complete opposite. I still want to know.

"He's amazing! Him and Alaric are very similar. Even in looks, but he has a lot more tattoos," she says with a little giggle. "He is a people person, and if he asks about your day or how you are— unlike other people—he genuinely cares. That's why everyone in the pack loves him. He's Alaric's beta, so most people go straight to

Darren with their problems, and he makes sure that he knows everyone by name, what their complaints are, and implements ways to fix any he can before they leave his office. He also has a serious coffee addiction and can drink it at midnight and still sleep." She pauses again briefly, waving her free hand.

"You're going to have to meet him to really know. Words doesn't do him justice. He's just an all-around good guy," she finishes. He sounds amazing, and if he looks like Alaric, he's sure to be handsome. Even though I have absolutely no romantic feelings toward Alaric, I can still admit that he's a handsome man, and Phoebe is one lucky woman.

Fortunately, we're interrupted in our conversation before I say that out loud. I don't know how Phoebe would react to another woman ogling her mate—sister or not.

"I asked Sarah to join us for an extra set of hands," Charleigh says, walking up the steps with a small woman following behind her, looking at the ground. I wonder what that's about. Every other woman I've met so far in this pack has been boisterous and outgoing. Seeing a woman acting so closed off reminds me of the women I met in Devin's coven.

"Sarah, this is my twin sister Sophia." Phoebe introduces me as soon as she mounts the steps.

"Nice to meet you," she says, seeming to struggle to make eye contact. Without thinking, I stand up and wrap her in a hug. I kind of need one right now, and I have a feeling she does too.

"It's nice to meet you too," I whisper in her ear and go to release her, but I guess I was right about her needing a hug, because she squeezes me for several long seconds before releasing me. I sit down on one of the benches and pat the spot beside me for her to sit.

"So, Sarah, tell me about yourself." I've never really been the shy type, and I'm bad about putting my foot in my mouth and saying things I shouldn't—which is probably why I received so many punishments—but other than a flash of shock on her face, she doesn't seem to mind.

"There's not much to tell. From what Phoebe has told me about you, my story doesn't seem much different," she begins with a shrug. Her words are straightforward, direct, but her voice is small, whisper thin.

"What do you mean?" I ask, confused.

"My father was a mage in Phoebe's ex-husband's coven. I'm sure I don't need to tell you what that is like."

I shake my head. "No. You don't."

"My mother died giving birth to me and my father blamed me my entire life. He cared about her—or thought he did. The way he talked about her wasn't typical, but the way he treated me was. At eighteen, I was given to Tanner's best friend Joe as a 'gift.'"

"Gift," I scoff.

"Exactly. For the first few years of our marriage, my entire life changed. I actually felt like I was in love with him and would do anything to please him. I didn't realize how much of it was fake—how much of it was a spell to make me feel that way—until he spent a week or two away."

"Wait. What? He made you believe you were in love with him?"

She nods sullenly. "Once I realized it, I rummaged through his office while he was gone and found the spell he was using. No one ever taught me magic on purpose, but I was able to counter it. Things got worse after that. I no longer found his...'quirks' cute. He was a vile man. Worse than Tanner in some ways, because of his standing in the coven. He wanted to be the high priest and..."

"So, he took it out on you," I provide, and she nods. "Where is he now?" If he's not already dead, I may just have to pay him a visit.

"Dead. He came after Aurora, and Phoebe killed him." Her smile slips away as she says it. "I shouldn't be happy that my husband is dead. What's wrong with me?" Her bright green eyes shine with sadness, and I wish I could take the feeling away. She's already stunning. If her eyes were alight with happiness instead of pain, there's no one alive who could resist her.

"Nothing." I grip her hands in mine. "Absolutely nothing. Whatever he put you through, he got what he deserved, and so did you. You're free now. No more looking over your shoulder. No more worrying about having dinner on the table or a spotless house. No anxiety over whether he's going to come home in a good mood or not."

Hope shines in her eyes through the unshed tears, and I can tell that she desperately wants to believe me, so I take it a step further and tell her about my life. About how Devin treated me—about the cage.

"Are you kidding me?" she spits, anger flaring in her beautiful green eyes.

"No. But, like you I didn't let what they did break me. We're free. Finally free and, even after only being here a day, I can tell that the men around here are nothing like them."

She nods. "I've noticed that too. But I feel like I'm waiting for the other shoe to drop. For one of them to come storming up the steps demanding payment for me staying here."

"That will never happen," I growl. "Phoebe would never stand for it, but neither will I. I have a feeling we're going to be good friends."

"You probably don't want to promise friendship to someone like me." She reverts back to her meek self.

I gently place my fingers under her chin, raising it up so she looks in my eyes. "Someone like you?"

She nods. "A mage."

I take a page out of Phoebe's book and tighten my hold on her, not to hurt her but to make my point. "Now you listen here. You may have been raised by a mage and married to a mage. But that's not what you are. I can feel it. In here." I place my hand on my heart. "If you were a mage, I wouldn't feel so drawn to you. I can feel how pure your soul is, and I know for a fact Phoebe wouldn't let you around her children if that's what she thought you were."

"But if I'm not a mage, what am I?" she asks, and it gives me pause.

"I don't know. But we're going to find out. Together," I tell her fiercely, and I mean it.

She nods, her eyes getting misty. "Thank you."

"You don't have to thank me. And if you ever want to talk to someone who knows—truly knows—what it was like, you can come to me any time. You're not alone anymore."

Her eyes go wide. "I really needed to hear that." she says, wrapping her arms around me and clinging to me tightly. I rub circles on her back, understanding now why I feel a connection to her.

When we break apart, I look around, noticing for the first time that the rest of the women have already made their way down to the clearing in the grass, leaving Sarah and I to have our conversation privately, and I'm grateful. I'm sure that everyone is going to know both of our stories eventually, but that was a private conversation between two people who have similar backgrounds and wasn't meant to be shared with others.

We make our way down to the grassy clearing, and Sarah sits next to Charleigh in one of the chairs. Phoebe walks over and places Aurora in her arms before joining me and Skar in the middle. Looks like we not only have the boys joining us but also an audience. Great.

"Okay Pheebs, you and Sophia work on getting the fire to come at will, and I'll continue working with the boys over here," Skar says to us before walking over to where the boys are already playing with their flaming hands. They look so happy and excited. I wish I felt like that instead of a ball of nerves. Everything that I know about phoenixes tells me that it should be impossible for them to have a phoenix flame. Not only are they male, but they're not nineteen. Maybe it's their father's magic that has allowed it to manifest.

I look back at Phoebe with a small amount of panic in my eyes. What if I can't get any flame to show up? What if here, in front of all these people, I fail to even set a small spark? What kind of phoenix would that make me?

"It's okay. Pretend that it's just you and me here," Phoebe says in a calm voice, and I take a deep breath in through my nose and exhale through my mouth, trying to visualize that it is just the two of us. To my utter surprise, it's working, and some of the nerves I was just feeling start to dissipate.

"Good. Now I want you to close your eyes and look inside for the spark of your magic. Mine is like a small flame that flickers in my chest. It's a deep crimson red with blue streaks spread throughout it. Let me know once you find it." I search inside myself for what she's talking about, but it's hard. How do you look for something without your eyes? I try thinking about all the times my flames have made an appearance, and I realize that each time my emotions have been high. If my fire is linked to my emotions, maybe I should try to provoke some in order to figure out where it is. I begin thinking of my time spent here with Phoebe, about last night's dream of us flying high in the sky. As I'm visualizing us flying in our phoenix forms, my awareness shifts to a small flame that flickers in my chest. It's a light orange with dark crimson streaks laced through it. The longer I stare at it, the brighter it gets.

"Okay, I found it in my chest like yours," I tell her with my eyes still closed.

"Now I want you to coax it to spread. Visualize it spreading from your chest, down your stomach, up your neck, down each leg and each arm. You have to put your will into it. You have to want it to spread. Don't fear it. It will never hurt you." I try everything that she's saying, but every time I get it close to moving, it seems to shrink back.

"I don't know what I'm doing wrong," I complain to Phoebe, opening my eyes.

"It's okay. It took me weeks to be able to coax it out. I was always worried that I was going to hurt someone at a subconscious level. It took me realizing that my fire will not hurt anyone who I trust. I'm still not sure why, but I can touch everyone in this clearing while in my phoenix form and they won't get so much as a red mark from a burn. When I touch someone I don't trust, they burn up within seconds. Skar explained it as my will. The magic in my phoenix form reacts to my will. So, if I don't mean any harm, it won't harm and vice versa." That makes me feel a lot better. Maybe, like her, I was worried about hurting someone, or maybe it's the years of conditioning from Devin not to use my flame. Either way, I need to find a way to get past it. If Devin is coming for me, and I am sure he is, this is fire is my only weapon.

"Okay, I'm going to try again." I close my eyes and, once again, start visualizing my flame. It comes much easier this time, but it still doesn't want to spread. "Come on, damn it," I say out of frustration before opening my eyes once again.

"Let's try something different." Phoebe steps aside and strips down to her bra and underwear. I look at her in question. "I'm tired of burning through all my clothes when I shift," she tells me with a shrug.

Maybe I should do the same? Who am I kidding? I probably won't be able to spark a flame, let alone shift. With that thought, my self-doubt creeps in.

"You should strip too. I have a feeling this is going to work," she tells me, so I quickly strip down to my bra and underwear too.

This better work, because otherwise I'm going to look like an idiot.

She walks back up to me, takes both my hands in hers, and

closes her eyes. Immediately, her flame begins licking up her skin, causing her to shift into her phoenix form. Just like the first time I saw her in Supernatural, I'm in awe. She's so beautiful.

I'm snapped out of my trance as her flames begin licking up my own arms, and I watch in amazement as my own start to form, dancing with hers. Within seconds, I feel the shift happen, and I look down to see my entire body engulfed in flames.

Remember this feeling. The feeling of power. The feeling of the heat. I hear Phoebe speak into my head.

Okay, I say back to her in the same manner, once the shock of her talking into my mind wears off, I close my eyes to make a mental note of how it feels to be in this form. I feel untouchable, like nothing or no one could hurt me. As I close my eyes, I can feel each of my individual flames as they do a seductive dance over my body. I can feel my wings stretch out and itch to take flight.

Can we fly? I ask her as I open my eyes.

She simply nods and shoots up into the sky. Once again, I'm completely enamored with simply watching her. I hope I look that majestic right now.

No more thinking. I just want to fly, and I will my wings to begin flapping, lifting me off the ground. This is amazing! I feel so free.

Phoebe and I fly over the entire pack land as the sun begins to set. It's beautiful. More beautiful than anything I've ever seen. The way the last of the red and orange colors touch the treetops is inspiring and reminds me of the two of us.

Despite my initial fear and my lack of practice, something about flying through the sky is incredibly familiar. There is no science or expertise to exercise. Once I am in the sky, flying feels as natural as breathing.

As we're flying, she points downward.

This is the border of pack land. Skarlyt and her coven have a protection barrier set up so that no one wishing us harm can cross.

I nod and, now that she's pointed it out, I can see a slight shimmer in the air, that must be the barrier she's talking about. We continue to fly the perimeter of the barrier and I see slight movement in the trees off to the north. I speed up, trying to fly closer to check it out.

We should get back, Phoebe says, and I turn away.

I thought I saw something, I tell her, gesturing toward the movement.

She looks at the area I pointed out. *Could just be some animals.* I nod, though that doesn't feel quite right. I turn and follow her back.

As the clearing comes into view, I watch as Skarlyt walks toward us, holding our clothes out. That's smart. For a moment, I worry that I won't know how to shift back, but once my feet touch the ground, my flames automatically recede, and I slip back into my clothes. Phoebe waits for me to be covered before shifting herself.

"That was amazing," I say excitedly, at the same time Seb and Alaric pop into existence on the deck.

That was quick. I look over at Phoebe and watch as her face goes from excitement of having Alaric home to panic. What's that about? When I turn to look at Alaric and Seb, I see why.

Instead of the happiness I expected to see on their faces, it's disappointment. What happened? Is Darren dead? No. He can't be.

Chapter Seventeen

Sophia

I stand frozen in my spot by fear. Is he hurt? Is he dead? If they don't have him, who does? Did I put him in danger by coming here? Have I put them all in danger? I try to shake those thoughts away, but they persist. How is it possible that I am so intensely afraid for a person who I have never even met? Is there something to Phoebe's theory about him being my mate? Or is this feeling just guilt over getting more innocent people hurt?

Once I am able to finally snap myself out of the what if game I was playing inside my head, I make my way over to where everyone is gathered. As I approach, Sarah comes to walk beside me and hands me Aurora.

"Here, it helps to hold her. She has this aura that can help heal any emotional breakdown I start to have. I think you need her more than me right now." As I settle her into my arms, I understand exactly what Sarah is talking about. It's like she's sucking the paralyzing fear and anxiety right out of my body and replacing it with only calmness and a feeling that everything will be alright. I stop in my tracks, looking from Sarah to Aurora.

"This is incredible. She's incredible," I whisper to Sarah,

glancing down at the beautiful girl in my arms as we join the group.

"He wasn't there?" Phoebe asks.

Alaric shakes his head. "No, one of the women said Devin brought him to Ontario to trade for Sophia." He finishes with a sad look in my direction.

I can't help the quick intake of breath that gets caught in my throat. Devin has him? And he wants to trade him for me?

"No way!" Phoebe exclaims. "We aren't trading Sophia for Darren. We have to find another way." I steel myself for the inevitable fight, ready for Alaric to hand me over to get his brother back.

"I know, love. We'll find another way," Alaric says, wrapping his arms around his mate, and I snap my eyes to his.

What? He's not going to trade me. Why not? I'm nothing to him. He only just met me. Mate's twin or not. This is his brother.

He must see the look on my face. "We don't abandon family. No matter what. We aren't giving up on Darren, but we aren't handing you over either. We'll figure out another way."

I nod sullenly. If Devin has Darren, I can only imagine the horrors he's facing because of me. And they are headed here. I led him here. I look down at Aurora, realizing that I'm not the only phoenix here and quickly make up my mind. I need to find a way to keep her safe. Her and Phoebe. If Devin even thinks that there may be other phoenixes here, no one will be safe.

"I'm going to start teleporting everyone back before the women alert the men that we were there," Seb says before vanishing and returning seconds later with Samara, who throws her arms around me and Aurora.

"They want me. I can't let them find out about Aurora. I need to make the trade," I whisper to her.

"I told you not to tell her," she roars, circling around toward Alaric.

"She deserves to know. Besides, it's not like we have any intention of making the trade," he says, forcing Phoebe behind him protectively.

"That won't stop her from making the trade anyway to protect all of you!" she screams at them before turning to me and softening her tone. "I should never have brought you here."

"Hey now, don't say that. We don't want her to make the trade any more than you do," Phoebe says defensively, attempting to get out from behind Alaric.

Even with Phoebe's calm tone, it does nothing to stop Samara and her lion's rage. "That doesn't matter. I'm taking her away from here, so she doesn't do anything stupid," she snarls, grabbing my hand and trying to pull me away.

"Samara," I warn, my flames already brewing in my chest. I try to smother them, the last thing I want is to hurt her and, right now, I don't trust that they won't.

"No!" Phoebe exclaims. "You're not taking her." Her flames quickly spread over her body, her emotions taking over as she steps toward Samara.

Samara raises her upper lip in a snarl, her eyes flashing gold. She doesn't like to be challenged, and there are far too many shifters nearby for this many displays of dominance. This is going to go bad if I don't do something.

I quickly hand Aurora back to Sarah and step between them, putting my hand on each of their chests with flames of my own licking down them. Samara looks down at my flaming hand, and I realize that Phoebe was right. I'm not hurting her. They aren't even burning her clothes.

"Soph. You can't stay. We both know what you're going to do," she whispers, hurt lacing her voice.

"We can try and find another way," I try to placate her. "Worse case, I'll lead them away from here." We both know I won't really do that. It will still leave Darren in Devin's hands.

Samara raises an eyebrow at me before her face shifts back into rage as she realizes my intentions.

"No," she growls. "We're leaving."

Phoebe's phoenix lets off a loud screech and I turn my attention to her. "Please, Phoebe, you need to calm down." She doesn't seem to understand me though, trying to step around me to get to Samara.

A few seconds later, Trev steps up to an extremely pissed off Samara, soothing her, and Alaric does the same with Phoebe. They are both nearly lost to their fierce protectiveness.

I don't listen though. I can't. It's not their decision; it's mine. If I have to choose between a life of imprisonment for myself or this beautiful girl that was in my arms, or Phoebe, or even Darren, I will choose myself every time. I've lived with it for twenty-eight years. I can live with it some more.

I turn to Sarah, sharing a knowing look. She knows what I'm thinking. She also probably has a pretty good idea of what's going to happen to me once I do, but I can see the understanding in her eyes. It's that shared look that cements my decision. I can't let them ruin anyone else's life. I'll make the trade and end them all before they can place a tether back on my body.

"It's not your decision. It's mine!" I shout to the group, halting their argument in its tracks.

Phoebe, having finally shifted back, spins out of Alaric's embrace and clasps my arms. "You can't. I won't let you," she tells me, sadness coating her voice. She knows as well as I do what my choice means, and she also knows why. She did the same thing herself when Tanner took Riley.

"You're my family! I'm not going to pretend I'm doing it for your brother, Alaric, because I'm not. I'm doing it for Phoebe and Aurora. I can't let the mages find out about them. The longer they are nearby, the more likely it is that they will learn about you. If they learn that there is another phoenix—a baby phoenix—they will stop at nothing. Aurora will never be safe." I take a deep breath.

"At least if I go willingly, they have no reason to stay here and hopefully will never find out about her. Think about it," I say, looking directly into Alaric's eyes. I know he agrees. I can see the resignation on his face.

"No!" Phoebe says once again, throwing her arms around me and squeezing me tight. "I just found you, I'm not losing you now." Then she releases me and rears on Alaric. "You hear me? I am not giving up my sister. Not for anyone. We. Find. Another. Way." Her screech comes out in her voice, and she can't seem to control the shift that overtakes her again. Next thing you know, we are both in flames.

I want to fly away right now, lead the mages away from here, but I know Phoebe will only follow and give away the fact that there is another, so I stay.

Phoebe, you need to understand. You made the same decision when Tanner took Riley. I try to reason with her.

No! There was no other way then. I'm stronger now. We can find another way, she pleads with me.

You may be stronger, but Aurora is defenseless. If they find out about her, they'll stop at nothing to get to her. I try again, hopeful that bringing Aurora up would help her see sense. Instead, it only seems to enrage her further. Her flames grow and deepen in color, and she lets off a terrifying screech.

No one will touch her. Or you, she screams through our link.

Okay, I concede. *We have some time to try and find another way. They aren't here to make the trade yet. That's the best offer I'm going to give you.*

She doesn't answer, just wraps her arms and wings around me, making our flames merge so that you can't tell where one of us ends and the other begins. I close my eyes and cry, relishing the feeling of love she is sending through our bond. Not once in my entire twenty-eight years on this earth have I felt this amount of love.

I continue to hold her and cry as I feel our flames die out and someone drapes some sort of fabric around us.

"I can't lose you," she sobs into my hair. The truth is, I don't want to lose her either, and that's why I think the trade is the best option. It's the only way to know for certain that nothing is going to happen to my family.

We are still hugging and sobbing when I hear an unfamiliar voice. "Sorry to interrupt." I turn toward the voice, seeing a tall blond man standing off to the side, looking toward Alaric.

"Drake. Good, you're here. We need to talk," he says, striding forward and clasping the newcomer's hand. If his pale skin wasn't a dead giveaway, the small fangs poking out of his mouth definitely are. This man has to be a vampire.

"Actually, I came to ask for your help," he replies, looking upset.

"Help? What happened?" Phoebe asks, stepping toward him and bringing me with her. I guess she's not ready to let me go either.

"Well, we were looking into some strange newcomers over the past couple of days, trying to figure out what they want, when we stumbled across a group of mages and hunters just outside of town. There's a pretty large group. The mages, I'm assuming, after seeing another phoenix, are here for you. But the hunters, they've taken notice of our coven, and we've already had three disappearances in the last two nights," Drake says.

The group around us exclaims in shock. Phoebe, though, looks around and asks the same question on my mind. "Hunters? There are always hunters around here."

Skarlyt steps up shaking her head. "Yeah, hun. Not the 'venison stew' kind of hunter. They're a group of humans who have made it their mission to get rid of anyone who is supernatural."

"What? How can they do that?" Phoebe asks.

"Like Skarlyt said, most of them are brainwashed or conditioned from birth to believe that any race other than humans is evil," Trevan answers, looking apologetic. "They believe that we go around killing humans, and, from their skewed perception, they're protecting them."

"What the hell are they doing with the mages then?"

"That's a good question," Skarlyt looks at Trev thoughtfully, but he just shrugs. "Hunters believe that any kind of supernatural is a lesser-being. We aren't human, so they don't worry about being humane. The mages want us to drain for fuel, so maybe the hunters just agree that's all we are good for."

"Drake," Alaric looks apologetic and overwhelmed. "I am not sure we can help you much with the mages knocking on our door."

"I was hoping that our women and children could stay in your bunker until this blows over. Only a few adults have gone missing, but everyone is terrified one of our young may be taken and killed or, worse, experimented on," Drake's face pinches in disgust at the thought. "We can't let that happen. I know it's not the best time right now with this newest threat you're facing, but we have no one else to turn to short of fleeing the area."

Alaric and Phoebe share a look.

"Of course," Phoebe says, "they are welcome here."

"There should be more than enough room down there for all of you." As Alaric answers, I watch Drake's shoulders relax in relief.

"We're already packed up. We have a refrigerated trailer loaded with enough blood to last us a week, so we don't need to leave." Drake clasps Alaric's hand in a sign of gratitude and commitment. "While we're here, we'll do whatever we can to help you with the mages."

"What were you going to do if we said no?" Phoebe asks.

"We didn't get that far. We had hope that you would say yes," Drake answers and Phoebe nods.

Just as Drake looks like he's going to leave, Skarlyt pipes up. "Oh Drake...Do the blood bags—"

He cuts her off. "No, Skarlyt. We do not need to talk about the feeding habits of vampires right now."

Everyone laughs; well, everyone except Skarlyt laughs. "Fine. I was just doing my scientific duty," she says with a pout and then she seems to be distracted by her own train of thought. "It just seems like the temperature change would change the arousing effect of feeding."

"Wait, is that a thing?" I ask, looking around. Drake and Alaric simply roll their eyes at me, but Skarlyt gets a super excited look on her face.

"From every vampire that has actually answered me when I ask that question, which is a lot, by the way..." She sends a pointed look in Drake's direction before continuing. "They all confirmed that when they drink directly from the 'source' they get aroused, which is apparently why they enjoy feeding while in the bedroom, if you know what I mean." She adds an eyebrow wiggle on the end for emphasis.

Drake interrupts our conversation. "All right. We all know what you mean. Now we're done with that." He gestures his hands in Skarlyt's direction. "I'm going to go collect my coven, and we will be here in the next hour or so. Thank you again, Alaric.

"Oh, and Skarlyt...I am bringing children, so try to keep the questions to a minimum," he adds in warning.

"I'm curious, not stupid," she says with a huff. "That's why I was trying to ask you."

He simply raises his eyebrow at her before turning to leave.

"I wish Gran was here," Phoebe whispers, melting into Alaric's side.

"Me too," he responds, placing a soft kiss on her head. "But what she's doing is just as important—if not more. If our experiences with the mages lately tell us anything, it's that all of the supernaturals need to band together. We need allies. I'm sure she'd take the first flight back if we asked her to."

Phoebe sighs. "I know she would, and I agree that she's doing important work. Maybe we should send the kids to her?"

Alaric shakes his head. "That's too risky. We can protect them better here for right now. If that changes, we can discuss how to send them to her." Phoebe nods.

"Okay, we've got a lot to do, and a short time to do it in. Let's get the bunker ready and get planning for what to do about the mages," Alaric says, turning back to us. Phoebe takes my hand and leads me back into the house so we can get dressed before helping.

"I meant what I said, Phoebe. If we can't find a way, you know I have to do this," I say to her once we are alone in her room.

She blows out a long shaky breath. "I know. I don't like it, but I understand. We need to train as much as possible over the next twenty-four hours, push our limits, see what we're really capable of."

"About that." Skarlyt barges into the room, adding on to a conversation I had not thought she heard. "I was going through Seb's grimoires while he was gone, and I found an entire section on phoenixes and what powers they possess. It's insanely cool. You two should come down to my room when you're done getting dressed." As she finishes, she simply sweeps back out of the room as if she were never there.

Phoebe shrugs, making me feel this is normal behavior for Skarlyt as I stare where she just was. That was a whole lot of information with little to no explanation at all. I hurry getting dressed and we make our way downstairs together.

Time to find out what this book says.

Chapter Eighteen

Darren

I wake up groggy, still in a cage. This cage, though, has an actual door. My mind runs through the dream, and I breathe a sigh of relief. Both Sebastyn and Sophia are safe with the pack. Now all we need is for me to get free. I close my eyes and realize that, for the first time in two days, I can feel my wolf. He's weak, but he's there.

You okay, buddy? I ask him. He doesn't answer, just lifts his head with a slight nod. I've never seen him like this. Whatever magic is in this stupid collar needs to go. I can't stand watching him suffer like this. I open my eyes and reach up to my neck, searching for a clasp. Just like before, I find none. How the fuck did they get this thing on me without a clasp?

Instead, I turn my attention to my surroundings and immediately recognize where we are. We're just outside of pack land. We are in the area between our pack and Axel's bear sleuth. This is not far from where Sebastyn and I made our tree fort when we thought we were old enough to run away. They must've teleported here once I was passed out because there's no way we got here this fast by driving.

I thought I'd have at least another night, one more dream, to figure out how to get Sophia to remember the dreams. If Sebastyn is with her, maybe she'll confide in him, and he'll realize what's happening.

I've almost run out of time. I can't let them trade me. I need to figure out a way to escape.

I strain myself to contact Alaric through our private link. If we're this close, he should be able to hear me.

Alaric! I say...nothing.

Alaric! I try again, and this time my wolf joins in, using all the strength he has.

Darren? I hear his response faintly. It almost sounds like he's underwater.

Yeah. I'm close to home; don't make the trade. I push through. I hope I sound clearer than he did.

Darren...It's hard to hear you. Did you say you're close to home?

Yes! Don't make the trade! My wolf helps me force the words to make sure that my message gets through.

We won't, but Sophia won't give us long. She promised us some time, but she will make the trade herself. I can tell that he's also using his wolf to push the words through as well so it's easier to hear him, although I wish I hadn't. She can't trade herself for me.

You can't let her do that. I'll find a way. They're draining my energy. I'll contact you again when I have more. I reply with the last bit of strength that I have. Between the tether and the amount I spent pushing through the contact, I'm depleted once again.

Stay safe. We're coming for you. It is the last thing I hear before everything goes black.

I know he's coming for me. He's my big brother. He's been protecting me my whole life. I just don't want them to get me back at the expense of someone else—definitely not Sophia.

I wake up what must be hours later, judging by the number of stars in the sky, as a bucket of freezing cold water is thrown on my head.

"What the fuck?" I growl.

"Time to wake up, dog," a strange man laughs. I haven't seen this one yet. From his black leather clothing, I wouldn't peg him as a mage. No. He looks more like a soldier.

Shit. It couldn't be. Could it?

I spin my head around, noting all the cages that have been placed around me, filled with people—no—supernaturals. I recognize a few: a teenager from Trixie's pride, a couple of adults from Drake's coven, even a bear shifter so large he is scrunched into a ball inside the cage. I only know he is a bear by his extreme size. How the fuck did they get him in there?

The man drops the bucket with a loud clang and bends down so he's at eye level with me, "You're one of the lucky ones. When we're done here, I get the pleasure of questioning you," he says with a snarl.

Like fuck he will.

I spit in his face, and he wipes it off quickly, standing and kicking my cage. "You're going to regret that," he says, turning and walking toward a group of people dressed similarly to him.

Hunters...It can't be.

I turn to the cage closest to me, seeing a young girl with brown hair, caked with dried blood and dirt.

"Psst," I whisper, trying to get her attention.

She turns and looks at me with wide eyes.

"How long have you been here?" I ask.

She swivels her head, looking around before answering.

"They brought us in while you were passed out."

"What's your name?"

"Margo," she sniffs, tears forming in her eyes.

"Where are you from, Margo?"

She wipes her eyes and nose on her shirt. "Trixie is my alpha."

With the tears running down her face, she looks even younger than I thought.

"How old are you, Margo?"

She begins to sob. "I just turned fifteen." Fifteen? What the fuck? A look of horror crosses my face. She's just a baby.

"Do you go to the Westwood Academy?"

She nods. "I snuck out to meet some friends in the woods. But I was taken before I got there."

Shit. There were other kids in the woods. I look around, not seeing any other teenagers apart from one. "Are they here too?"

She shakes her head. "No, only Oscar." She nods toward a young man who I recognize as a senior at the school. "I hope that doesn't mean the rest are dead."

"It doesn't," I tell her, though I have no way to be sure of that. I try to reach my hand through the bars to touch her, but I get a zap of electricity.

"What the fuck?" I growl, pulling my hand toward my chest and cradling it.

"The bars won't hurt you unless you try to reach through the spaces between them. That guy over there kept trying. That's why he's out cold." She gestures with her head over to the bear shifter, and I nod, only comforted by the fact that I can see his chest rising and falling.

"We're going to get out of here, Margo. I promise," I tell her, knowing that's not a promise I should make, but it seems to lift her spirits. She wipes her eyes and nose once again with her shirt before giving me a curt nod. I'm not sure if she believes me. Hell, I'm not sure I believe myself, but I believe in Alaric and my pack. If it's possible, it will be done.

"Have you tried to mind link anyone?" I ask her.

"I tried to reach my alpha, but there's something blocking it. My lion is exhausted."

I nod. "What about your parents? I couldn't get through the

pack link either, but I was able to use my familial link to reach my brother." Her eyes widen before closing, and I can tell she's trying.

Her eyes open quickly. "I told my mom. It was hard to hear her, but I told her what happened."

"Good. Don't worry. My brother will come." Even if he can't save me, he may be able to save some of the others.

She opens her mouth to respond but shuts it quickly, her panicked eyes looking behind me. I turn my head and watch Devin walk over to my cage.

"Hopefully, your brother is smart enough to make the trade. It hardly matters. Whether the trade is made or not, your pack won't last the week," he snarls.

"What is that supposed to mean?" I ask.

He chuckles. "It means exactly what you think it does. Whether your brother trades you for Sophia or not, we can't allow them to get away with kidnapping my daughter."

"She wasn't kidnapped. She ran away. She ran away from you," I snarl.

He nods. "Yes, but the others don't need to know that. I thought I had broken this rebellious streak of hers—seems I was wrong. I'm going to enjoy showing her the error of her ways."

I try to reach through the bars to clasp at his shirt despite the pain. Damn him.

Seeing my pain at trying to get through the bars, he steps away and laughs. "You'll never get through. Better you resign yourself to your fate." With that said, he walks away, and I slump down in my cage. I sit there for a few minutes, angry tears brimming in my eyes.

"Who's Sophia?" Margo asks.

I turn and look at her, my face softening. "She's my sister-in-law's twin sister, and I think she's my mate." It is the first time I have said it out loud, but I already know it is true.

"But that man said she's his daughter. How are you mates with a mage's daughter?" I sigh, not wanting to answer but needing something to occupy my time. I start with finding out about Sophia from Skarlyt and end with the kid-friendly version of the dreams I've been having.

"Wait. Who is your brother?" she asks.

"Alaric, the alpha of the Westwood pack."

"Wait. You're Beta Darren?" she asks, disbelief in her tone, and I nod.

"That's me."

"You were supposed to be my teacher this year, but it was changed at the last second."

I nod again. "I needed to go look for Sophia, so I asked my friend Heydon to step in for me. How are classes going anyway?"

"A lot of the shifters are disappointed that you aren't their teacher. They said that next to your brother, you are the strongest shifter around."

I chuckle. "No. That would be my sister-in-law, Phoebe."

"The phoenix?" she questions.

"Yup. Once my nephews are old enough, she's going to start teaching a class as well. Although, she doesn't think she has anything to teach."

"I wish I never snuck out," she whispers, and I long to reach through the bars and comfort her.

"We can't change our mistakes, but we can learn from them and try to do better in the future."

"Gods," she chuckles, "what a *teacher* thing to say."

We spend the next hours talking about anything and everything. She tells me about her family and her friends, her classes at the academy, and what she wishes was different. She gives me a lot of things to think about and even more to worry about, the way kids always seem to do.

Chapter Nineteen

Sophia

P hoebe, Skarlyt, and I all end up downstairs in her room. It's amazing in here. From the outside, you would think that it's a small room, but once you walk in, it's the size of the entire main floor.

"How is the room this big?" I ask, as I'm spinning around to get a good look at everything.

"Magic," Phoebe and Skarlyt reply at the same time.

"You know, for someone who was raised by mages, you don't seem to know a whole lot about magic," Skarlyt says, and Phoebe smacks her on the arm.

"What? It was just an observation. Besides, she'll get to know pretty quickly that I tend to speak my mind, and I hardly ever mean offense. If I'm trying to be mean, you'll know it," Skar says with a shrug and a wink in my direction. I can't help but laugh. It is so refreshing to not have to worry about saying the wrong thing or not being able to talk at all.

"It's okay. I'm actually enjoying seeing women speak their minds. All the women I grew up with were drones and unable to say anything out of turn. And you're right, for someone who was raised by mages, I don't know a lot about magic. At first, they tried integrating me to their coven, allowing me to be around when they were practicing magic, but after they realized I wouldn't be so easily brainwashed, they did everything they could to keep me secluded. So, no, I don't know much, and what I do know I'm sure is very different from how you use magic," I tell Skarlyt. She seems surprised but simply nods and goes back to searching for the book.

"Ah, here it is!" she exclaims, holding up a huge, old-looking book, and flipping it open.

"Here, it says that phoenixes should be able to not only produce flames but also direct flames to fly as a sort of projectile. It also says that a fully matured adult phoenix's screech can knock a grown man unconscious." Wow.

"If that's the case, do you think it's like our flames? It will only hurt people we want it to?" At their furrowed brows, I continue. "Earlier Phoebe screeched pretty loud, but it didn't hurt any of us."

They both nod in understanding. "I don't know. But it would make sense," Skarlyt says, turning her attention to the book. "This book doesn't have too much in it but it's more than we had. I think most of your powers are going to be trial and error unfortunately."

"But what if we screech during a fight and knock everyone unconscious, including those on our side?" Phoebe supplies, and we both turn back to Skarlyt.

"I guess we should try it before any fights to make sure then," Skarlyt says and Phoebe nods.

"Maybe we should try practicing..." Phoebe begins to say but is quickly interrupted by the boys.

"There you are, Aunt Sophia. We wanted to play with you," Riley says, coming up to give me a hug. I look at Phoebe and Skarlyt. As much as I want to practice and learn more, I really want to spend time with them. At the end of the day, I really don't know how much time I'm going to get with them.

Phoebe obviously sees the conflict on my face because she says, "Why don't you go play with the boys tonight? We can start training in the morning."

The boys don't even wait for me to agree before they are pulling me out the room and up the stairs. "It's after bedtime, so not too long," Phoebe yells after us.

The boys and I spend the next two hours exploring their play-room, and they showed me how to play all types of video games. Turns out I'm pretty good at Mortal Kombat. Who knew?

By the time Alaric steps into the room, Ryker is staring into space, unable to focus.

"Time for bed, boys."

"Aw. Do we have to?" The boys whine but rub their eyes and yawn immediately after, making me chuckle.

"Alaric's right, boys. Time to get into bed. I promise we'll play again soon."

"Tomorrow?" Ryker asks hopefully.

"We'll see," I tell him, pulling him with me to the bathroom where they both brush their teeth.

After stripping down to their underwear and crawling into bed, Alaric and I take turns wishing them good night and tucking them in.

"Aunt Sophia?" Riley calls out as I get to the door.

"Yeah, buddy?"

"I love you," he says, and tears instantly begin flowing from my eyes.

I rush back over to him, wrapping him in my arms. "Oh, Riley. I love you too—more than there are stars in the sky."

I walk over to Ryker and whisper the same. "That's what Mommy always says," he murmurs, and I hug him tighter.

"I'll see you boys tomorrow," I tell them before closing the door and heading down the stairs.

I walk out on the back deck and see Sarah feeding Aurora.

"I thought Phoebe was breast feeding her?" I question after noticing the bottle.

"She does, but she took a break and pumped so that she could continue training with Skarlyt, and I think she realizes how much I just need to hold her. With the mages so close, my anxiety is running rampant, and I can't seem to get a handle on it," she finishes with a slight look of embarrassment. I put my hand on her arm.

"I completely understand. I only know a little of your past, but them being this close makes me want to run and hide somewhere where they'll never find me. But then I look at this gorgeous little girl and I think about what her life would be like if they find out about her." She nods in understanding, and we both start to watch Phoebe in her phoenix form, flying above the lake. It makes my own want to break free to fly with her, but I don't want to distract her. I hear her screech loudly and feel a warm breeze blow toward us. Wow.

I watch in awe as her flames grow outward, making it look as if she is simply a ball of fire or a star going supernova. After a few seconds, I see the flames start to retreat into her, but instead of remaining shifted, she seems to have depleted her strength and begins free falling.

Everything seems to move in slow motion, and she's showing no signs of trying to correct her fall. That's all it takes for me to be up out of my chair and completely shifted, flying toward her in seconds. For a minute, I wonder if I'm going to be fast enough to catch her before she hits the water, but at the last second, I grab onto her arm, pulling her body flush against mine.

Phoebe? I try to connect with her through our link. Nothing.

Phoebe! I try, louder this time. Still nothing. Without knowing what I am doing, I feel my flames grow and let loose an earth-shattering screech, watching as my flames move out of my body with a force so strong that I watch the tops of the trees sway. After a minute, I feel my flames begin to settle inside me once again and move back toward Skar. As I land, I shift back, settling on my knees, and lay Phoebe down.

"Come on, Phoebe!" I shout as I begin to shake her.

"It's okay; she's just depleted. We pushed it too hard today. She's breathing. Look," Skar says coming and rubbing my back, pointing toward Phoebe's chest where I can clearly see it rising and falling.

"What was that?" Alaric says, running out of the house, picking up his pace when he sees Phoebe's form laying on the ground in front of me.

I can't help the tears that are streaming down my face, which isn't helping Alaric's panic as he drops to the ground and scoops her up into his arms.

"What happened?" he looks between Skarlyt and me. I want to answer, but anything I try to say gets stuck in my throat.

Luckily, Skarlyt answers for me. "She was training, and I think we pushed her a little too hard. She's okay, just drained, Alaric." When she finishes, she moves over to him and places her arm around him. "You bring her inside, and I'll make her a tonic to help her energy levels," she adds, ushering him toward the house and grabbing me by the hand to bring me with her.

Once we're out of earshot of him, she rounds on me.

"What was that?" she asks, more out of curiosity than anger.

"I honestly don't know," I tell her because I don't. I've only fully shifted twice before today and needed Phoebe's help both times. Whatever that was out there was not something I've ever experienced before.

"I think you were able to expand your flames like Phoebe was trying to do, but she didn't get anywhere near the power you just emitted. What were you feeling?" she asks.

"Why does that matter?" I question her back.

"Because we've already established that, in the beginning, your phoenix form is linked to your emotions. Whatever emotions you were experiencing just then amped up your power to a level I've never seen, not even in the strongest witch I've ever met."

"Fear. I was scared. At first, I thought she was going to catch herself, but, when I realized she was unconscious, I acted. I didn't think about it; it just happened. One second, I was sitting, talking with Sarah, and the next I was holding Phoebe and letting out all the fear of her being hurt," I tell her honestly.

She nods, turning to continue pulling me down the stairs. "We need to figure out how to tap into that without the life-or-death situation."

As she's pulling out different ingredients, she points toward the book we were reading earlier. "Flip the pages until you find the one titled 'Tidal Flames.'" I do as she asks and look at the picture on the page. I see a phoenix with a ring of fire around her, pushing outward, similar to what just happened with me.

"That's what it's called," I say in awe.

"Yeah, and I don't even think that picture depicts the strength of what you just did. It was amazing. If Phoebe wasn't unconscious right now, we'd be celebrating," she says as she adds water to the powder she has just ground up, straining it into a cup.

"All set," she announces and hurries up the stairs to Phoebe and Alaric's room.

We prop Phoebe up, and Skarlyt carefully pours the potion in her mouth.

"Ugh, that's gross," Phoebe complains as she is coming to.

"Thank Mother Moon," Alaric says, cuddling Phoebe closer to him.

"What happened?" she asks.

"You used up too much power, and Sophia shifted and saved you, but after, she set off a tidal flame large enough that Alaric felt it inside the house," Skarlyt says, and Phoebe looks at me with a mix of excitement and awe. I simply shrug my shoulders, trying to play it cool. I'll talk to her more about it when she's feeling better.

"Why don't you pump again, and Sarah and I will keep Aurora for the night?" I ask as I offer her Sarah's and my services, but I know Sarah won't mind. I would offer my own, but other than cuddles, I really don't know much about babies.

Phoebe goes to protest, but Alaric cuts her off.

"That would be great. Thank you."

With that, I give Phoebe a quick hug and head to let Sarah know what I just signed her up for.

Chapter Twenty

Darren

I watch as they purposely let a vampire overhear their conversation and then "accidentally" leave the keys nearby. If he thinks that it was just dumb luck, he's sorely mistaken. He's now a pawn in their little game, just like the hunters.

I've noticed that the hunters seem to revere the mages, thinking they're some sort of deities instead of the evil, corrupt monsters that they should be hunting instead of us. It's strange, and it makes me question what lies the hunters were told. How could they hate all supernaturals but work with the mages at the same time? Don't they realize what they're doing?

About twenty minutes later, the same guards that left the keys, walk closer to my cage.

"He took the bait," one says.

"Of course, he did. Just got a report that the entire coven moved onto pack grounds."

"Good, then all the scum are in the same place. It will be easy pickings, especially the little ones." They both chuckle at themselves, making me feel sick to my stomach.

What kind of monsters are they that would be happy about

hurting children? It gives me hope. I can only guess that Alaric and Drake came to some sort of agreement that helps keep both groups safe, but it might not be enough. These mages are far more powerful than the ones we've faced before, and I'm not sure how well our barrier will hold up.

"It won't be much longer now," the first man says, clapping the other on the shoulder before they move out of hearing distance. Shit!

Realizing that I'm running out of time, I try to reach Alaric again. I'm not up to full strength, but I've got to try.

Alaric? I close my eyes and push the word out through our bond, gathering strength from my wolf.

Darren! he exclaims with excitement.

We don't have long. They're keeping me tethered, so I'm not sure how much energy I have. But they are planning to attack even if Sophia gives herself over. We have to do something. I try to get the words out fast so that we can say everything that we need to.

Fuck. I figured as much. We're trying to come up with a plan. Other than using Phoebe and Sophia in phoenix form, we haven't come up with much.

Shit. I know how he feels about Phoebe joining the fight, but he has to know that we might not have a choice.

These mages are strong. Stronger than any others I've met. We're going to need to use her, Alaric. I don't like it either, but it's a fact. I don't think we can beat them without her, I tell him, hoping that despite his protective nature, he agrees.

I know. Okay, how many are there with you? How many mages, hunters, and captives? Good. He knows about the hunters and captives. That saves a conversation. I glance around, trying not to attract any attention. I know that I've counted most of the mages and hunters, but the number of captives seems to continually increase. When I first woke up here, there was just me, Margo, Oscar, the bear shifter, and a few vampires. Now I see five vampires, a few bear shifters, and a couple more teenage mountain lions from Trixie's pride.

I've counted about fifty mages and just as many hunters, but the number of captives keeps increasing, including four teenagers from Trixie's pride. I relay as much information as I can to him, but I can already feel myself starting to wane. It's no wonder Sophia couldn't remember our dreams if she was having this much power pulled from her for the last twenty years. It's shocking she could do anything at all.

Shit. Okay. I can feel your energy dropping, so last thing. Do you know where you are? That's a good question. I look around again and remember that earlier I saw the tree where Seb and I ran away to when we got mad at our parents at ten years old. We thought we could build our own tree house and live off the land without them, all over something stupid that I can't even remember right now, but I can still see the branches nailed into the trunk as the start of our ladder.

Tell Sebastyn that we're right by our tree house. He'll know where we are.

Okay, Darren. Stay safe. We're coming for you. I know he is, but, given the amount of strength it's taking just to keep my head up, I fear I won't survive until he does.

"You should try and get some sleep, Margo," I whisper to her, watching her yawn.

"I can't," she whines.

"They're coming for us. You need to be ready," I tell her.

"They are? But they don't know where we are," she says, and I smile.

"Yeah, they do. You see that tree over there with the pieces of wood nailed into the trunk?" I point, showing her the tree I'm talking about, and she nods.

"My best friend, Sebastyn, and I built a fort into that tree when we were younger, and I just linked with my brother. They know exactly where we are, and they're coming."

Her eyes widen, and her body begins humming with excitement. "Really?" Shit. I was hoping to settle her nerves enough to get some sleep, but I'm afraid I just had the opposite effect. Now she's going to be wired and waiting for the cavalry to arrive.

"Yup."

"Do you think my parents are with them?" she asks hopefully.

"I told Alaric about you and the others, so I expect that he'll be reaching out to Trixie and Axel. The vampires are already there. Between the pride, sleuth, pack, and covens, there is a huge army ready to come for us."

"Good. I hope they kill every one of them." Her words give me pause. I was thinking the same thing, but to hear them come out of the mouth of a child...maybe that's not the best thing.

I sigh. "Margo, you know that most of these people, especially the young ones, are only this way because of how they were raised. Maybe some of them can change." The argument falls flat even to myself, but I have to try.

"It doesn't matter. If they can stand around and watch what the others are doing without realizing there's something wrong with this picture," she gestures to the cages, "then they're not redeemable. Keeping kids in cages, even keeping adults in cages, like they're animals is wrong." She sounds much older than she is, and I nod.

"You're right, of course. But how do we know what they're thinking? They could be just as scared as us and not know what to do," I say, gesturing to a female hunter standing off to the side who is wearing a look of disgust and sadness on her face. The sadness shows when she looks at the cages and then morphs quickly into disgust when she looks at the group she's with.

Margo watches her curiously for a few minutes, her brown

eyes softening, obviously seeing the same thing I do before she steels herself.

"It doesn't matter. She's not doing anything about it, so she's just as bad as they are." I let out a sigh, knowing I'm not going to be able to change her mind, and make a mental note to create a class at the academy to discuss this very topic. No one knows the inner thoughts of others or what has been or is being done to them to force their compliance. I think about my time with Devin and shudder. If all mages are capable of getting into people's heads like that, I don't know many people who would be able to resist doing as instructed just to make the images stop.

"Darren?" A groggy voice calls from behind me, and I turn, meeting the eyes of Granger, a bear shifter from Axel's sleuth.

"Whoa, there buddy. Go slow," I tell him as he stumbles while trying to sit up.

"What's going on? Who are all these people?" He gestures around us.

"It's a mixture of hunters and mages." The rumble in his throat shows me his bear is very much present and a lot stronger than my wolf. Maybe they didn't put a big enough drain on his cage. Bad move.

"How long have I been here?" he asks, scrubbing a hand down his face.

"Margo said you got here while I was sleeping but passed out from trying to put your hands through the bars and getting shocked," I explain, gesturing both to Margo and the spaces between the bars.

"I don't remember that. The last thing I remember is patrolling around the sleuth and going to investigate a noise. Then nothing," he says, confusion lining his strong features.

"They captured quite a few of us," I tell him, and he nods, looking around with sad eyes before landing on Margo and the other teenagers.

"Kids? They took kids?" he growls, and I nod sullenly.

"Any other bears?" he asks but turns to look around anyway.

"A couple over there." I point toward the other bear shifters I saw.

"Thank the goddess they're not kids. Does Alaric know you're here?"

I nod. "Yeah, I was able to link him because of the familial bond and told him. He knows where we are. The vampires are already there, and I'd bet both Axel and Trixie will be there soon if they're not already."

"Good," he snarls, turning back to look around, and I do the same.

A few minutes later, Devin comes walking back up. "It's almost time, dog. We'll see how much your brother loves you."

Almost time? Sophia said she'd give them time, but I guess no one knew when the mages would make their move. I hoped that they would have time to rally. Shit.

"Not enough to trade me for Sophia," I snarl.

"Pity. I had hoped he was smarter than that."

"He is smart and loyal. Two things you know nothing about. He loves his family fiercely and would never trade one member for another."

His face morphs into one of confusion.

Shit. Maybe I shouldn't have said that.

"What do you mean one family member for another?" He questions and I smile at him.

"Exactly what I said. You're in for a rude awakening if you think this is going to be an easy win. Sophia will never be yours again," I growl the last part, knowing it's the truth. No matter what happens to me, Alaric and Phoebe won't let him get his hands on her.

His upper lip curls in disgust just before everything goes black. *Please, Mother Moon. Keep my family safe.*

Chapter Twenty-One

Sophia

"Phoebe? What is it?" I am shaken awake by my twin sister, and I squint into the meager light of the nightlight in the corner. I look over at Sarah and Aurora, ensuring that we haven't disturbed them. Upon seeing both wiggle in their sleep from the sound, I carefully extract myself from the bed, and we both make our way to the door.

Once we're in the hallway, Phoebe whispers, "We received a message from the mages. We need to go get Skarlyt and Sebastyn."

"Skarlyt's downstairs," I reply with a yawn. I try to read her expression, but I am not sure just how bad the message was.

Soundlessly, we make our way downstairs and find Skarlyt fully awake, sitting at her workbench with the book about phoenixes open before her.

"What took you guys so long?" she asks.

"What do you mean?" Phoebe asks, and we look at each other in confusion. We literally just woke up.

"Were we supposed to meet you down here for something?"

"The goddess woke me up with a dream about an hour ago, urging me to go over this book some more," she shrugs as if a goddess waking her in the middle of the night is perfectly normal. "I was expecting you two a while ago. Oh, and Seb's on his way with coffee."

That is so much to unpack.

"Okay, first. Wow. The goddess woke you up with a dream? You're going to have to explain that one to me another time. Second, awesome. Seb is my new favorite person," Phoebe says back to her with a smirk, obviously completely expecting Skarlyt's response.

"Hey! He can't be your new favorite person. That is reserved for me for all time. You told me so last month. No take backs." I let a small chuckle escape my lips, glancing in the direction of her bedroom where I'm assuming Lennox and Kayne are sleeping and cut it off quickly.

"It's okay. I put a sound barrier around this room when I woke up so that I didn't disturb them. Seb has some seriously cool tricks up his sleeve. It makes me wish I went traveling with him," she says, looking both excited and regretful.

He went traveling. That's so cool. I've always dreamed of seeing new places. Mental note: ask Sebastyn about where he went and what he did.

"Maybe you still could. Once Kayne is old enough, you could go as a family." I try to cheer her up. She thinks on it for a moment before a small smile spreads across her face.

"I guess you are right," she admits.

"That doesn't sound right," Sebastyn says as he walks in, holding three coffees. Alaric walks in just behind him holding two. "I wasn't here, so I don't know who could have been right."

Alaric rolls his eyes.

"Okay, what message did the mages send?" I ask, ready to set aside the casual conversation now that everyone is here. I need to know.

"The mages sent a message?" Skarlyt and Seb both say in shock.

"Yes," Alaric answers. "That's why all the normal people came here. They gave us twenty-four hours to hand over Sophia, or they are going to kill Darren and attack the pack."

I suck in a breath, anger brewing in my veins. Even my coffee has lost its appeal. How dare they? How dare he? I've always known Devin was a monster, but this...

I look around the room at my newfound family, and determination to keep them safe sets in. I place my coffee down and walk toward the door.

"I'm going to take him down...He's never seen me without a collar. He's in for a rude awakening if he thinks he can threaten the people I love."

Phoebe grabs my arm just as I'm about to walk out of her reach.

"Don't. Not yet. Give us twelve hours. Please?" she begs.

I look around the room and then back at her. I'm still determined to trade myself to save them, but when she gives me those puppy dog eyes, I deflate a little with a curt nod. I can give them twelve hours but not a minute more. Not if it means putting the kids in danger, and not just my niece and nephews, but all the kids here. The vampires brought all their children with them, and I've seen a few dozen shifter children running around the pack. So many little lives that haven't even had the chance to begin.

We walk back in the room, and I fade into the background, still seething about Devin's ultimatum. How can I make them choose between me and their pack, their family? I know if I voiced this, Phoebe would argue that I'm their family too, but it's not the same. They only just met me. It's been just over twenty-four hours. How can they care that much about me already? But as soon as I think about how I feel about them, I know the answer. Ever since I met

Phoebe, the boys, Aurora, even Alaric and the rest, my soul feels like it's finally found where it belongs.

We all watch as Alaric places his coffee mug down and closes his eyes for a few minutes. I'm not sure why we're all staring at him, but I'm guessing that something is happening. Maybe he's talking to Darren in his mind, like Phoebe does with me. After what seems like forever, he snaps his eyes open and immediately finds Seb's.

"He says he's near your tree house. Where is that?" Alaric says curtly toward him. I don't know him well, but I can tell that it's stress that makes his tone so curt. Instead of answering, Seb zips away and pops right back into the room, holding a map and laying it flat on the table.

"He's around here," he explains, circling a wooded area to the west with a pencil. "I can't draw the exact spot on the map, but I could teleport there."

"No, we can't. Darren said there's about one hundred mages and hunters combined. They have prisoners, including a few teenagers from Trixie's pride," Alaric says before adding to Skar, "Could you give her a call and see if she can come over. Better yet, go get her so they don't see her coming in? Might give us an edge if they don't know our numbers."

Skarlyt nods before picking up the phone and calling someone.

"Hey, Trix. Sorry to wake you. Get dressed; I'm coming to get you really quick." She pauses for a second, ready to hang up before adding, "Oh yeah, don't freak out, but I'm going to teleport into your kitchen and meet you there." I hear an excited voice on the other end before Skarlyt pops out of the room.

"Okay, someone needs to fill me in on everything that just happened. I feel a little lost," I say, meeting everyone's eyes.

Once again, it's Alaric who answers. "Darren reached out through our familial bond. I'm assuming since the mages don't have those types of bonds, they weren't expecting it, and it's so strong that the tether couldn't block it completely. It's still taking a lot of energy out of Darren when he uses it, which is why the conversation was so short. Thanks to him, we now have a general idea of where he is and how many there are.

"As for Trixie and the teenagers from her pride, I was actually going to invite her over when all this is done to introduce her to Samara. She is the alpha of the local mountain lion pride. The fact that she's recently lost some pride members to the hunters means the bears likely have too.

"Seb, why don't you reach out to Axel to see if he's missing anyone, and maybe he should come here too, provided you two can get along long enough to teleport him here and back," Alaric finishes looking at Seb.

"He always starts it," Seb huffs, pointing an accusatory finger before teleporting away.

"Does Samara know that there's a pride here?" I ask Alaric, reeling from this new knowledge.

"I'm not sure," he replies. That's all it takes before I'm rushing up the stairs, out the door, running across the lawn, and banging on the guest cottage door. I'm bouncing on the spot, unable to contain my excitement. She's never going to believe it. I never thought about trying to help her find another pride to join, but her lion would probably like that. I've been told shifters need their packs, or prides, to stay sane. Luckily, her lion has considered me part of her pride, so she's been able to keep the insanity at bay.

Trev answers the door. "Sophia? Is everything okay?"

"Everything is perfect, Trev," I say, squeezing past him to go deeper into the cottage. "Actually, things are kind of shit right now I guess." It takes me only one try to find the right door. Inside, Samara rests on the rumpled bed. I rush over and jump on the bed with her in it.

"Soph? What's going on? Did something happen?" she asks, sleepily.

"Guess what?" I ask, still bouncing with excitement.

"I..." she goes to answer, but I can't wait.

"There's a mountain lion pride near here! And guess what else?" I interrupt.

Once again, she opens her mouth to answer, but I don't wait.

"The alpha is on the way to Alaric and Phoebe's house right now!" I say as I pull the covers off of her.

It takes her a minute to catch up to the revelation I just dropped on her, but once she does, I see the surprise and excitement in her eyes.

"What?" she says as she jumps out of bed and begins throwing her clothes on.

"What's happening?" Trev asks from the doorway.

"Sophia said there's a mountain lion pride in the area and that the alpha is on the way to the house right now. We need to go. I need to meet them," she says.

"Her," I inform her with a nod and watch as the smile on her face grows even bigger.

"Yeah, Trixie. I assumed you knew," Trev says, and we both freeze and turn toward him.

He looks like a deer caught in the headlights under both of our stares.

"How would we know?" Samara asks.

He shrugs his shoulders, scrunching up his face, obviously unsure what the correct answer is.

"I'm sure he's had other things on his mind since he just met his mate," I say with a wink. Samara smiles at me with a nod before turning back to the task at hand.

Once Samara is dressed, we hurry back to the house with a still-confused Trevan following.

"Wait," she says, grabbing my arm and turning me to face her. "What if they don't want me?"

Now she's just being silly.

"Samara, you know as well as I do that you're amazing, and they'd be stupid not to want you." I give her a pointed look. I know how nervous she must be, but it's true. They'd be stupid not to want her. She was one of the most dominant shifters in her pride, and her parents were the alpha pair.

"She's right, my love," Trevan adds. "Trixie is daunting, but she's not stupid. She'll see how much you're worth."

She lets our words set in for a minute before nodding, and we continue to make our way toward the crowd convened in the basement of the alpha house.

I lead the way into Skarlyt's area and immediately notice the gorgeous brunette with olive skin standing next to her. Samara freezes at the door, and I watch as her lion makes an appearance in her eyes and sniffs the air. She stares straight at the newcomer who is doing the same.

Alaric, noticing the stare down that's happening, breaks the tension. "Trixie, this is Samara and Sophia." She doesn't say anything, just walks toward us, her eyes shining. Even I can see that her lion is close to the surface, but her eyes seem dull compared to Samara's. Samara and Trixie circle each other a few times in silence, making me wonder if there's going to be some sort of fight before Trixie breaks it.

"Where are you from?" she asks Samara.

"Halifax. My pride was wiped out ten years ago," she explains, with sadness lining her voice.

Trixie nods, and her tone is terse but not threatening. "I heard about that. I thought there were no survivors."

"Only me," Samara tells her.

"I'm sorry to interrupt, but we have some big things to discuss and a very short time in which to do it," Alaric says. I turn to look at him and can see that he really doesn't want to be interrupting this, but he's right, we don't have the time for this.

"You're right, Alaric," Trixie says, turning her focus over to him and away from Samara. "Before Skarlyt and I came, I checked in with the pride and confirmed that there are three teenagers missing. All fifteen, three males. Their parents think they must've snuck out because they thought they were asleep in their rooms..." As Trixie finishes, I hear a rumble come from Samara. Trixie's eyes glaze over briefly, and she sighs. "One of the parents just reached out. Their daughter linked them earlier saying she's with Darren. They have been trying to get contact back, so that's why I am just finding out now. So, there are four in total, three males, one female. She's also fifteen." A small growl comes through her voice, obviously upset at the situation.

I walk over to a seething Samara and place my arm around her shoulders. In my excitement for her to meet Trixie, I forgot that there were teenagers captured.

She's been there my entire life and knows what I went through, and I can only imagine what's going through her mind right now. The fact that the same monsters that killed her family and hurt me all my life now have other shifters as captives must be hitting a nerve for her.

As I begin to scan the room once more, I notice that Trixie's neck is bent to the side in submission with a shocked expression on her face. What the fuck?

Samara also looks stunned and reigns in her lion quickly, allowing Trixie to stand upright. Uh-oh. The look on Trixie's face is a mix of awe and rage. I guess she didn't expect Samara to be more dominant than her.

"Sorry," Samara says, not looking away. As a matter of fact, she doesn't really look that sorry at all, but she wouldn't have said it if she wasn't. That's not who Samara is.

Trixie just waves it off, breaking eye contact first and returning to where she was standing beside Skarlyt.

Next thing I know, Sebastyn breaks the tension by popping back into the room with a large mountain of a man by his side. He is well over six feet tall and makes this enormous room seem small. He is full of muscles without an inch of fat on him. There's no question in my mind that this is the bear shifter alpha we were waiting for.

"Okay, good. Everyone is here. Let's get to it," Alaric says, and everyone finds a spot so they can hear and see him.

"First, Trixie and Axel, you aren't the only ones who have had members taken. Darren is a captive, and so are a few of our vampire allies," he says before adding, "Actually Seb, do you think you can go get Drake? He should probably be here too. I'd send Skarlyt, but I don't think he'd actually come with her." He chuckles, trying to make light of the situation that we find ourselves in.

As I look around the room, I realize for the first time since hearing the message from Devin that I might not have to make the trade. Maybe with the amount of people in this room and their packs, prides, covens, and whatever the bears call themselves, we may be able to win without having to sacrifice anything or anyone. At least that's what I'm starting to hope, but I know what hoping gets me: disappointment.

Maybe this time is different.

Chapter Twenty-Two

Sophia

Alaric begins explaining everything that we know thus far once Drake enters the room. I try to pay attention to everything he's saying, but my flames start licking up my arms. I shake them out, trying to extinguish them before anyone notices, but the more I wave and panic, the bigger they get and the more they spread.

Phoebe notices first and hurries over to me, taking my hands, turning them over in her own. Bad idea, she shouldn't have done that, because now it's not just me that's on fire. We're both quickly becoming engulfed in our own flames, unable to tame them.

"What's happening?" I whisper to her.

"I don't know," she says, her eyebrows pinched in confusion.

"The barrier!" Skarlyt shouts from across the room. Raising her hands to the sky and closing her eyes. Maybe that's it, maybe our inner flames sensed the danger and decided they needed to come out.

"The kids," Phoebe says to Alaric. It's Seb that jumps into action, though.

"I got them," he says and blinks out and back with one boy and then the other before coming back a third time empty-handed.

"I can't find Aurora," he exclaims. For a split second, I watch as Alaric and Phoebe start to freak out before I remember.

"She's in my room with Sarah." Everyone deflates, and Seb leaves and comes back first with Aurora, handing her to Alaric, and then with Sarah.

"Okay, our timeline has just been moved up. I don't even know what the plan is, but I need to know. Are you two with us?" Alaric says, looking toward Trixie and Axel. They look at each other and then back at him with a nod.

"Okay. Seb, teleport Axel back and have your sleuth come around the west here," he says, pointing to the map. "Skar, take Trixie back and take your pride to the east here," he adds, again pointing to a separate area on the map. I watch where he is pointing and realize that he's forming a box to trap the mages in. The only spot that won't be covered is to the north, but if I'm reading the map correctly, there is a large lake there so they wouldn't be able to escape that way anyway.

The two are gone and back in seconds. "Darren..." Alaric begins looking around, seeming to have forgotten for a second that Darren isn't here. "I mean Skar, can you wake up Lennox and have him sound the alarm please. Get everyone down here that needs to be.

"Drake, can you have all your able-bodied members come outside?

"And Seb, I need you to go get your coven and, most importantly, your mom. We need her for the kids," Alaric says. Everyone is moving in a rush around the room, seeming to have forgotten that Phoebe and I are still on the verge of shifting. The boys, though, do notice and walk up to the two of us, placing their own hands on ours, creating beautiful flames with a range of colors from deep crimson red to a sunflower yellow. If we weren't in danger right now, I would stare into them forever. As it is, we are in danger, so I snap out of it, sinking down into a crouch and grabbing the boys into a hug.

They look up at me with worried eyes. "You boys protect your sister and I'll protect mine," I whisper into their ears and feel them nod. I don't want to let them go, but I know that they'll be safer in the room with the other kids, so I pull back and am quickly replaced by Phoebe. Once they've shared a nice long hug, she stands, and they begin to move toward the safe room. I look at Phoebe and realize that her flames have died out in the time she was hugging the boys. Looking at my own hands, I notice the same. Huh. That's weird, but I'm not going to complain. As cool as it is when I can coax my flames out, I don't want them to start coming out without permission. I would like to maintain some type of control.

I stand back against the wall and watch as all sorts of people make their way down. It is more people than I thought lived here, but I haven't really had much time for exploring. I'm still observing when Sarah walks up to me and gives me a hug.

"Don't do anything stupid, okay? You're stronger than they could've ever expected. This is your chance to show them what you're capable of."

With how meek she normally is, I was not expecting that kind of pep talk from her, but it did the trick and has my inner flames rushing up to meet her in determination.

"I promise. I will go show them for the both of us," I say and give her one last squeeze before urging her into the safe room.

I never thought in a million years that I would call a mage someone I cared about, but then again, Sarah isn't really a mage, is she? She is far too pure to have actually corrupted her soul. I wonder how many other women in the coven are like Sarah and are simply too afraid to get away. I quickly shake that thought out of my head. None in Devin's coven that's for sure. I tried, I really did, when I was younger to make friends with some of them, but they're brainwashed. They genuinely believe that is the way life is supposed to be.

Samara comes to join me after Sarah leaves. "She's not like the other women in the pack, is she?" I forgot she wasn't here for the whole Sarah conversation. How do I explain this to her so that she won't go all crazy?

"She's a mage," I say quickly, grabbing onto her shoulders as a growl comes out, and she starts to move forward toward the door. "Wait," I plead, and she looks at me. Just like before, I can see her lion looking back at me, impatiently waiting for an explanation. "She was raised like me but forced to marry at eighteen like the rest. She is sweet and kind and definitely does not deserve to be lumped in with those monsters, but until we find a way to break the link she has to them, a mage is what she technically is." I slip everything out as fast as possible and feel her deflate a little. Not completely because, let's face it, we're still in danger, but enough that I am comfortable releasing her shoulders, knowing that she's not going to rush over and kill Sarah.

"When this is all over, sit down and talk to her. Let her tell you her story. I promise she is not like them," I say again, hoping to really drive it home. I watch as the glow begins to recede from her eyes and she nods at me. Whew.

"But if she is like them in any way," she begins.

"She isn't," I tell her adamantly. "But if she is then we will ask the coven for help purifying her soul."

Samara growls, not agreeing, but nods seeing the look on my face. There is no way that Sarah is like them so I have nothing to worry about, but even if she was, I would do absolutely anything in my power to fix it.

When the trickle of people finally stops coming down the stairs, we make our way up and out to the back deck where I can already see an extremely large number of people gathered. Alaric makes quick work of breaking everyone into teams and directing them where to go, pairing vampires, witches, and shifters into each group to work together. Once everyone starts to dissipate, though, he turns to Phoebe and me.

"I need you two to stay hidden until I give the signal."

I go to protest, but he gives me a look.

"Listen, I know this is your fight more than anyone else's, but if he sees you, he won't hesitate to start killing people to get you to go to him. If you're hidden, he might wait, and it will buy us time," he finishes with a pleading look. I have to admit it sounds like something Devin would do, so I reluctantly nod. Phoebe and I walk to our designated spot in the trees where we can wait. We each climb one, hidden in the branches but high enough that we can see everything. In between the trees just on the other side of the shimmering barrier, I see movement, lots of movement. Exactly how many mages did Devin bring?

I watch and hold my breath as Alaric walks between the trees, calling out, "Where's my brother?"

I'm still holding my breath as I see Devin crest the trees followed by a bunch of men I recognize as members of his coven, one of whom is dragging someone behind them by a leash.

"Right here," Devin responds, gesturing toward the battered man being dragged behind. I suck in a breath. What have they done to him? "Now where is my daughter?" he adds with a sneer.

Alaric seems frozen for a moment, staring at his brother before allowing his anger to fuel him. "Your daughter? Don't you mean the woman that you stole after you killed her parents? Or the woman that you locked in a cage for most of her childhood? Or did you mean the woman who ran away from you out of fear that you were going to turn her into a breeding mare?" Alaric yells with more venom than I've ever heard coming out of anyone's mouth.

Yes! I've never had anyone stand up for me that way before, and I admit it feels pretty fucking good.

Devin looks shocked only for a second before he strides up to Darren, pulls his head back by his rumpled dark hair, and lets his magic course through Darren's body, causing him to convulse. The growl that comes out of Alaric seems to shake the ground, and even the trees we're sitting in sway for a minute.

"Now that I have your attention...You will give me my daughter, or I will continue to test out my new forms of torture on your beloved brother," Devin responds, letting Darren's head drop down. At the same time, I see movement from the east and west approaching. This must be the bears and lions closing in.

The problem is that Devin seems to have noticed as well, and he quickly erects a gigantic dome over his entire group, making it so that no one can enter.

"I should've known better than to expect a dog like you to have any sense. You want to watch me torture your brother? Obviously, you do. I'm going to enjoy this," Devin says, pulling out two small knives from his back and slicing one through Darren's left chest. A sob gets caught in my throat at the sight.

As if sensing me, Darren raises his head, looking straight at me. Our eyes connect, and I recognize him immediately.

"Mate," I whisper, my phoenix waking and flames rushing down my arms. So, he is my mate. While I'm still dumbstruck, Devin takes the other blade, slicing it through the other side of his chest. I see the blood wicking into his already tattered shirt.

I can't watch this anymore.

"Stop," I yell, climbing down the tree and making my way to the barrier. "Just stop. Let him go, and I'll cross," I tell Devin as I come closer.

"There you are, my darling daughter. How I've missed you," Devin coos at me. "But I'm afraid I can't let him go just yet. How do I know that once I let him go, you will actually cross?"

"You have my word," I spit back at him, not daring to glance in

Darren's direction. The last thing I need is to draw more attention to him than there already is.

"Sophia, dear, your word doesn't mean anything anymore, not since you decided to run away from me, and after everything I've done for you," he says softly, ensuring that only those closest to us can hear him.

"You will cross, and I will release him, and not a second before," he announces louder, and I know him well enough to know there is no use arguing. He won't be swayed. There is no reasoning with him when he gets like this. I just hope that either he keeps his word, or I'm strong enough to kill them all when I cross. If I were a gambler, I'd wager everything that he's not going to keep his word, so I steel myself, gathering up as much emotion as I can to try to prime my flames.

I turn to Alaric. "Thank you for everything. If I don't make it back, you keep them safe." I whisper low enough that only he can hear. He nods, and I turn around, walking toward Devin.

Here I go.

Devin meets me at the border and pulls me through the border as soon as I am near enough and back hands me across the face. Instead of cowering or looking at the floor like I've always done, I hold my ground and keep eye contact.

"You are making a fool out of both of us with this rebellion," he whispers the words to me, laced with venom.

"Now let him go," I spit at Devin, still doing everything in my power not to look toward Darren, even though my entire body is craving to go into his arms and claim him as my own.

"Why should I? You're already across. Besides, he seems to mean something to you. He might come in handy keeping you in line." As he finishes, he runs the blade down Darren's cheek, drawing blood the entire way.

Before I can do anything, I hear a phoenix screech above me

and look up in time to see Phoebe completely decimate the barrier that Devin erected, allowing the bears and mountain lions access.

There's a flurry of activity as I watch the bears and mountain lions attack from each side, going after the hunters and mages. They do not hesitate, and I see blood shed almost immediately.

I'm satisfied that they've got it handled, so I turn back to Devin, who is looking around in complete and utter shock before raising his eyes to my twin with a murderous look on his face.

"Another phoenix?"

Oh hell no. He's not going to lay a finger on her. "Devin," I growl out, bringing his attention back to me, locking us in a staring contest. I can hear the carnage sounding around us, and I'm sure he can too, but I can't focus on anything but the man in front of me. The one who's made my life a living hell, and if he gets his hand on my sister, he will do the same to her. "This fight will not be worth it for you."

"You think I'm worried about losing a few men?" He looks disgusted with my ignorance. "I know better than to get caught up trying to protect one person." He points toward Darren, still at his feet, as an example of this type of failure.

It's then that I make the biggest mistake of my life. I follow his motion and risk looking down at Darren. His brilliant blue eyes are studying me, and I get lost in them for a moment too long. Whatever passes between us in that look is immediate and instinctual, and it doesn't escape Devin's notice. Before I can think of my next move, two things happen in quick succession. First, Devin drags his blade across Darren's throat. Then, he grips my arm roughly and teleports us away.

I'm still screaming when we arrive. I am in the basement of the house I've lived in my entire life, wrenching my arm away from the man who just murdered my mate.

I always knew Devin was a monster, but this...I know I shouldn't be surprised, but I am. Amid the shock, thoughts—

horrible thoughts—start to trickle in. I didn't even get a chance to talk, touch, kiss, or love the one man that the goddess created for me. Tears begin to fall from my eyes, and they only increase when I think of Alaric, Phoebe, and the boys. Alaric just watched his brother die. Phoebe will have to explain his absence—my absence—to the boys. My sobs increase, and I sink to the floor, placing my head in my hands.

"What have you done?" I ask between sobs, but the question is mindless. I know Devin doesn't understand the weight of his actions. "What have you done?"

"What are you crying for, girl? I'm the one who just lost most of my coven due to your little stunt!" Devin spits at me, dragging me to the cage and throwing me inside.

"Maybe some time in here will remind you of your place," he says, walking back up the stairs and slamming the door.

How could I have been so stupid that I actually allowed myself to hope for a better life? I thought I had learned my lesson about hoping. Instead, here I am, once again locked in this cage with no future ahead of me. It is like I have woken up from a dream, finding myself exactly in the awful situation I was when I fell asleep.

I can't help thinking it would have been less heartache if I never ran away in the first place. At least my mate would've still been alive, even if we would never be together.

Now I just need to hope and pray that Samara and Phoebe don't get any bright ideas about rescuing me. Neither of them should be anywhere near here.

Chapter Twenty-Three

Darren

Mate, my wolf whispers.

I lift my head, searching the area for who he is talking about. My breath catches when I lock eyes with her hiding in the trees. Sophia. The dreams don't do her justice. Her strawberry blonde hair is blowing in the wind. Even at this distance, I can tell her expression is pained. I'm so lost in my thoughts of her that I can hardly feel the mage dragging the knife across my chest, drawing blood the entire way.

Mate, my wolf says again when I hear her voice yelling, instructing Devin to stop. I follow her movements as she jumps down from the tree, pulling all eyes to her hiding place. I watch with wide eyes as Sophia, with her hair blazing down around her shoulders and her light eyes aflame with rage, steps up to the border separating the pack from the mages.

Mate, my wolf says again, and I blow out a breath as I watch her standing proud and furious, like an avenging angel, before this army of mages and hunters. My wolf doesn't have to remind me. She's perfect.

"There you are, my darling daughter. How I've missed you."

Devin's tone makes my skin crawl. The way he says "daughter" with a promise of punishment makes my heart begin to beat faster. There is rage in my veins and fear. He has already put her through too much; she will trade herself for me.

"But I'm afraid I can't let him go just yet. How do I know that once I let him go, you will actually cross?" he adds, and I can't help the growl that escapes my mouth. He continues his stare down with Sophia. He doesn't acknowledge me, but there's a twitch in his hand, still trapping my shoulder, that makes me think I just fucked up.

"You have my word," Sophia spits back at him with her hands clenched in fists at her sides. I can tell that she's feeling the pull of the mate bond just as strongly as I am, but she's doing a much better job at hiding it.

"Sophia, dear, your word doesn't mean anything anymore, not since you decided to run away from me, and after everything I've done for you." This he says quieter, as if he's embarrassed to admit that she ran away. Her getting away likely does make him seem weaker in front of the other mages, who pride themselves on keeping their wives and daughters in check.

"You will cross, and I will release him and not a second before," he finishes, and I know he's lying. He's not going to release me. He's going to use me to hurt her and keep her compliant. After my growl, and the fact that she's willing to trade herself for me, he's not stupid enough not to connect the dots and realize that we mean something to each other. I just hope he doesn't know exactly what it is.

She turns toward Alaric, saying something in low tones so others cannot hear her.

Alaric, stop her, I try to scream through our bond. She's going to cross, and it's going to be all my fault.

Alaric, stop her! I force through once again, but if he hears me, he doesn't show it. He simply nods at her with a forlorn look, and she turns around, walking through the barrier.

Devin meets her at the border and immediately grabs her arm, pulling her across in a rough motion. He cocks his hand back and backhands her across the face, and her lip splits open immediately. The rumble in my chest gives me hope that, with the need to protect my mate being so strong, my body is healing. Soon, maybe, I'll have enough strength to break this tether. Once that happens, I'm going to enjoy every single second of tearing this fucker to pieces.

Instead of shrinking away or submitting, she holds her head up high, maintaining eye contact while demanding, "Now let him go." Surely, she knows that he has no intention of letting me go, surely she realizes that this was just a trick to get her on this side.

"Why should I? You're already across. Besides, he seems to mean something to you. He might come in handy keeping you in line." As he finishes, he runs the blade down my cheek, drawing blood the entire way.

Still, I don't feel anything as I continue to look at Sophia. Her being this close is making it more difficult to stay still. All I want to do is scoop her up and run to safety, keeping her out of harm's way. Between the collar on my neck, the leash attached to the back of my head, and the amount of energy being drained, I know I won't make it two steps, so I stay in my spot. Our best bet now is giving her a chance to burn these fuckers to ash.

Next thing I know, I hear a loud phoenix screech above me and look up to see Phoebe completely shifted and destroying the barrier that the mages erected around us. As the barrier comes down, I hear a series of growls and roars coming from each side. Looking to the left and right, I recognize Trixie's pride and Axel's sleuth coming through, attacking any who get in their way.

I'm distracted from watching the carnage that the bears and mountain lions are committing by Sophia growling out, "Devin, this fight will not be worth it for you." I snap my head around to her. That has to be the hottest thing I've ever heard in my life. My cock seems to agree because, despite the number of injuries throughout my body, it's hard as a fucking rock and straining against my pants to get out.

"You think I'm worried about losing a few men?" His words are laced with scorn, but I do not hear what he says next.

Sophia turns to meet my eyes, and I get lost looking into them. Finally, after all this time, I feel the longing in my chest start to fade and love for this woman quickly fills up my heart. I know very little about her, and she knows even less about me if she still can't remember our dreams, but suddenly she's my entire world, and I know I was right in thinking that I would die willingly for her to never feel any kind of hurt again.

I feel something sharp slide across my neck, and I watch as her face shifts to one of horror, hear her scream, and feel the shift in the air as Devin teleports her away. The next few seconds go by in excruciating slowness. My hand tests the skin at my throat and pulls away coated in blood. My blood. There is no pain; there is only curiosity, shock. I try to come to terms with the truth of the world around me: Sophia has just been taken somewhere by that monster, and I'm going to die here.

I slowly turn to face my brother, my eyes finding him with ease. I watch as his wolf forces the shift and howls in pain before rushing to my side, nudging me. Weakly, I raise my hands, resting them in his fur. I so badly want to tell him that he was the best big brother anyone could have asked for, that I love him, and that he shouldn't blame himself. I want to ask him to find and protect Sophia for me, to tell the boys and Aurora all the funny things we did as kids, to keep my memory alive.

I hear Phoebe come to land close by and I try as hard as I can to turn to look at her, but I can't. I want to tell her that I love her too, that she's the best thing that has happened to our family, that the light she and the kids have brought with them has made this life so much more than I ever thought possible.

My eyelids are heavy from the blood loss, and I feel someone's arms slipping under my own, laying me down, and a liquid being poured on my neck and in my mouth. Warmth spreads across my body, and I feel someone removing the collar from around my neck. I don't see what the point of that is, but if they feel the need, it's not going to matter to me soon because I'm going to be dead.

Just as I'm thinking my goodbyes, I start to feel my body healing. What the hell? My eyes fly open, and I sit up fast, realizing that all the aches and pains that were previously coursing through my body are now gone. Other than slight dizziness from sitting up too fast, I feel amazing. Better than I have in days.

"Sophia?" I whisper, looking from Alaric in wolf form to Sebastyn to Phoebe. Seb shakes his head, and Phoebe, wreathed in wicked flames, takes to the sky with the loudest screech I've ever heard her produce.

I look back toward Seb. "She's my mate," I tell him, and he just gives me a solemn look with a nod. "We have to get her back."

Again, he gives me a nod, showing he's on board. Good. Now we just need to figure out how.

Sebastyn is helping me stand, but my legs are still wobbly from disuse, when a woman comes stomping up to us, anger evident in her stride.

"Where is she?" she asks, her pointed jaw tense. I look over at Seb in confusion. He only blows out an exasperated breath.

"Who?" I ask the woman, trying to remember if I know her. Her dark skin and long coiled brown hair are familiar enough, but I think I would know someone holding onto this much anger by name.

She just continues to stare at me, visibly seething with rage.

"She means Sophia," Seb tells me quietly with a nudge.

"Of course, I mean Sophia," she shouts at us. "Who the hell else?"

"Samara," Trev says, walking up behind her calmly and putting his arms around her. She relaxes enough for me to actually answer. This must be Sophia's best friend. The one who's pride was slaughtered by Devin because they were friends. I soften my gaze as I meet her eyes.

"Devin took her," I tell her.

Her eyes widen and then immediately begin to fill with tears.

"You," she says, breaking free of Trev's arms and pointing her finger in my face. "You should have minded your own damn business, and we would have been free." Trev tries to interrupt her, but her eyes are glowing gold. "If you hadn't gotten caught, she'd still be here."

She is in my face and looks ready to murder me when Alaric shifts back. "Samara, that's not fair. Nobody wanted this," he tries to reason.

"I told you," she says, her finger now pointing at him. There's venom in her voice, derision and pain mixed. "I told you this would happen, and I told you to stop it." Now she's yelling at Alaric. What's weird is, even though he's rumbling in his chest, he's letting her.

"You know as well as I do that no one could've stopped her," he reasons again.

Trev pulls her back into his chest, and tears start streaming down her face. "You don't know what he's capable of. What he's going to do to her for running away. I never should've brought her here," she sobs, turning to cry into Trev's chest.

"Actually, I do. When Devin had me, it was one of his torture methods. He showed me his treatment of her over the years." I pause, calming my wolf who is snarling and ready to murder everyone now that he has his strength back and knows that our mate is gone.

"We're going to get her back." I fill my voice with determination. She simply shares a brief look with me before turning back to Trev, dismissing me. "She's my mate," I add, and she spins around to look into my eyes.

"What did you say?" She searches my eyes for the truth, and I nod.

"Yes, and I'm getting her back one. I promise."

"Okay," she whispers, turning away, shifting quickly, and jumping into the fray. I look around at the battle raging around me and can see immediately that we're winning. There are only a couple of small groups of mages and hunters left, but I don't know how many were able to run or teleport away. I spin on my heel, calling on my wolf to enact some revenge.

The captives are over there, I link Alaric, turning my head in the direction of the cages.

Got it, he responds, not wasting any time and rushing in that direction.

I meant what I said. We're going to rescue Sophia—no matter what. We just need to finish whatever is going on here quickly first.

The mage who first found me in the woods, who stunk of magic, runs in front of me. He is retreating from a group of vampires that are currently falling upon a hunter that was guarding him. It's his bad luck.

I make a break for him. He sees me as I get close and tries to erect a barrier around himself, but Matt, a witch from the coven, gets there first, slinging the silver lasso around him and preventing him from accessing his magic.

I latch my teeth around his neck and give it a shake, breaking it and killing him instantly. They say mages are immortal, but it's different if they are cut off from their power source, unable to bring themselves back from the brink of death.

I am dropping him, shaking his blood from my muzzle, when a

blast of magic lands close to my back paw. It is close enough to knock me to my side without actually hitting me. I jump back up and find the offending mage immediately. He's looking betrayed at his own hand, as if his aim went wrong of its own accord. I race toward him, but his hands are already raised again.

I duck, taking his legs out from under him. He falls backwards, the wind knocked from his lungs and his spell interrupted. Before I have a chance to make my next move, an enormous bear shifter takes my place, landing with a thick, liquid squelch on the mage's chest.

I must've taken a lot longer with him than I realized because, as I look around, our small group is standing in a circle. I rush toward them, shifting back.

"What's the plan?" I ask, pulling on a pair of shorts that Alaric hands me.

"Sebastyn is going to take us four first and then come back for more help as we need," Phoebe says, gesturing to herself, Samara, me, and Alaric.

I nod ready to go get my mate before anything else can happen to her.

Chapter Twenty-Four

Sophia

I'm sitting in the cage, still sobbing over all the events of the last hour. So much has happened that I almost feel numb. I found my family, and I lost my family. I found my mate, and I lost my mate. I was free, and I'm a captive once again. I don't know what Devin has planned for me now, but I know it won't be pleasant.

I pick up my stick dolls and hug them to my chest, wishing for a way out, wishing that I never left in the first place, wishing that there was something I could do to fix this. I let the tears fall down my face. They heal the split in my lip as they slide down my face, and I wish they hadn't. At least the pain from that was distracting me a little.

I know I need to pull myself together, but my brain is sluggish from shock and grief. I glance around the room, paying special attention to the cage. I know there's no visible door and they use magic to open and close it. There's no door to force, but I know one entire side of the cage slides up and away when they throw me in here. Maybe there's something I can do that side.

I reach inside, the way Phoebe showed me to, and search for

my flames. It takes longer to calm my mind, but I find my orange and red flames. Just like before, they are in the center of my chest, but they are dull, burning low and weak.

Come on, flames. We need to get out of here, I say to my flames, and they flare up for a moment as if they understand me. They fade quickly, though, settling into a weaker flame than before.

Damn it! Damn this cage. I bang on the bars in frustration before sinking back into the corner, letting the tears flow again.

I keep trying to summon the flame but coaxing it out accomplishes nothing. We are both feeling weak and exhausted.

Please, I beg. *I can't do this without you.*

I hear the basement door open and slam shut. I keep my eyes clamped shut, but I know it is Devin stomping down the steps.

Flames, I plead. *This may be the only chance we get. We can't let him tether us again.*

With each step that brings Devin closer, I become more and more frenzied in my attempts. From outside, a strange noise cuts all the way down into the basement. A few days ago, I wouldn't have recognized it, but now I know it is a phoenix screech, my sister coming to save me.

"Well, dear daughter," Devin spits at me, now only a step away from my cage. "Seems like you made some friends. I usually don't approve of company, but we can let the phoenix stay." He grins down at me, looking like the cat that stole the canary.

Shit. Phoebe should never have come here. If they get her too, it's over. Doesn't she realize that?

"Where is she?" I hear a man's voice shout. It is followed by a crashing sound that may be the door being knocked in. The noise draws Devin's attention, and, instinctually, I try to draw it back to me.

"You're not going to get away with this," I growl. "As soon as I get out of this cage, I'm going to end you."

He laughs as if I just told the funniest joke he's ever heard.

"I think I'll capture her first, then make you both watch as I get rid of the pesky shifters you two seem to collect."

"Devin!" Another, more familiar, voice comes from upstairs. Samara? "Come out here, you coward."

No, no, no. What were they thinking bringing her here? Devin must realize who it is as well. A shocked look flits across his face, but it is gone almost as quickly as it appears.

"Seems I didn't take care of the shifter problem as well as I thought," he sneers, bending down to look at me through the bars. "I think I'll start with that little bitch instead. Make you watch as I end the mountain lions once and for all." Standing up, he turns and walks back up the stairs.

No. Think, Sophia. Think.

Phoebe. I close my eyes and reach out to her, hoping that our bond is stronger than the shielded cage. If Darren and Alaric can do it through the tether, I have to believe we can as well.

Sophia? Thank the goddess. Are you all right? she asks in relief.

I am, but you and Samara need to leave. All of you need to leave.

No. We came for you. We're not leaving here without you, she replies with determination in her voice.

Well, shit. I may have only just met her, but I've seen enough to know there's no swaying her once her mind is set on something. We are both stubborn, but I don't think anyone can get in her way.

I need to come up with another plan. Wait...When we first met, Skarlyt said our flames should be able to destroy any spells the mages use. Phoebe was able to destroy my tether, and she could destroy their shields also. If I can coax out my flames, I may be able to destroy this cage. If I can get free, at least I can help. We may stand a chance with two untethered phoenixes. I am not sure if Devin thought the cage would be enough or if he just didn't have another tether ready, but I may give them the element of surprise.

I close my eyes and search inside my chest once again, finding my flame. It is burning slightly brighter than before, but the sounds of multiple fights breaking out in the front yard causes me to lose my concentration.

Okay, Sophia. You can do this.

I let the sounds fall into the background and return my focus to my flames. This time, it only takes seconds before I find it. Just like last time, it flares, seemingly excited, trying to spread, only to shrink right back down again.

"Ugh," I groan out in frustration, hitting the bars.

"Darren, over here!" I hear another voice—Skarlyt?—shout. Her voice is near enough and loud enough that it breaks through my focus.

Darren? But I watched him die. Didn't I? If Darren is here, I really need to get this to work. Devin is not going to make the same mistake twice. He'll make sure he really is dead this time.

Phoebe? Is Darren here? I ask.

Yes. We got to him in time.

Thank the goddess. He's alive. If I can get out of here, I do actually have a chance at a life. There's no way in hell I'm letting Devin take that from me a second time.

With renewed purpose, I close my eyes once more, talking to my inner flame.

Come on. Our twin, mate, and friends are all going to die if we can't make this work. I know we can do it.

My awareness tingles as if it actually understands me, and I watch as it doubles its efforts to spread and surface.

Yes.

The flames spread outward, beginning to form in my hands and slowly making their way up my arms. It takes longer than when Phoebe helped me, but my shift comes over me in a wave. In a moment, I am overtaken by flames, and the cage is melting into a puddle around me. I stretch my wings and body out, momentarily savoring the feeling of not being crouched in that cage, before flying up the stairs and out the door.

As I make my way outside, I notice that Devin has erected a barrier around the house. Most of the mages went to Parry Sound with him, so he doesn't have much support. He is feeding energy into the barrier at the same time Phoebe is tearing it down, and neither of them seem to make any headway. I look around, seeing Samara, Alaric, and Skarlyt before locking eyes with my mate. Last time I saw him, he was dying, a mess of blood and bruises. Now he's standing tall, looking like he was made in the image of the gods themselves.

I drink him in, his tall, muscular frame with tattoos going up both arms and spreading out over his chest. Holy fuck! If I was in my other form, I'd have to change my underwear because they would be drenched. He has to be the sexiest man on earth; he's like a Big Mac that I want to eat up, except I'm the one dripping sauce.

Movement from behind him snaps me out of my ogling and reminds me that we're fighting for our lives. I watch as two of the men I grew up with attack him by hurling energy blasts at his back, catching him off guard and sending him to his knees.

Oh hell no. Not again. I refuse to watch my mate die a second time.

I let the rage and fear pour through me, flying up to meet Phoebe at the top of the barrier.

Sophia. I hear her sigh in relief, but I don't let my happiness at seeing her stop me. I let loose all the feelings inside of me. The fear for my mate, the rage toward Devin, the desire for the freedom to be with my family and my mate, it all pours out until I explode. I let loose an earth-shattering screech, followed by a tidal flame that puts my previous attempt to shame. It destroys the house, the barrier, and all the mages within close proximity without touching any of our allies. I let out a breath of relief and fly to my sister's side, and my flame spreads from me to Phoebe and ignites a tidal flame in her as well. The next thing I know, she's detonating beside me as well.

I watch as her head slips back and her beautiful crimson and blue flames shoot out in wave after wave, ensuring that all of our enemies are gone.

I search the ground for any sign of Devin, but he is nowhere to be found.

Have you seen Devin? I ask Phoebe as her flames return to normal. At least she didn't drain her powers again this time.

No. Not since before we erupted, she says, looking around.

We need to find him, or we'll never be safe, I tell her and begin to fly around to search for him.

He can't escape. If he does, I'll be looking over my shoulder for the rest of my life. My mate, family, and friends will be in danger. My children, if I have any, will always be looking over their shoulders too. That's not the kind of life I want for myself or any family I have.

Chapter Twenty-Five

Darren

Seeing Sophia in phoenix form takes my breath away. She has a lighter shade of flames than Phoebe, ranging from a burnt orange and a sunflower yellow. She looks almost like the sky at dawn, and I cannot look away.

I am so lost staring up at my gorgeous mate flying overhead that I don't immediately hear the two assholes sneaking up behind me. After they throw a couple of cheap shots my way, I watch in awe as Sophia lets out a wave of flames so strong it pushes me back. My knees scrape along the grass, but I am completely unharmed by the blast. Within seconds, Phoebe is doing the same. Amazing.

Again, I'm so distracted by the wonder of my mate and her sister that I am not aware of Devin before he grabs me from behind and places a knife to my throat. Not this again. I don't know how he survived both blasts, but I don't suppose it really matters now.

"Sophia!" he screams, getting the attention of everyone around.

"You and that other phoenix will come peacefully, or I will

finish the job this time," he says, moving the knife slightly so it nicks my neck. Blood trickles down my chest.

"Never," Alaric growls out as both Phoebe and Sophia screech, landing in front of us in their phoenix forms.

Sophia takes a step forward, but Phoebe grabs her arm and pulls her back. They share a look like they are communicating, and I recognize that they must have a link like Alaric and I do. It makes me look forward to the day I share a mate link with her. Because I fully believe, after seeing her in action, that we will get our happily ever after, and this fucker is going down.

Phoebe nods as Sophia walks up to Devin and me.

"Good girl. I knew you'd see reason," he says to her.

She doesn't stop though. She continues walking up to us and places her flaming hands on Devin's, passing the flames to his skin. I feel the heat from the flames, but it doesn't burn me. It feels like a warm caress on a winter day.

Devin steps back in shock and screams.

Sophia shifts back and says, "You will never harm my mate or my family ever again."

I don't get the satisfaction of seeing what I'm sure is the shock on his face, but I'm okay with that. After it's done, I can finally hold Sophia in my arms.

I don't even get the chance to stand up before she tackles me to the ground and places her mouth on mine. So, this is what it feels like to be complete. I wrap my arms around her, pulling her even closer to me. We've kissed in our dreamscapes, but this feels different. Better. Real.

I run my tongue along the seam of her lips, trying to get her to open up and let me in. After a moment, she does just that, and her tongue begins a slow, tentative dance with mine. Her hesitation makes me think that she's never done this before, but that doesn't match her confidence from the dreamscape. I guess everyone is braver in their dreams. Because of her tentativeness, I stop myself from rubbing my fully erect member on her very naked pussy while she's straddling me. We have yet to even speak to each other, but already, I feel the beginning of the mate bond snapping into place—which should be impossible.

Heaven. I hear a woman's voice in my head. What was that? It wasn't my wolf, and I don't think any of the women in the pack would be saying this was heaven. I pull back and look into Sophia's eyes.

"Was that you?" I ask her.

She looks confused. "Was what me?"

"Did you just say 'heaven' in my head? Through our bond?" She looks embarrassed and begins to stand up. "Please don't. I agree; this is heaven." I feel her relax slightly back into my arms with a nod.

It doesn't last long, though, because our perfect twosome quickly becomes a dog pile when Samara tackles Sophia, wrapping her in a hug, and is joined by the rest of our ragtag family.

"Don't you ever do that again," Samara declares. Sophia just nods and falls into a fit of laughter. I'm not sure anyone knows what she's laughing about, but it doesn't stop everyone from joining in. We must look like a bunch of idiots—a pile of naked and half naked idiots.

As usual, Alaric gets to be the fun killer. "Let's go home," he announces, watching the smoldering house for evidence of further trouble. Although it is ruining our fun, I agree with him. I've been away from home for far too long, and I want to get my mate somewhere nice and private.

As we all stand, Seb takes off his shirt and hands it to Sophia to cover up. I shoot him a look of thanks. My wolf protests momentarily at the thought of an unmated man's shirt on her body, but, as much as I'd love to be able to stare at her beautiful body for hours on end, I'd rather not have the rest of the pack doing the same.

Seb and Skarlyt make quick work of teleporting us all back to the house, where we are greeted by not only our pack but also Trixie, Drake, and Axel. It seems like all of their packs, sleuth, and covens headed back home already.

"Once you guys left, most of the mages teleported away. and a lot of the hunters ran. We were going to chase them but decided to tend to our wounded," Axel says, filling us in quickly about what happened after we left.

"I don't think they'll be back any time soon," Trixie adds, and Drake and Axel both nod. They seem confident that we've seen the last of them, but I'm not so sure. I think that the mages and hunters are like a hydra. You cut off one head, and two more grow in its place. At least that's been our experience thus far.

"Thank you all for coming to our aid," Alaric says, clasping Trixie's hand before moving on to Axel and finally Drake.

"We're allies," Drake says, evidence of the extreme changes our relationship with the vampire has undergone in such a short time.

"Still. It means a lot. Allies or not." Phoebe steps up, molding herself into Alaric's side, and I pull Sophia into mine.

Finally, when everyone seems to have settled, Axel, Trixie, and Drake say their goodbyes and head home. We do the same, our large group heading to Alaric and Phoebe's.

I am walking up the steps when I hear two little voices. "Uncle Darren! Aunt Sophia!" We both only have enough time to open our arms before two little bodies are launched into them. Now I'm especially grateful to Sebastyn for giving Sophia a shirt.

"We missed you," Riley says while Ryker adds, "Don't do that again okay?"

Sophia and I chuckle.

"We don't plan to," I tell them, giving them both a tight squeeze. As we release them, Alaric and Phoebe come walking up with Aurora.

"There's my gorgeous girl," I say, holding out my arms for her and peppering her face with kisses.

"Hey, no hogging the niece," Sophia chimes in, wrapping her arms around the both of us and nuzzling Aurora.

This is it. This is my idea of heaven. Looking around at the small amount of people that are left in the house, I realize this is our family, maybe not all by blood, but by choice.

One by one, it seems that everyone is feeling the love in this room, and they come to join in our hug. First are the boys, then Phoebe and Alaric. Skarlyt and Lennox are next, but only slightly before Seb and a very reluctant Sarah who gets as close to Sophia as she can, sharing a soft look. Seems like they became friends in the short time I was gone. Good. They both need that.

Next come Charleigh, Ashton, Cybil, Felicia, and Josh. I think our group hug is complete, but Sophia raises her head to look around the room for something. She finds it when her eyes land on Samara and Trev, and she waves them over. At first Samara seems hesitant, but Trev pulls her forward, helping her squeeze through the people to get up close to Sophia.

"This is our family, Sam," I hear Sophia whisper to her with unshed tears lining her eyes.

Samara glances around at the large group in this hug and whispers back, "Yeah, it is. And it's perfect."

We all linger in the hug, and, after the last few days, I don't blame any of us. Hell, after the last year, we deserve to savor a little bit of joy.

Everyone takes turns saying their goodbyes and heading off to their respective houses until it's just us and Sebastyn with Alaric, Phoebe, and the kids.

"Okay, boys, off to bed," Phoebe tells them, and their faces fall.

"But Mom...Uncle Darren just got back," Ryker whines.

"And I'll still be here in the morning when you wake up, I promise," I tell them.

And Sophia adds, "If you go to bed now, we can show Uncle Darren all the cool things we found on our walk, or maybe we can have a *Mortal Kombat* tournament." She gives them a wink.

I nod, and they excitedly give hugs and kisses goodnight, rushing up the stairs satisfied with the promise of tomorrow.

"Okay..." Phoebe starts with a pointed look at her sister and then me. "Someone going to tell me?" I know what she wants to hear, but I don't know what the point is. She can obviously tell that we're mates.

"Darren is my mate," Sophia says excitedly, turning to look into my eyes.

"I knew it. See, I told you," she says waving her finger in Alaric's face and doing her "I told you so" dance around him.

"Yes, you did, love. You were right," he relents.

Sophia and I share a confused look before turning back to them.

"Phoebe told me that you two were mates the day that Sophia got here. I didn't agree or disagree," he says, pointedly. "I just stated that Sophia's dreams of the pack could be related more to Phoebe than to the fact that you're mates." Phoebe just sticks her tongue out at him and continues dancing, causing Sophia to giggle.

The sound shoots straight to my cock, making it twitch with lust.

"All right. I'm taking Sophia back to my cabin," I announce, handing Aurora to Alaric.

I pull Sebastyn aside while Sophia hands out her hugs and ask, "Is there any way to share my dreams with Sophia?"

He looks from me to Sophia and back again. "She doesn't remember?"

I shake my head. "No."

"That makes more sense then. I'll be right back," he says, popping away and returning a few seconds later with the crystal ball. "Just say 'I'm a fart knocker,' and it will show you," he says with a smile.

"Really, dude?" I ask, though a chuckle slips out. He shrugs his shoulders before walking over to Sophia to say his good nights.

I wrap my arms around Alaric, Phoebe, and Aurora, whispering good night to all three. Alaric squeezes my shoulder when I step back, and I give him a nod, knowing his meaning without him having to say anything. Neither of us want to voice what could've happened tonight or how lucky we are to be together. All that matters is that we are.

With a promise to be back in the morning, I grip Sophia's hand and lead her to my cabin.

"I have something to show you," I say, stopping to sit on a secluded bench and pulling out the crystal ball.

"What is it?" she asks, with a mixture of excitement and nerves.

"You don't remember, but we've met before. A few times in fact," I tell her, and she steps back in disbelief.

"What do you mean?"

"We've been meeting in our dreams every night for the past week."

"I think I would remember that. I remember dreaming of a black wolf sitting by the lake and flying above a pack of wolves with Phoebe, but I don't remember meeting you."

I let out a sigh and pull her close. "Watch." I quickly whisper "I'm a fart knocker" under my breath and pray that she doesn't hear me. If she does, she doesn't get a chance to say anything as she stares into the crystal ball. I move my hand over it the same way that Sebastyn did to turn up the volume, and she leans closer, in awe of what she's seeing.

She looks up at my eyes a few times before quickly looking back at the ball as it jumps from one dream to the next. When they're over, she looks up into my eyes, tears threatening to spill over in hers.

"I'm sorry."

I place the crystal ball on the bench and place my hands on either side of her face, raising her chin up so I can see her eyes. "For what?"

"For not remembering. If I would've remembered, none of this wouldn't have happened."

I kiss her cheeks and then her mouth. "Everything happens for a reason, love. Besides, we don't know what would've happened. We can only guess. At least we're together now."

She nods. "That's true."

"Come on. Let's get you home," I say, standing, grabbing her hand and continuing toward our home. I am leading the way, hoping that she likes it. If she doesn't, I'm not opposed to changing anything and everything that she wants. It's going to be her home too after all.

Chapter Twenty-Six

Sophia

I'm so nervous. The way he was kissing me earlier shows me he has way more sexual experience than I do, but that's not saying much. Even most kids get their first kiss long before age twenty-eight.

But as far as first kisses go, I can't imagine there has ever been a better one. He was so confident and smooth, taking the lead, probably not realizing how little experience I truly have. Although, if what I saw in that crystal ball was true, we've already shared many kisses in our dreams that I don't remember. A small smile slides onto my face while running our dream meetings through my head. Not once did he get upset or mad that I didn't remember when I woke up. Instead, he kept a record of them, and, whether it was to show me or not, it was still sweet.

My stomach begins to churn in anticipation of what's going to happen once we reach the cabin, and, right on cue, my self-doubt starts to seep in. What if I'm no good? What if my lack of experience repels him, and he wants someone with more? He's my mate, so he probably won't leave me. What if it just disappoints him and ruins our first night together? What if....

I am snapped out of my thoughts by Darren placing his hands on either side of my face. "Hey. Whatever it is that you're thinking about, it's going to be okay. I promise."

I want to believe him. Everything in my body wants to believe him, but how can he be so sure without knowing the issue? He starts walking again, and we arrive at an extremely secluded cabin on the lake. Alaric and Phoebe's home is just visible through the trees, and the outside of this house looks almost identical to theirs. It's smaller but still two levels, with the wrap-around porch on the ground level, allowing for a perfect view of the lake.

He stops, turns to face me, and reaches under my legs and arms in order to carry me across the threshold. I wrap my arms around his neck, savoring the feeling of his coiled shoulder muscles. He stops in the kitchen, placing me down on a stool.

"Would you like a coffee?" he asks. A normal person would say no way. It would ruin sleep for most people, and we have plenty to talk about without sharing a refreshing drink, but coffee is one of my favorite pastimes, so I nod my head.

As he gets to work setting up the coffeemaker, I get a good look around. I was right. The layout inside is almost identical to Alaric and Phoebe's, with exposed wood beams and flooring. It's gorgeous. Their house is decorated in what I would call showroom furniture, like you would see in a magazine, but this house is more lived in, with a well-used lazy boy sitting to the side of a large blue sectional couch with deep pockets that looks perfect for snuggling up and watching a movie.

"Milk and sugar?" Darren asks, drawing my awareness back to him. Again, I nod. I don't think I've ever been this quiet. Well, not since I've been in Parry Sound anyway. I was always quiet around Devin and his friends out of fear of retribution for speaking out of turn. Right now, I'm quiet because I don't know how to tell this sexy-as-sin man that I'm a virgin.

"Whatever you're nervous about, you don't need to be," he

tells me with a chuckle while placing my coffee in front of me. I let a small, nervous giggle slip past my lips as well. "I know we just met, but there's nothing—"

I nod but don't respond, grabbing my mug and taking my first sip of the most delicious coffee I've ever tasted. I moan in ecstasy simply from the taste and am shocked when a rumble starts in his chest.

Oh goddess. That sound sends sparks straight to my core, making the insides of my thighs dampen with proof of my desire for this man. I squeeze my legs together, trying to decide how to broach this subject. How do you tell someone that you are desperate to kiss and touch that you've never had any sort of sexual encounters with anyone except for yourself and you aren't even sure you were doing it right?

He sniffs the air, scenting my obvious desire, and rounds the island, coming toward me. I swivel on the stool so that I'm now facing him, and he slips in between my legs, cupping my chin. I get lost in his blue eyes for a second before he's claiming my mouth again. This time, I don't hesitate, and I slip my tongue through his lips, matching his passion, showing him exactly how much I want him. As he snakes his hand up my thighs, moving toward my center, he lets out another rumble upon meeting my wetness and pulls back.

"Oh goddess, you're so wet for me," he says gruffly, before resuming our kiss and inching his fingers toward my clit with small circular movements, quickly bringing me to a frenzy. What was it that I had to tell him again? Oh, that's right.

I reluctantly jerk back from our kiss. "There's something I have to tell you first," I say fast, still breathing heavily with need.

He gives me a concerned look but takes a step back. Once he's far enough away that I can think clearly, I try and think of how I want to say this.

I cannot think of any better way, so I decide to jump right in. I just blurt it out. "I'm a virgin."

A smirk crosses his face until he notices the amount of anxiety that must be plastered all over mine and steps back up to his spot between my legs.

Cupping my face with both hands this time, he places a gentle kiss on my lips. "Then we'll go slow or do nothing. Whatever you want. I'm willing to wait if that's what you want," he tells me.

"Goddess no. I don't want to wait." It comes out of my mouth before he's even taken a breath. Can I seem any more desperate? But he doesn't seem to take it that way or, if he does, he likes it. He just steps back, taking my hand in his, and leading me up the stairs and into the only room on the right. The upstairs is set up the same as Phoebe's except there's only one room on each side. I step into the room and look around.

I am expecting a man's bedroom. You know: dirty clothes strewn all over, dirty dishes on every available surface, but that's not what I find. In front of me is a beautiful bedroom with a four-poster bed with sheer blue fabric hanging like curtains pulled to the corners and a midnight blue comforter. Much like Phoebe and Alaric's, it has an open concept closet and bathroom, showing his neatly placed clothes, sparkling clean sinks and shower, with the most gorgeous claw foot tub in the corner that I know I'm going to enjoy using. He lets me explore for a few minutes, and I'm standing in front of the bed when he comes up to me from behind, wrapping his arms around my middle and kissing the side of my neck.

I lean my head back and savor the feeling as his fingers once again find my clit, increasing pressure on his circles, quickly bringing me to orgasm.

"Darren," I cry out with my release as my knees go weak. He spins me around, lifting the shirt over my head, leaving me bare before him. He takes his time, moving his eyes from bottom to top, drinking in my naked form.

"You're so beautiful," he says to me, before merging his mouth to mine once more and lowering us onto the bed.

"Wait," I say as he lowers his body over mine, and he straightens back up.

"Is everything okay? We can go slower if you want," he tells me, and I can see the honesty on his face.

"No, it's not that it's just..." How do I say this...

"Whatever it is, you can tell me." He reaches down and strokes my cheek.

"I've never seen...I mean, I've never been with anyone, so I've never seen a man naked up close before," I say quietly, looking down at my twisting hands in my lap. He grips my chin lightly, raising my face until I'm looking into his eyes once more before he steps back and slowly removes his pants.

I watch in awe as he undoes his button, then his fly, watching as the slight bulge in his pants grows as it's released from its confines. He pulls them down, and I immediately realize the lack of underwear. Oh, my goddess. It seems as though I blink and suddenly there's a long thick cock standing straight at attention, and I lick my lips.

I look back up in his eyes, watching the heat and desire smolder in them and assume that the same is reflecting in my own. I reach out my hand to grip his member but stop short. What if I do it wrong? He seems to recognize my tentativeness and places his hand around my own, guiding it to wrap around him. It's so thick that my thumb and fingers don't meet, but it doesn't seem to matter as he slowly guides our hands to stroke him from base to tip, inciting a moan to slip from his own mouth.

I wonder if I can taste him. I decide to risk it. He's been so patient with me, and I know he will correct me if I do it wrong, I move my mouth toward him and slip my tongue out of my mouth to lick the small amount of pre-cum glistening on the tip.

"Mmm." It tastes so good. I open my mouth wide and slip my

lips around him, following the same motions that our hands are making, and it has him moaning even louder this time.

I watch his body for cues on what I'm doing, realizing that he really likes it when I swivel my tongue around the tip in between sucks.

"Stop, angel. I won't last if you keep going like that," he says, and I pull my mouth back with one last lick. "Besides, it's only fair that I should get to taste you as well." With the last statement, he pushes me back onto the bed, quickly settling his mouth between my thighs. He places a few quick swipes of his tongue before going straight to my clit and moving his tongue in quick motions from left to right. I thought the feeling with his fingers was good, but this is amazing. As my legs begin to shake, showing my impending release, he slips one finger inside of me, causing me to jerk. He doesn't slow though; he just moves his finger in and out of me in time with the movement of his tongue.

Just as my release begins to crest, I feel him slip another finger inside, scissoring them, stretching my insides in preparation for him.

"Darren!" I scream as my core clenches down on his fingers. As my orgasm begins to slow, he moves up my body, still moving his fingers in and out.

"I need you," I say breathlessly to him.

"Not yet, angel, we need you to be ready," he starts kissing his way up my body, only stopping to lavish my breasts with attention. Sucking my nipple into his mouth and tugging on it gently, he makes me squirm and moan before continuing on to the other one and doing the same.

He finally arrives at my mouth, and I grip his head firmly, pulling him to me, and sucking on his bottom lip. "I need you now, Darren," I tell him again, continuing to squirm, moving my hips in time with his hand.

He must sense that I mean business this time, so he extracts his hand. But, instead of lining himself up with me, he rolls onto his back, bringing me with him so that I'm straddling his waist.

"This way, you control the pace. If it hurts, you can stop or slow down," he explains, seeing the confusion on my face. Oh, that makes sense and is so sweet.

I bet none of the mage men Devin wanted to give me to would've been like this. I shake the thoughts of Devin from my head and focus back on the present. Devin is gone, and he's never coming back.

I move my hand down, gripping him tightly and lining him up with my core. As I move my body down, I am met with resistance and a pinch of pain, so I pause. I know the first time hurts and expect that, but I'm now wondering if me being on top is the best idea. If it hurts too much, I may just give up and stop altogether.

I have a moment of panic, but I look into Darren's eyes, seeing the love, desire, and lust shining back at me. I begin to move slowly downward again. There's still some pain, but. thanks to the extreme amount of wetness, he is gliding in smoothly. Once I'm fully seated and he's all the way in, I pause again, allowing my channel to stretch to accommodate him.

"Not yet, angel," he tells me when I go to move again, and he grips my hips, holding me in place. He slowly moves my hips forward and backward for a few strokes. I wish I could say it feels amazing. I want to so badly, but I can't. The pressure and pain, though subsiding, are still there. He loosens his grip on my hips, and I begin to move up and down slowly.

After a few strokes, he takes his thumb and begins circling my clit with increased pressure and speed, distracting me from any pain and allowing me to focus on the pleasure. It doesn't take me long before I'm shattering onto him, and he follows me over the edge and spills his seed into me.

We lay there for a few seconds, breath ragged and hearts speeding, before he gets out of the bed and gently lifts me, bringing me into the bathroom with him and drawing me a bath. He fills the water with some Epsom salts before slipping in behind me.

"The bath will help with the soreness," he says, pulling my hair off to the side and rubbing a warm washcloth over my skin. I feel a tear slip out of my eye at the tenderness he's showing me. I never imagined that I would be able to have a man this tender and caring for my own. I was resigned to, at best, a life alone or, at worst, with one of the mages. More of my tears slip free, hitting the water.

After a minute, my core begins to lose its tenderness and starts to feel normal once again. I look down in confusion before wiping my face and realizing that it must be my tears. I slip my hand down under the water to touch myself to feel if the tenderness really is gone. Yup, it is. Perfect.

I spin around to face Darren and straddle him again, gripping his already-erect cock in my hand and lining myself up for round two.

"Angel, we don't have..." he starts, but I impale myself on his cock with a moan. Oh, I was right. The water is making it feel much better, and I slowly move my hips forward and back, up and down, finding the right angle where he hits that amazing spot he did when his fingers were inside me.

Finally, this is how it's supposed to feel, and I let the moans slip out of my mouth with each downward thrust. Darren finally seems to catch on to the fact that it isn't hurting anymore, takes over, and begins to thrust his hips up, picking up speed and adjusting his angle based on my moans. Water is spilling out of the tub, but neither of us seem to care, too caught up in the pleasure of this moment.

After only a few of his powerful thrusts, I'm tumbling over the edge with my orgasm, enjoying the feeling of fullness with each pulse of my walls. He follows me again, but this time his canines drop down and sink into my neck at the same time my flame flares to life, marking him as mine. All the spaces between the Greek key tattoo that surrounds his collarbone are filled in with my orange and yellow flames.

He extracts his teeth from my neck and gives the mark a few soft licks. I reach down and cup a bit of water, pouring it over my shoulder. I watch as he goes from shocked to confused to content.

"A tear or two may have slipped into the water earlier," I explain to him, and he gets a concerned look. "Don't worry. They were happy tears," I add and give him a soft kiss as I lift myself up, letting him slip from within me.

"Okay," he replies, brushing my hair off to the side again and getting out of the tub.

Reluctantly, I stand up as well and walk into the waiting towel Darren has for me. I raise my arms, allowing him to wrap it around my body.

"Can we finish our coffees before we get into bed?" I ask.

"Of course, we can. Let me get you something to wear first," he kisses me on my head before going into the room and coming back with a large shirt that will make a perfect night gown.

We finish our coffees and slip into bed, snuggled together, my back to his front, in complete and utter bliss.

"Can we have a double mating ceremony?" I ask with a yawn.

He spins me to face him. "Whatever you want, but with who?"

"Samara and Trev. After they slaughtered her pride, she never thought she'd be able to have one, so it's kind of a big deal for her. Plus, she's my best friend," I tell him.

He nods. "Of course, we can." His reply registers as I am already drifting off to sleep with a smile on my face. For the first time in my life, I feel complete and may actually get my happily ever after. I guess my life really is a fairy tale.

Chapter Twenty-Seven

Sophia

Waking up wrapped in the arms of my mate has got to be the best thing in my life thus far. Never have I felt more loved or wanted than feeling the hardness of his cock poking me from behind and his arms holding me tight.

"Good morning," he says, placing a soft kiss on my neck.

"Good morning," I whisper back, turning in his arms, placing a kiss on his mouth. I intended for it to be a soft good morning kiss, but it becomes heated quickly, with him flipping me over onto my back and lining himself up with my entrance.

As he pushes in, I break our kiss with a moan. Goddess, this has to be the best way to wake up ever.

We spend the next while exploring each other's bodies, and when we're both finally sated, we fall back down beside one another.

"That was incredible," he whispers, and I nod in agreement.

"So, what happens now?" I ask, wondering what day-to-day life looks like for us. I've never dared to dream about a life where I was free to make my own choices, have a mate, friends, start a family, maybe even get a job.

"What do you mean?"

"I mean, what does daily life look like for us?" I wave my hands in an overly exaggerated manner.

"Whatever you want. I do have to go to work at some point though," he says, turning toward me.

My mouth drops open in shock, though I'm not sure why. Most people have jobs, so it makes sense for him to have one too.

"What's your job?" I ask

"I actually have two. I'm the beta for the pack, so I deal with a lot of the issues around here that Alaric is too busy for, and I also teach at the Westwood Academy."

"You teach? And what's the Westwood Academy?"

He gets this big goofy smile on his face, and I can tell he's really passionate about it. "I could tell you, but I can do even better. Why don't I show you?"

Now it's my turn to smile. I don't know what it is about this man, but his moods are infectious. He gives me a soft kiss before pulling the covers back and hopping out of bed. "I just asked Alaric to send some clothes over for you. Until then, there's a toothbrush in the bathroom. Why don't you have a shower while I make us coffee and wait for your clothes?"

He doesn't need to tell me twice. "Have I told you that coffee is the way to my heart?" I ask, walking over to him and giving him a kiss on the cheek.

"Mine too," he says with a wink before throwing on some sweats and heading downstairs.

I walk into the bathroom, taking my time to brush my teeth before getting in the shower and look at myself in the mirror. I look different. Not so vastly different that you wouldn't be able to recognize me, but different enough that I can tell something has changed. The only thing I can think of is that I'm finally free. The bags under my eyes are gone, and I seem to have put on a few pounds, my ribs no longer poking out through the skin of my waist. I'd almost say I was beautiful.

I rinse my mouth out before hopping in the shower, turning on the dozens of jets lining the wall and ceiling. I find a razor on the shelf and contemplate whether I think Darren would mind if I used it or not. I quickly decide he wouldn't and get to work shaving my legs, armpits, and girly bits in anticipation for another round, or five, with my mate later.

Darren still isn't back yet by the time I'm done with my luxurious shower, so I throw on the black bathrobe hanging on the door over my towel and head downstairs. Once I reach the landing, I hear the excited voices of Riley and Ryker and rush down the stairs.

"Boys!" I exclaim, opening my arms wide for them to rush into. I don't think I'll ever stop being so excited to see them.

"Auntie Sophia!" they say at the same time, rushing from Darren's side and into my waiting arms. Darren has a look of shock and betrayal on his face, but I know he's not serious and stick my tongue out at him behind their backs. He gets a smirk on his face and walks over to Phoebe, snatching Aurora out of her arms and nuzzling into her with a pointed look in my direction.

So that's how it's going to be. I move my fingers to my eyes and point at him, so he knows it's on, and we both giggle.

"Are you two fighting over my kids?" Phoebe berates us with a smile of her own.

I pull back from the boys sheepishly while both Darren and I say, "No."

"Sure, you weren't," she laughs. "Here, I brought you a few sets of clothes until we can go into town shopping." She hands me a bag full of clothes. I peek inside, and I notice some still have the tags on.

"Uh Phoebe, some of these are brand new."

"Yeah, my mate seems to think I need more clothes than I actually do, so he went a little overboard when I first got here. I gave Samara a bag too," she says with a wink and a smile at Alaric.

"Well, then, thank you, Alaric," I giggle and rush up the stairs to get dressed. The quicker I'm dressed, the quicker I can steal Aurora away from Darren.

I rush through pulling on clothes, leaving the empty bag and pile of clothes on the bed before rushing back downstairs. I walk over to Darren, stepping up on my toes going in for a kiss while snaking my arms under Aurora and pulling her toward me.

"Hey! No fair," he says, as I slip away. I just stick my tongue out at him once more and snuggle into Aurora.

"Good morning, my gorgeous girl," I whisper, placing soft kisses on her face.

"Alright, boys. You be good for Uncle Darren and Aunt Sophia," Phoebe says, and I snap my head up to look at her.

"What?" I ask, looking between her and Darren.

The man in question comes up beside me, wrapping his arms around both Aurora and me. "The boys are supposed to start at the academy next year, so we're going to give them a tour as well. With their powers being unpredictable at times, Phoebe is having to home school them this year." I look at him before turning toward the boys, both their bodies vibrating with excitement, and I smile.

"By the way. Samara said to let you know she was going with Trevan to meet his family but will be back in a couple of days." Phoebe says, and I nod. I wonder why she didn't tell me herself.

"She said she, and I quote, 'didn't want to interrupt your sexy time'," Alaric says with a wink, and I blush while Darren smiles.

Phoebe steps up to me, and I reluctantly hand Aurora over to her, still not confident that I've pressed enough kisses on her tiny little head but promise myself to make up for it later.

I sigh, and Phoebe chuckles. "She'll still be here when you get back."

"I know," I pout.

"Besides you'll have us, Auntie Sophia," Ryker adds, coming over and wrapping his arms around my waist. I lean down and pepper him with kisses as well while Phoebe and Alaric walk out the door.

"You're very right," I say, and he giggles.

"Aunt Sophia," he warns, and I pull back.

"What? Are you too old for kisses from your aunt?" I challenge.

"Never," he whispers, and tears mist in my eyes.

"Good answer," I tell him, pulling Riley into our little hug. "What about you, munchkin? Are you too old for kisses from your auntie?"

"Nope. I'm just the right age," he says proudly, and I quickly lavish him with the same number of tickles and kisses that I did his brother.

"Alright, you three. Time to go," Darren says, breaking us out of mini-love fest. I sigh, and the boys clap excitedly. What I wouldn't give to have been in their life from the day they were born. It hasn't even been a week, and they already feel like a missing piece of me that I didn't know was missing.

Each boy takes one of my hands, and we begin to make our way to the door.

"Hey! What am I? Chopped liver?" Darren pouts. Riley looks up at me with concern in his eyes, and I give him a nod with a smile. He rushes behind us and clasps one of Darren's hands, and he smiles down at him. Maybe one day this will be us with our children. My smile widens at that thought. Maybe one or two kids would be nice. I always dreaded bringing new life into the world because of Devin and his cronies, but now, being here, maybe it's possible.

"You guys ready to go?" Sebastyn asks as we step out of the house.

"When did you get here?" I question.

He chuckles. "Just now."

"Hey, man. Are you actually considering teaching?" Darren asks, hope lacing his voice.

"Yes, he is," Skarlyt calls out, walking out of the forest, hand in hand with Lennox. "And I have something to talk to you about, Darren."

He looks shocked momentarily before a huge smile graces his face, and he clasps Sebastyn on the back. "I knew I'd wear you down," he chuckles.

"Or my sister would threaten me," Sebastyn mumbles back.

"If this is the end result, it doesn't matter which," Darren laughs.

Skarlyt reaches up on her tiptoes, placing a kiss on Lennox's mouth. "I'll see you later," she says to him, walking over to us with a clap. "Let's get this show on the road."

Skarlyt reaches out to me at the same time Sebastyn reaches out to Ryker and I clasp her hand. Within seconds, I'm deposited on the immaculate front lawn of what can only be described as a castle. There is a big main building made of brick with windows strewn throughout. Directly in front of me are stone stairs, leading up to a huge doorway with the words 'Westwood Academy' over top. To the left and right there are circular towers, reaching up above the highest tree. Wow.

My mouth is still hanging open in awe when Darren and Riley arrive with Skarlyt and Sebastyn.

"What do you think?" Darren asks. I try to turn my head toward him, but I can't look away.

"It's amazing. But how?" How isn't this seen by humans and satellites? Wouldn't it be dangerous having all of our kids in one place?

"It's cloaked. No one can get here or even see it unless they already know where it is. If a human were walking through the forest right now in this direction, they wouldn't see anything, not even us, and a sense of foreboding would flow through them, making them avoid the area completely." That's just... wow.

"How do the students get here?" I ask, looking around for a parking lot or bus. Anything that would transport them here.

"The shifters run in their animal form, the vampires run as well because it's only a few kilometers away from each pack, pride, coven. The witches though..." Darren begins, but Skarlyt steps up.

"Those with strong air magic float themselves and a few others here. Some of the parents have to help out. Since Sebastyn has mastered teleporting now, we are hoping we can teach them to start teleporting themselves."

"Actually, when Devin had me, I was in a cage next to a teen named Margo, a mountain lion from Trixie's pack. She made some suggestions that I think we should discuss."

"Who's we?" I look at them confused.

"The board. We make all decisions about the school together. Skarlyt, Axel, Trixie, Roderick, that's Drake's father, and either me or Alaric make up the board. Trevan will sit in a meeting if there is a Fae student in attendance, but we don't have any this year. We're hoping to include all supernaturals across the globe, but no luck yet."

"That's amazing," I whisper, going back to look at the massive building in front of me.

"What suggestions?" Skarlyt asks.

"Well first, she thinks that students, local or international, should be staying here during the school year. She argues that it will help with 'inter-species' relations and also improve the tardiness complaints," Darren says, and Skarlyt nods.

"Any chance Margo's got a vampire boyfriend she's hoping to cozy up to?" Sebastyn laughs. "Help 'inter-species relations' my ass."

Skarlyt rolls her eyes. "We brought housing up when we first opened, and everyone shot it down."

"Yes, but another suggestion she made should help with that. She said we should have a student council with one representative from each faction and each grade to sit in with the council meetings once a month to bring up issues that the students believe are important."

"Giving the students a voice," she says with a nod.

"Exactly."

"That's smart," I add. Every child wants to be heard, whether it's about something small, like what color to paint the washrooms, or something more serious.

"Ready, boys?" Darren says, reaching out his hand to Ryker while Riley takes mine.

We spend the next two hours walking around the main building of the school. Turns out there are three levels, each with over twenty classrooms, and a large gymnasium.

"Off to the side, there are the mechanic bays for the apprenticeship classes," Darren says, pointing to a couple of buildings through the windows that look like large barns.

"Lennox agreed to teach that class by the way," Skarlyt says, and Darren beams.

"Perfect. That will help the older kids get jobs," Sebastyn says.

We continue walking toward a set of downward stairs, taking them slowly. When we get to the basement, Darren and Skarlyt begin talking excitedly. "We could convert this entire basement into dormitories for the vampires," she says, and he readily agrees with a nod.

"But I think we'll still have to expand the other two," he suggests. "Right now, we have it separated by boys and girls in each tower, but maybe we should go further than that. Especially for mature students."

"Mature students?" That catches my attention.

"Yeah. We have been trying to incorporate college and university classes catering to the students who will be taking on higher roles within their faction. My goal is to even expand to having medical school and veterinary classes."

"But that's way off. Although Felicia may be able to teach some of those classes and Charleigh could teach some psychology classes." Skarlyt adds excitedly.

"That's not a bad idea," Darren agrees.

"What about you boys? What do you think? Do you like the school?" I crouch down and ask them.

"Can we start tomorrow?" Riley asks and Ryker nods in agreement.

We all chuckle. "Not yet, but soon. Maybe we'll even find more phoenixes so Aunt Sophia and your mom can teach a few classes," Darren says, and I look up at him before looking back down at the boys.

"I do like kids," I admit. Maybe that can be my purpose.

They take us on rounds through the dorms, each floor housing four suites, each with four bedrooms, a living room, a bathroom, and a small kitchenette, and I have a thought. "What if you build small cottages on the grounds for the mature students? I can't see nineteen or twenty-year-olds wanting to be in the same dormitories as eleven and twelve year olds."

"That would certainly fix the issue of space," Darren says, looking at Skar.

She nods. "I think we need to call a board meeting."

With the tour done, we return to the pack, heading straight for Alaric and Phoebe's. Once we get there, I catch up on my Aurora snuggles, and we talk about the academy. At one point, Sarah even joins us, and Phoebe demands that she teach a class on making her body care products and cleaning supplies. Sarah doesn't agree right away, but she doesn't turn it down either. With a little encouragement, I could see this working out perfectly.

I glance around the room as I snuggle Aurora in my arms and marvel at my life. I'm not sure how it could get any more perfect.

Chapter Twenty-Eight

Sophia

I t's been two weeks since Darren and I claimed each other, and, although we've spent time with our friends and family and at the academy, most of our time has been spent perfecting our 'wrestling' as the boys have taken to calling it after interrupting us the other day. It's really Phoebe and Alaric's fault for telling them they could come see if we wanted to go over for dinner. It didn't help that the boys didn't even knock. In all honesty, they could've knocked, but we wouldn't have heard them over the sounds of our lovemaking.

It's gotten so much better since that first time, and I have also found that I kind of like being spontaneous and maybe even the added thrill of possibly being caught. Okay, not kind of. I love it. Like now, I'm standing in the kitchen doing the dishes, and Darren thinks that I don't see him prowling around the island toward me. I know what he's going to do. Why else does he think I've taken to wearing dresses and skirts around the house?

I am acutely aware of his presence behind me when he drops to the floor, spinning around, placing his head under my skirt at the perfect level with my core, and immediately sucks my clit into his mouth, making me drop the dishes in the sink and cling to the counter. It only takes a few swipes of his tongue before my juices are spilling down his chin with my release. He stands up, wiping his mouth off, grabbing my hands and holding them behind my back as he thrusts inside of me in one smooth motion. He begins hammering into me the way he knows I like, causing me to explode over and over again until he follows me and spills his seed deep inside me.

Once he removes himself, I spin around and wrap my arms around his neck and merge my mouth with his.

"Okay, angel, let's not start this again. Your friend is going to be here any minute to get ready," he says between kisses.

"She's probably doing the same thing," I try to reason, but he shakes his head. "What if you help me shower?" I ask with a raised eyebrow.

"That sounds like a fantastic idea," he races me up to our room, tossing clothes along the way.

We explore each other's bodies quite a few times in the shower before I hear Samara call my name from downstairs.

"Be right down," I call out to her as Darren is thrusting in and out of me, up against the shower wall.

I place my arms on his shoulders for leverage and begin meeting him thrust for thrust, knowing that he won't last long if I do. We both are falling over the edge soon after, and we finish showering to get ready for our mating ceremony.

Coming downstairs dressed in Phoebe's mating dress, the white to red ombre that Sarah took in for me, I see Samara wearing Charleigh's matching one and smile. In all the movies, it's always heartwarming when the daughter wears her mother's wedding dress. This is obviously different, but it means so much.

"The guys are all getting ready at the big house, and the rest of the girls will be here soon. I just wanted a few minutes with

Sophia if that's okay," Samara says, looking at Darren for the last part.

"Of course. I'll see you soon," he says to me, placing a kiss on my forehead before heading out the door.

"So, I wanted to tell you before anyone else," she begins.

"Oh, my goddess, you're pregnant?" I ask. She looks shocked.

"No. Not yet anyway. What I wanted to tell you is that Trev and I talked about it, and. after meeting with Trev's family and his court and then with Trixie and her pride...Well, we decided that we're moving here to Westwood pack land permanently," she says.

I start jumping up and down in excitement. Even though the pride and Trev's court aren't far, I had still been wishing that there might be some way she could stay closer.

I stop abruptly. "But what about your lion? I thought you said she is too dominant to recognize Alaric as her alpha."

"We've been shifting together a lot more in the last week, and I've come to an agreement with my lion. We will recognize Alaric as our alpha. She's learned to trust him. She says if he fucks up, we can always just eat him," she finishes with a laugh, and I join in.

I grab her, pulling her into a hug. "I'm so happy," I whisper into her hair.

"Me too, Soph. Me too," she whispers back.

We are interrupted by Phoebe, Charleigh, Sarah, Skarlyt, and Felicia coming through the door. We spend the next hour getting ready, laughing, and drinking a bottle or two of wine.

"So how are classes?" Skarlyt asks, stepping up and placing a flower crown on my head.

"Great. I'm with the younger grades for right now, since I'm still trying to get a handle on my own powers, and it's fantastic."

"I'm glad. The kids really seem to love you," she says, as she pins the crown in at the sides before moving to Samara. "So, when are you going to start teaching a class?"

Samara scoffs, "On what?"

"How about survival skills? If any of these kids got lost, they need to know how to survive in the forest. Or worse, if they were to be taken and escape, they need to know how to either survive long enough for help to get there or how to save themselves," Skarlyt supplies.

I smirk to myself. Skarlyt and I had schemed, hoping to use this as a way I could still see Samara every day if she had chosen to go live in the pride or Trev's Court. Turns out I didn't need to, but I really do think it will be good for her. I can't see her enjoying working at Supernatural with Trev.

"You think so?" Samara asks, and Skarlyt nods. "What about you?" she asks, looking over at me.

"I think it's a fantastic idea and perfect for you." The way I say it, maybe a little too eagerly, has her eyes narrowing and glancing between both Skarlyt and I.

"What did you do?" she urges, looking directly at me.

I wave my hand in dismissal, but she continues her staring. Finally, I sigh in defeat. "Okay, okay. I brought up to Skarlyt that I think you would make a great teacher and that maybe we could incorporate survival classes at the academy." I begin to sweat under her gaze, knowing that she's putting the pressure on to ensure she gets the whole truth. If there's one thing Samara hates, it's being kept in the dark about things. A close second is being given handouts, which is exactly how she is probably feeling about this job offer.

"Fine. It was because I was worried you were going to move to the pride or the Fae court or whatever, and I wanted you to get a job at the academy with me so we could see each other every day." I say it all so fast some of the words blend together but, from the small smile gracing Samara's face, she gets it.

"Okay," she says with a slight nod.

"Okay?" I ask, surprised that she put in all that effort, staring at me, exerting her dominance, just to agree.

"Yup. I already knew that you had done that. Trev's on the board, remember? All new classes and teachers need to be agreed on by every member." My mouth drops open in shock, and I round on Skarlyt.

"You knew! I was so worried and stressed out about it this entire time, and you knew. You could've told me."

"But you're so adorable when you're stressed. Besides, Samara made me promise," Skarlyt says, and I huff, crossing my arms over my chest and pouting.

"Come on. No pouting on the day of your mating ceremony," Phoebe says, coming to stand in front of me with a smile on her face. "It's time to go."

As a group, we head down to the lake to meet the men. I requested that our ceremony be held on the shore with the reflection of the moon over the lake. In most of my dreams before coming here, that is what I saw. No one complained and most thought it was an amazing idea. Phoebe and Alaric's and Skarlyt and Lennox's ceremonies were also held at the lake at night, but they were farther inland, on the grassy area. I wanted it—no—needed it to be on the shore. When I showed all the girls the spot the other night with the crescent moon hanging high in the sky, they all agreed that it's perfect. We quickly pulled the men in, putting their muscles to work. There is now an archway and aisle fashioned out of fallen trees and vines on the shore that will serve as a permanent fixture from now on.

As I round the corner to the top of the aisle, I stop. There at the end are Darren and Trev. Darren is wearing khaki pants and a white button up, with the sleeves rolled up, showing off his tattooed arms, and the top button undone, showing off my mate mark. Goddess, this man is sexy, and he's all mine.

I resume walking until I reach the end, and Darren takes my hands in his and whispers. "You look beautiful."

"You don't look so bad yourself, handsome," I tell him with a wink before we both turn to Alaric. Seeing that we're finally ready, he jumps right into the ceremony. I'm guessing since there's four of us, he doesn't want to waste time. Perfect.

"Do you, Sophia, take Darren as your bonded mate?"

"I do."

"And do you swear allegiance to the Westwood pack and me as your alpha?"

"I do."

He then moves on to Darren.

"Do you, Darren, take Sophia as your bonded mate?"

"I do."

"And do you reaffirm your allegiance to the Westwood pack and me as your alpha?"

"Let me see," Darren starts, earning a growl from his brother. "I do," he adds on.

He then goes on to ask the same of Samara and Trev and, although I was worried for a minute, even Samara's lion made an appearance when swearing allegiance to Alaric, which was surprising.

Just one thing left to do, so Alaric speaks.

"In front of Mother Moon and the witnesses here, I declare Sophia and Darren as well as Samara and Trevan bonded mates. May she bless your unions."

With all the formalities complete, we dance and laugh the night away. For the first time in my life, the future looks bright. It looks full of love, family, and friendship. There may be some heartache thrown in here and there, but I know that, no matter what, I won't be facing it alone.

Epilogue

Sarah

I'm standing in the shadows, watching everyone having a great time at the mating ceremony. Everyone except me. As much as I want to join in their revelry, I can't. The pit of anxiety that constantly lingers in my gut prevents me from doing anything remotely fun. That is, unless I'm holding Aurora. There's something about her...no matter how stressed or anxious I am, holding her makes me feel like I can take on the world.

Out of the corner of my eye, I see a beautiful woman with long, sandy blonde hair, high cheekbones, olive skin, and bright green eyes. She looks identical to the only picture of my mother I have. When I turn to get a better look, she's gone. It's been happening more and more lately, and I'm concerned that I might finally be having a mental breakdown. With everything I've been through, I am certainly due for one.

For as long as I can remember, I've dreamed about myself as a young girl, dancing and twirling in a forest with my mother. It always felt more like a memory than a dream. If so, it is a single happy memory from a childhood that I hardly remember. When I dream about my mother and the forest, which is more often than not lately, I wake with a sense of longing for the woman I never met and cannot be sure is real

The one time I asked my father about it, he lost his shit. I was only a child, but I should have known. He couldn't stand it when I did or said anything that made him think of my mother. He made sure I knew that I had killed her coming into this world, and I should be grateful for the life he had given me. What life? It was always on the tip of my tongue to ask, but I knew even then what would happen if I spoke out of turn.

Even after leaving the coven, I've logged in to check my emails and voicemails, wondering whether or not my father was concerned about where I went. Instead, I've received nasty messages from just about every other member of the coven. They have called me every name you can think of, blamed me for Joe's death, and accused me of being a traitor—the reason why their magic is failing them.

The one message I did receive from my father outlined my only path back after Joe's death. I could either return home immediately and marry one of the widowed men of the coven or be disowned. As if, "disowned" isn't exactly what's best for me. As if it isn't what I want.

It is what I want.

Right?

The fact that I still check the messages, unsure what I am hoping to see, shows that I must care at least a little.

"Would you like to dance?"

I'm ripped from my train of thought by the soft, smooth voice of Sebastyn, Skarlyt's brother. He's spoken to me before, of course, but I do not respond. I have nothing worth saying. If I don't say anything, my words can't get twisted up and used against me.

My silence doesn't mean I haven't appreciated him from afar. Since the night he met me at Pittock and accompanied me the rest of the way to Parry Sound, I have felt my eyes pulled toward his toned, tanned, slender body. That night was a nightmare in more ways than one, but I can still remember being comforted by his easy, forgiving silence and his graceful, careful movements.

His hand is extended toward me, some of his many tattoos peeking out from his long sleeves, as he waits for an answer. I can barely force myself to meet his bright blue eyes, so I focus on the strands of straight, midnight black hair that hang in front of them.

He is beautiful and sexy, and something in my body begs me to say yes, take his hand, and let him whisk me away. Instead, I shake my head and shrink back.

I watch as his entire body deflates at my rejection.

"Maybe another time," he says, lifting my hand and bringing it to his lips, pressing a feather light kiss to it. I'm sure a blush spreads across my face at his act, as I can feel my cheeks grow hot.

"Seb, come dance with me," one of the more beautiful witches coos at him, going so far as to grab his hand and drag him away from me.

All I want to do is pull him behind me and claw her eyes out for daring to touch him, but I don't. I lower my gaze and watch as he's pulled out onto the dance floor with another woman. He looks my way more than once, but when I see the familiar way she touches him, the way their bodies fit so neatly together, , I decide I'm done torturing myself for the night.

I turn away, catching the hazy image of my mother just as she fades again. The celebration will go on for hours still, but I am exhausted and ready for some quiet.

Sebastyn Moon is obviously preoccupied and way out of my league. Sebastyn Moon is not my concern.

* * *

Want more from the Westwood Pack?
Of course, you do!

Find information Book 4, Magical Mate here:
https://fdfairauthor.wixsite.com/website

About the Author

F.D. Fair is the author of the Westwood Pack Series. As an avid reader of Paranormal Romance Novels for the past 20 years, she turned her love of everything paranormal into steamy True Mate novels with a twist.

F.D. Fair lives and works in southern Ontario, Canada and

spends her time when she is not working or writing with the loves of her life—Her husband and 3 boys.

She is as weird as they come but is proud of it. Embracing her weirdness makes for some great stories.

Sign up for FD Fair's Newsletter:
https://dashboard.mailerlite.com/forms/76323/
5809623843156931o/share

Make sure to stalk her...

Instagram:
https://www.instagram.com/f.d.fairauthor
Facebook:
https://www.facebook.com/profile.php?id=1oo0716886485 16
Goodreads:
https://www.goodreads.com/author/show/21734156.F_D_Fair
Twitter:
https://twitter.com/FdFair
Bookbub:
https://www.bookbub.com/authors/f-d-fair

More from Foundations

Vengeance Marked by S.J. Pierce

GET IT HERE: https://www.sjpiercebooks.com/full-width-page-2/

International Bestselling Author SJ Pierce brings a "heart-pounding" and "electric" story to the Paranormal Romance genre that's interlaced with twists, turns, HEAT, and thrilling suspense. This one's a must-read...

Complete series available now!

When the woman of your dreams looks like a

demon…that's never a good sign.

Isaac doesn't know it, but his dreams of a woman with black eyes are actually a premonition. So, when he meets her in real life, sans demon-eyes, he knows something isn't quite right. But he also has a hard time staying away. What do these dreams mean? And why, despite their sizzling chemistry, can't he shake the feeling it will all end in catastrophe?

Probably because he also knows she's hiding something.

When the man you crave is also the man you've been sent to kidnap…things get messy.

The ones who created Alyx are watching her every move, which includes her forbidden meetings with the man she's been sent to spy on: Isaac…who also doesn't know who or *what* she is. So, when her creators finally summon to fulfill her purpose and capture him, she knows they're not the only ones she'll have to answer to. When all of mankind hangs in the balance, there is no room for error, and her draw to Isaac had her stumbling from the start. It's only a matter of time before things start going to hell.

Literally.

If only she'd followed the rules…

Fans of Gena Showalter and Christine Feehan will devour this EPIC end of the world, FORBIDDEN ROMANCE series. One-click today to get your binge-read on!

If you like **PARANORMAL ROMANCE** *books, or supernatural, you will love this.* - **Michelle's Paranormal Vault of Books ★★★★★**

WOW! *What an awesome beginning to a new series!* - **Nomi's Paranormal Palace ★★★★**

A **CAPTIVATING BOOK** *right from the start.* - **Mandy, Goodreads ★★★★★**

Foundations Book Publishing

Our mission is to exceed the expectations of our authors and the reading community with an uncompromising commitment to quality, individualism and personal pride. We measure our success one book at a time.

You can find more great works in multiple genres including Romance, Literary Fictions, Thrillers, Suspense, Young Adult, and more!

Visit us at FoundationsBooks.net